Shakespeare in the Theatre: The American Shakespeare Center

SHAKESPEARE IN THE THEATRE

Series Editors
Bridget Escolme, Peter Holland and Farah Karim-Cooper

Published titles
The American Shakespeare Center, Paul Menzer
Nicholas Hytner, Abigail Rokison-Woodall

Forthcoming titles
Patrice Chéreau, Dominque Goy-Blanquet
Trevor Nunn, Russell Jackson
Cheek by Jowl, Peter Kirwan
The King's Men, Lucy Munro
Mark Rylance at Shakespeare's Globe, Stephen Purcell
Shakespeare and the National Theatre, 1963–1975:
Olivier and Hall, Robert Shaughnessy

Shakespeare in the Theatre: The American Shakespeare Center

Paul Menzer

Bloomsbury Arden Shakespeare
An imprint of Bloomsbury Publishing Plc

B L O O M S B U R Y

LONDON • OXFORD • NEW YORK • NEW DELHI • SYDNEY

Bloomsbury Arden Shakespeare

An imprint of Bloomsbury Publishing Plc

Imprint previously known as Arden Shakespeare

50 Bedford Square	1385 Broadway
London	New York
WC1B 3DP	NY 10018
UK	USA

www.bloomsbury.com

BLOOMSBURY, THE ARDEN SHAKESPEARE and the Diana logo are trademarks of Bloomsbury Publishing Plc

First published 2017

British Library Cataloguing-in-Publication Data
A catalogue record for this book is available from the British Library.

ISBN:	HB:	978-1-4725-8498-4
	PB:	978-1-4725-8497-7
	ePDF:	978-1-4725-8500-4
	ePub:	978-1-4725-8499-1

Library of Congress Cataloging-in-Publication Data
A catalog record for this book is available from the Library of Congress.

Series: Shakespeare in the Theatre

Cover image: John Harrell, Chris Johnston, Christopher Seiler, and Gregory Jon Phelps in *The Blind Beggar of Alexandria, 2009*. Photo by Tommy Thompson.

Typeset by Fakenham Prepress Solutions, Fakenham, Norfolk NR21 8NN
Printed and bound in India

CONTENTS

LIST OF
ILLUSTRATIONS

SERIES PREFACE

Each volume in the *Shakespeare in the Theatre* series focuses on a director or theatre company who has made a significant contribution to Shakespeare production, identifying the artistic and political/social contexts of their work.

The series introduces readers to the work of significant theatre directors and companies whose Shakespeare productions have been transformative in our understanding of his plays in performance. Each volume examines a single figure or company, considering their key productions, rehearsal approaches and their work with other artists (actors, designers, composers). A particular feature of each book is its exploration of the contexts within which these theatre artists have made their Shakespeare productions work. The series thus considers not only the ways in which directors and companies produce Shakespeare, but also reflects upon their other theatre activity and the broader artistic, cultural and socio-political milieu within which their Shakespeare performances and productions have been created. The key to the series' originality, then, is its consideration of Shakespeare production in a range of artistic and broader contexts; in this sense, it de-centres Shakespeare from within Shakespeare studies, pointing to the range of people, artistic practices and cultural phenomena that combine to make meaning in the theatre.

Bridget Escolme, Peter Holland, Farah Karim-Cooper

PREFACE: IN THE FIRST PLACE

In 2007, during the celebrations of the 400th anniversary of the founding of Jamestown, the Annual Meeting of the Southern Anthropological Society met in Staunton, Virginia, to discuss 'Memory and Museums', since Staunton is 'itself, a living museum of nineteenth-century industrial Virginia enhanced by the American Shakespeare Center/Blackfriars Playhouse and the Museum of Frontier Culture.' The Anthropological Society did not mean to make history, but the notion that a 'living museum' of nineteenth-century industrial Virginia could be 'enhanced' by a reconstruction of a sixteenth-century English playhouse produced the kind of preposterous history in which theatre specializes. In the sentence's elision, the years slide away. Times change place, places swap times and worlds collude.

This is a book about times and places and the ellipses that align them, the way particular locations can fold time, scrunch it so that unlikely periods come into contact. Staunton, Virginia, a small town in the heart of the Shenandoah Valley, boasts a full portfolio of such places. Along with the Blackfriars, the Frontier Culture Museum – down the road – and the Woodrow Wilson Birthplace – up the street – triangulate the coordinates of the memory industry, at least the Staunton, Virginia branch. The Frontier Culture Museum honours a time when central Virginia *was* the frontier, when the Allegheny mountains just a few miles to the west barred further expansion. The 'living history museum' itself sprawls across Staunton's rolling outskirts and hosts reconstructed houses and barns from England, Ireland and Germany, which exemplify the vernacular styles that Virginia's white settlers copied. It is merely, maybe, coincidental that the chief builder of the new Globe in London and of the Sam Wanamaker Playhouse, Peter McCurdy, spent some early years in Staunton overseeing the remantling of these dwellings. Retracing the colonial trajectory, McCurdy came to Staunton well before he embarked on the Globe to establish some English homes there, or here. Staunton may be a 'living museum of nineteenth-century industrial Virginia', but twenty-first century Staunton is alive with industrialized memory.

The Frontier Culture Museum's homes-away-from-home represent some of the dislocations of Staunton, a city that specializes in recreations of places that were not there in the first place. A book about Staunton's Blackfriars – and the American Shakespeare Center (ASC), which built and operates it – could do worse than start at the *other* end of the street, therefore, with another home-away-from-home: a reconstruction of Anne Hathaway's Cottage in a part of Staunton called 'Newtown'. The ASC had nothing to do with the replica of Hathaway's Cottage – it is a mild embarrassment to the Center – although it never would have been built had it not been for the Blackfriars. Hoping to capitalize on the playhouse, a local sought to cash in on some collateral business from the thriving memory factory at the other end of town. (As of the writing of this book, the business was up for sale. People have their limits.) The city boasts, then, a Frontier Culture Museum of buildings from elsewhere, a replica of the Warwickshire home of Shakespeare's wife, and a recreation of the indoor playhouse that hosted some of his late plays. None of these sites were ever in Staunton, of course, not originally at least; but they are now. Evacuated of presence, these recreations all reject original places and originary things, participating, in Julia Reinhard Lupton's terms, in a 'Protestant spirituality [...] given new lift by the promise of an Americanized Shakespeare who can be truly everywhere.'[1] In Newtown, USA, recreations are even better than the real thing.

Memory is mobilized by absence, and Staunton's various memorials all embody that absence differently, the Blackfriars most radically since no one and nothing were ever there in the first place. Just because – or perhaps mainly because – the Blackfriars was built on the site of an old carpet factory, and not the site of the London Blackfriars, the building consolidates a swarm of histories and temporalities and fabricates something new. Lacking original presence, 'the Paternal reference',[2] the Blackfriars acts as a temporal centrifuge, concentrating but also separating one time from another, one history out of other histories. This project untangles these different histories although, in practice, the ASC ties them into a tidy knot. For the purposes of organization, the book treats these histories as discrete, although they are not: the 'deep' history of early English theatrical practice; the 'local' history of Virginia; the recurrent revolutions that make up the history of Shakespeare and performance, etc. The larger argument that follows here is that these various histories eddy around the Blackfriars, creating crosscurrents and riptides, swells and undertows. Over twenty-five years or so, the ASC has learned to navigate these waters through a range of theatrical practices. Among many other talents, the company knows how to tread water.

This book is written in, and about, three tenses, then, three cases of the historical past: early modern theatre history; the 'revolutionary' history of Shakespeare and performance; and the history of Shakespeare in Staunton, Virginia. It nests the Blackfriars within those histories to make sense of the weirdness that is the American Shakespeare Center and in particular the Blackfriars Playhouse. It tries to make the unlikely phenomena of a Blackfriars recreation in central Virginia seem likely – even inevitable – while honouring its oddity. The introduction that follows this preface therefore explores the litany that takes place on the threshold of every Blackfriars performance. The invariable and unvarying pre-show ceremony at the Blackfriars – which also previews their shows on tour – does far more than offer safety tips and courtesy reminders. It works to align the multiple times and varied places the Blackfriars occupies – the pre-show speech may be invariable, but it makes the project seem inevitable. This book focuses significant attention on the Blackfriars 'retail experience' since – as Chapter 3 develops – 'Blackfriars Performativity' in part derives from a tension between the contents of the play and its dense historical bracketing at ASC shows.

Chapter 1 turns first to the history of Shakespeare in Virginia and Shakespeare in Staunton. It explores some of the dark passages between Old World and New, including some noxious colonial histories performed in Shakespeare's name. If colonizers called upon Shakespeare's name to endorse their expansionist fantasies, the colonized called upon him as well for a libertarian rebuke. Chapter 1, then, locates some dire histories, but also some redemptive ones, as well, when the disenfranchised found expression through Shakespeare's plays. This redemptive tale is not one of Shakespearean timelessness, but rather of the way the timely production of one of his histories gave voice to the ambitions of Staunton's marginalized community. Ultimately, the chapter returns to the peculiar institutions in whose shadow Staunton's Blackfriars operates, locating the playhouse in the cut of Virginia's deep history.

Chapter 2 turns to another tradition, the tradition of Elizabethan revivalism of which the ASC is only the most recent entry. 'Revolutionary Nostalgia' argues that those who forget history get to repeat it and that revivalism is fuelled by the power of selective memory, selective forgetting and deliberate amnesia. The chapter places the ASC project within a tradition of other revivals not to construct a genealogy of Elizabethan revivalism, but rather to argue that what aligns these projects is their collective profession to have been the first revival. A second revival is not a revival. It is a repeat, even a retread. The Elizabethan revival always recurs, each time for the first time.

The chapters that follow turn from history to practice, from the various traditions in which the ASC operates to a couple

of conventions that distinguish their brand. The chapters that
follow turn from an examination of historical sources to first-
hand observations of the ASC in action. 'A History of Light'
examines the central theatrical, even ideological, commitment
of the ASC across the last twenty-five years: a principle the
company calls 'universal lighting' that insists that actors share
the limelight with the audience. This simple convention has
complex effects – and Chapter 3 argues that universal lighting
is less a technology than an histrionic practice. 'Blackfriars
Performativity' is a complex communion of actor and audience
enabled – though not guaranteed – by universal lighting. The
wash of light in which actors and audiences commune at the
Blackfriars constitutes, therefore, the central dynamic of ASC
performance regardless the play, the players or the playhouse.
Whatever changes have taken place across the history of the
institution, the light has remained constant.

Chapter 4 examines another central ASC practice, the
'Actors' Renaissance Season,' a three-month affair at the
advent of every year during which the ASC drills down into
early modern theatrical practice and non-canonical plays. By
doing so, this book argues, the season stages an insurrection
within the ASC's larger remit, offering up a dynamic model
of theatre-making marked by discrepancies in style – and
an unevenness of aesthetic success – that contrasts with the
smooth professionalism, even the 'timelessness', of the rest
of the year's programming. As such, it seems both contained
subversion, but also a 'research and development' department
for the company's ongoing investigations of staging practices
and non-canonical Renaissance plays. In taking on the non-
or even anti-canon of Renaissance drama, the season also
closely cultivates academic concerns, pivoting out of scholarly
research while also contributing to it. Born of exigency,
levying academic work, the season now adumbrates the ASC
project and even forms a kind of contained history of the
company's origins.

This book concludes with a conversation with the ASC's
founders, Jim Warren and Ralph Alan Cohen. It offers them

various quotes from the book for their critique, a way of embedding in the project a conversation between inside and out. It gives Warren and Cohen a chance to challenge and even outright disagree with some of the book's observations about their practices. This is by design and the transcript of the conversation has been edited for length, but not to diffuse any contentions. At best, it lends the book balance, as well as a meditation on intention since it records a tension between what the founders *intended* to communicate with and about their endeavour and what one witness – the author – makes of it. It is also an attempt to let the two men responsible for the formation and success of the company have the last word on it.

*

The occasion, or occasions, for this book are two anniversaries. The year 2013 marked the twenty-fifth anniversary of the company's formation, a 1988 performance of *Richard III* under the name 'Shenandoah Shakespeare Express'. The other anniversary falls in 2016 and commemorates fifteen years of the Blackfriars Playhouse. The two anniversaries fittingly mark the two histories of the company: the first a history of a touring Shakespeare company with an emerging but not original ambition to build a replica playhouse; the second history of a resident company that performs at the 'world's only re-creation of Shakespeare's indoor playhouse', but maintains a touring company that honours its origins. Those two histories are neatly telegraphed by the company's two names: 'Shenandoah Shakespeare Express' for starters, the 'American Shakespeare Center' at present. (In between, for a couple of transitory years, the company was known as 'Shenandoah Shakespeare'.) The transition from the one name to the other, as the company worked out its identity and its ambitions, forms one thread of this book's narrative, and features prominently in Chapter 2: 'Revolutionary Nostalgia.'

One other occasion for the book's preparation is Arden's launch of a series of books on Shakespearean stages and stagers intended to chart the coordinates of the major agents and agencies producing Shakespeare today. The rationale for this book is not, then, just two arbitrary numbers – 25 and 15 – but rather the fact that the 'ASC' produces more Shakespeare and Renaissance drama than any other institution or venue in North America today. Indeed, it might be possible to extend the claim abroad. The ASC is a repertory house and nearly always has at least three titles rotating throughout a given week. The company produces twelve to fifteen individual titles a year from the repertory of Shakespeare's plays and that of Renaissance drama. (I deliberately separate those canons here to follow the ASC's lead, which I take up at length in Chapter 4.) That alone may be rationale enough for this book, but the company produces those plays in one of the world's most beautiful, or at least unique venues, what Andrew Gurr calls: 'One of the most historically important theatres in the world.'[3] That this recreation playhouse, with its repertorial churn, sits in a small town in the Shenandoah Valley in central Virginia is, itself, interesting enough. That the company's claim to be 'The American Shakespeare Center' is not only not implausible but rapidly becoming a self-fulfilling prophecy – name as destiny – further distinguishes the company as worthy of sustained critical attention.

One brief book cannot cover everything and, thus, much of the ASC's work goes untreated here. The precise details of the SSE/ASC's founding and the means by which they raised sufficient interest and capital to build a Blackfriars recreation have been told, and retold, elsewhere.[4] Instead, this book focuses its critical attention on the company's various histories and various staging principles. In doing so, it almost wholly ignores the company's significant commitment to educational outreach and the significant work of its educational team. Formed unapologetically as an academic venture by an unapologetic academic, the ASC has always had a commitment to offering workshops, colloquia, conferences, and 'Actor

Scholar Councils' that connect communities of teachers, players, scholars, editors, and dramaturgs of Shakespeare and performance. It is, in many ways, an academic institution, an educational venue, as much as it is a professional theatre. Indeed, when the Blackfriars opened in 2001, the neighbouring institution Mary Baldwin University started a graduate programme in Shakespeare and Performance, largely at the initiative of Ralph Alan Cohen, who still teaches for that programme. Chapter 4 explores in more detail the association of the ASC with the world of academia – particularly as it manifests in the Actors' Renaissance Season – but along with its commitment to the light, the ASC's commitment to enlightenment has proved its most durable feature. The book on that aspect of the ASC remains to be written.

The allusion to Mary Baldwin's graduate programme in Shakespeare and Performance gives me an occasion to set the 'terms and conditions' of this book's use. It requires of its author an unusually explicit disclaimer. I have been associated in one way or another with the ASC since 1990, when it was the SSE. First as fan, then as employee, then as board member, now as the director of the Shakespeare and Performance graduate programme at Mary Baldwin University, which operates in partnership with the ASC. (On more instances than I am willing to admit, I came across a line in an early grant proposal and thought, 'who wrote that!?' only to discover that I had.) Currently, however, I draw no paycheck from the ASC nor do I sit on any associated boards. However, the graduate programme I direct exists because of the ASC. While this association grants me unusual insight – I hope – into the company and unrivalled access to its operations past and present, it also means that I am implicated in its history. More than implicated, I am complicit. I wrote some of the materials that I critique in the coming pages, having served as the company's first fundraising officer in the early 1990s. As such, I packaged and presented the SSE's mission to prospective donors, foundations, and government agencies. If I played a small role in the company's success, I bear some responsibility for historical and ideological claims I now find suspect. I have attempted throughout to maintain a neutral tone – C. S. Lewis's injunction to 'avoid eulogistic and dyslogistic adjectives' has been a guide – but I have failed.

Love may be blind, but true love lets us see fault as clearly as favour, perhaps even more so. It's not an exaggeration to reveal that I 'love' the subject about which this book pretends to be neutral. Nevertheless, I have tried to be neither overly laudatory nor excessively critical. This book, in short, is neither wholly from the heart nor completely from the spleen. One fundamental assumption of this book, in fact, is that the ASC is *exactly* what the founders want it to be – though Chapter 5 gives them the opportunity to correct that impression or address what they take to be its current deficiencies and future directions. This book attempts to honour the institution by taking its claims and its project seriously, recognizing its contributions, noting its incoherencies, but above all attempting to locate and position it within the early twenty-first century landscape of Shakespeare and performance. The Blackfriars Playhouse in Staunton, Virginia, is a notable location – equal though not equivalent to Stratford; London; Washington, DC; Ashland, Oregon and other sites currently generating the energy that sustains the remarkable boom in Shakespearean production across the last twenty-five years. Those years overlap with the emergence of the ASC. Perhaps that is a coincidence. Probably it is not. But then just one argument this book makes among many is that 'coincidence' is what history looks like when you're standing too close to it.

Paul Menzer
Staunton, Virginia, 15 March 2016

The Blackfriars Playhouse at dusk, with the Stonewall Jackson Hotel in the background. Photo by Pat Jarrett. Used by permission

*Dedicated to Jim Warren, Ralph Alan Cohen,
and the staff of the American Shakespeare
Centre who work so hard off-stage to
make the on-stage work so good.*

Introduction: Locations

Thresholds of history

Something strange and boring happens before every show at the Blackfriars Playhouse in Staunton, Virginia – though it is deliberately strange and only technically boring. Eight times a week, five minutes before 'curtain', after fifteen minutes of well-played acoustic music and just before a brisk presentation of a play from the canon of Renaissance Drama – or a play by William Shakespeare – an actor delivers a pre-show speech. These talks perform the standard work of the modern theatre: they tell you how to locate the nearest exit in the unlikely event of a fire, remind you to turn off your cell phones and urge you to buy stuff, not least tickets to other shows. (Pre-show announcements in American theatres borrow their dramaturgy from the airline industry.) But woven seamlessly into this preamble is something you won't get on the flight out of Dallas: a very brief lecture on early modern theatre history. These lectures begin with a variant of 'here at the Blackfriars we do Shakespeare a little differently' and urge you to do some further reading, specifically in the programme where you will find a list of 'Shakespeare's staging conditions'. The pre-show talk – and the material it guides you to – is handled with such winning aplomb that only a pedant could object to the loose treatment of theatre history. But the aim of the pre-show is not accuracy. The actors are just setting the clock. Here, on the threshold of every performance, the American Shakespeare Center (ASC) threshes out the skeins of time that entangle anyone who sets foot in their playhouse, built, in 2001, in a small town in the Virginia Piedmont to

resemble a seventeenth-century Jacobean playhouse that originally stood on the banks of the Thames in the neighbourhood
of Blackfriars in London, England.

Deliberately strange. Technically boring. 'Strange' in the
sense of 'estrangement'. The actor invokes difference to stabilize
the temporal instability at the heart of the enterprise. The aim
is to alienate the audience into easy accord with the multiple
temporalities that they have let themselves in for. 'Boring' in
the technical sense that Bert O. States means when he describes
it as 'too much time-awareness', which extends in this instance
to an awareness of time passed.[1] This initiatory rite of boring
estrangement – or estranged boredom – is performed with a
cocked-hat insouciance that belies its own complexity. It may
seem as banal as a pre-flight enjoinder to buckle your belt
(low-and-tight), but something more important is at work for
these actors. They're feeling with their fingers for a cut in time
so they can hang out in history for two or three hours.

The pre-show talk goes on for a while, so long that it can
be hard to remember a time before it began. Maybe that's
the point. To make the audience forget *when* they are, since
forgetting *where* they are will prove impossible since the lights
will stay on throughout the play. Those lights illuminate a
splendid recreation of the original Blackfriars – or a splendid
best-guess reconstruction – and so constantly remind the
present audience of the theatrical past. The fabric of the
playhouse works hard and well to locate the audience in the
past without claiming slavishly to reproduce it. Since the
sense of place is so firmly fixed, the actors open the show by
winding their watches. Performances at the Blackfriars are
doubly coded with *this-was* and *this-is*. This book will argue,
ultimately, that we might treble that double code, since we can
see in the ASC's history a prediction of where Shakespeare and
performance is heading. Like Robert Greene's brazen head,
Blackfriars' performances speak three times, saying 'Time is',
'Time was' and 'Time is past'.

The repeat customer will notice that this opening chat
recurs every night with clockwork precision. It sounds off

the cuff but it is purely by the book. There is in fact a script for it, though the ASC's seasoned actors have committed it to memory. An actor's ability to speak without script imbues the performance with all the more charm: the pre-show lesson in theatre history is not a management dicta handed down to the actors but a company line, a genealogy that reaches from the Blackfriars troupe all the way back to 'Shakespeare's company', as the programme calls it (which would have been news to Shakespeare's fellow sharers, not to mention the Lord Chamberlain, not to mention the king). Through its nightly repetition the pre-show chat slowly reveals its true ambition, which is to overcome its banality as a necessary prelude to the performance proper. It is not an announcement, it is a liturgy, in the sense of 'an inscribed set of performatives written to require repetition where repetition is *both* reiteration of precedent *and* the performance of something occurring "again for the first time".'[2] At this moment – or at these moments – the ASC makes its own time.

All theatre is museum theatre and what's on display is time. To quote States again, theatre is a 'stylization of time', time made shapely, and what we watch when we watch is time made apparent, even when our consciousness of that time produces productive boredom.[3] Every performance in every theatre, explicitly or not, marks its own relationship with time through any number of framing gestures. As an organization with an allegiance to the theatre historical past, the ASC faces unusual pressure to be upfront about the scales of time at play in its house. This moment before the play, as an actor stands before us in period costume and tells us to locate the illuminated exit signs that flank the *frons scenae* – painted to resemble the Italianate faux finish of an indoor Jacobean hall – beneath the light of iron chandeliers fitted with electric bulbs, to not mention the company's relationship with the past would be to ignore the obvious. There's an elephant in the room, and it's history.

Rebecca Schneider, in *Performing Remains*, has written brilliantly about theatre and re-enactment within the twentieth-century 'memory industry'. She cites Gertrude Stein who, when speaking of *Hamlet*, refers to the play's 'syncopated time', which gave her the jitters.[4] For Hamlet, the time is out of joint and he, the unlikely bonesetter. Institutions like Shakespeare's Globe and the American Shakespeare Center have faced from inception sceptics unsettled by theatrical untimeliness, of the unsyncopated time announced in the architecture of their reproduction playhouses. W. B. Worthen has written persuasively about the way the Globe, at least, took on these early questions.[5] I will not recapitulate those arguments here, but abbreviate them (reductively) by calling them mainly a matter of time. Above all, critics worried that the Globe or Blackfriars had a naive sense of time, a condescension since these institutions have an extremely sophisticated sense of how people might like to spend their time (and what they might spend on it). Above all, the Globe and Blackfriars unsettled sceptics by provoking questions about just what kind of theatre was going on there, and just what kind of theatre history underwrote such projects. For both institutions challenged the 'logic of the archive' – a logic made of *logos* – by substituting for the document the 'body-to-body transmission of affect and enactment' more familiar from the practices of re-enactors (such as the Civil War re-enactors who practice in fields not far from Staunton's Blackfriars).[6] To the critics, the work at the Globe and later at the Blackfriars looked alarmingly like re-enactment – an oxymoronic *ersatz* theatre – and the playhouses embarrassingly like archives that tried to contain but also resuscitate embodied practice. Above all, the question that hovered was just what kind of theatre – and theatre history – was going on here? Was it theatre at all?

In response to this prevailing question – and sometimes in the face of ridicule – the Globe (from its opening in 1997) and the Blackfriars (2001, though the ASC got a running start by touring for a dozen years first) both evolved practices that synched up their tangled temporalities and disabled questions of historiography that attend productions at their respective houses. At the Blackfriars, at least, the company grew quickly adept at disarming sceptics with an offhand historicism, even a wilful philistinism on questions of authenticity. They evolved a kind of improvisational history that justified expedient practice – the ASC adheres to the practices it likes and demurs from the ones it doesn't (there are no hautboys or pavanes at the Staunton Blackfriars). They also quietly backed away from the term 'Original Practices' (now trademarked by the Atlanta Shakespeare Tavern, who the ASC feel are welcome to it). And if a programme note got this or that bit of historical detail wrong, getting it right was never the point.

The pre-show announcement is considered at length here since it constitutes the premier instance of the way the ASC ushers audiences across the threshold of history. And it does so charmingly, easing the audience from one time scale to another so effortlessly that the spectator may not even notice they've been shifted. The company was not always so good at it. A reviewer suggested in 1992 that, 'I do get the feeling that they talk down to the audience […] although that impression may come from hearing the explanation that the lights won't change, the actors play more than one role, etc., three times last week'. The company stuck to it with dogged determination, since what the pre-show is selling is a version, even a vision, of the past. After twenty-five years, it has got it pitch perfect. At the Blackfriars, before every performance, the present has to catch up with the past in order for the play to unfurl into the future. The pre-show talk is a buffering device the audience sits through while it waits for the performance to load.

*

This book is primarily about two things: time and place. Theatre takes both, and what it gives back is largely determined by how it coordinates the two. The following pages work through the various scales of history and geography that the ASC plays within to locate its time and place in the landscape of contemporary Shakespeare and performance. What it is after, in its first half, is a 'Blackfriars Historicity'. There are always at least two scales of time and place at work at the ASC's Blackfriars. There is the deep history and distant geography of the original Blackfriars on the bank of the Thames, a building itself haunted by its monastic past and its own role in parliamentary politics (not least the central part it played in the politics of Reformation England). That history echoes across the years and resounds, diminished yet clear, in the new Blackfriars in Staunton, Virginia. At the same time, that echo encounters a loud local history – primarily Virginia's colonial history and its role in the American Civil War, which bloodied the Valley that cradles Staunton. From the pre-show talk to the writing on its walls (and in its programmes), the Blackfriars brackets its plays with citations of early modern theatre history. But there is always another history at work, or in play, here, and while the ASC does not summon it, it comes without calling. The local histories of race and blood sometimes accord, but as often do not, with the history the ASC more explicitly courts. To a large extent the ongoing work of the American Shakespeare Center is to see that these sounds don't baffle one another, producing dissonance or, worse, silence.

Plays at the Blackfriars take place, then, in the cross-hatched history of England and America – and between the now and then. The ASC's coordinates are marked therefore by difference. The time is now and then, the place both here and there. ASC performances are *not* re-enactments, but they're not *not* re-enactments.[7] Furthermore, 'The Blackfriars' is not in Blackfriars, in fact is far from it. This is why the pre-show used to open with an invocation of difference: 'We do Shakespeare a little bit differently.' Than what? Or whom? (Or where? Or when?) At first blush, the ASC does Shakespeare a little bit differently from what they imagine you might expect from a theatre in twenty-first century America, although the architecture of the playhouse alone tells you that. After all, very few places look anything like it, almost none. But the invocation of difference implies a deviation from the imagined standard of theatrical presentation in the early twenty-first century. This idea, of course, grows increasingly hard to sustain since, at least in the Shakespeare industry, many organizations have loosely embraced some aspects of early modern revivalism. (When is the last time you saw a play by Shakespeare truly framed by a proscenium arch?) Nevertheless, the 'difference' the ASC insists upon smoothly segues into an insistence on sameness, though one that ends up drawing our attention to difference once more. For after the inaugural claim to difference, the pre-show litany draws attention to some early modern playing practices the ASC attempts to emulate, what the programme calls 'Shakespeare's Staging Conditions' (again, an historian would want to argue that these staging practice were not proprietary to Shakespeare, but that kind of history's not the kind of history the ASC's trying to make). As it turns out, the ASC does Shakespeare 'a little bit differently' by doing Shakespeare the same as Shakespeare did. At least a little bit. For the details of Shakespearean sameness laid out in the programme inevitably return to difference.

First, some background on the pre-show convention that this introduction is picking on: the American Shakespeare Center began life as a touring company in 1988 as 'Shenandoah Shakespeare Express', a quasi-collegiate-*cum*-professional troupe playing in auditoria, cafeterias, classrooms, bars, out-of-doors and even the occasional proscenium theatre tricked out in thrusty drag. The company's *raison d'être* was, and remains, a commitment to Shakespeare's staging conditions, an idea – an ideal – that an adherence to the conditions under which Shakespeare produced his plays would enhance their modern expression. The company's approach was originally judged by its founders (Jim Warren and Ralph Alan Cohen) to require some explanation, which actors provided in a pre-show preamble. In 2001, the company took up residence in the Blackfriars Playhouse, and the theatre-historical portion of the evening has now dwindled to just two or three important points, since much of the material is now obviated by the architecture and adumbrated in the programme. For instance, the actors – and the programme to which they refer you – detail some of these staging practices, though without ever calling them 'original'. What is remarkable in the material is the middle course it steers between fidelity to the past and the license it takes with it. For instance:

> Doubling: Shakespeare's *Macbeth* has more than forty parts; Shakespeare's traveling troupe may have had fewer than fifteen actors. Like the Renaissance acting companies, the ASC doubles parts, with one actor playing as many as seven roles in a single show. Watching actors play more than one role, an audience can experience another aspect of Elizabethan playgoing – the delight of watching a favorite actor assume multiple roles.[8]

Even the casual observer will notice that the ASC employs eleven actors, and they are not travelling but in residence, evidenced by the fact that they're standing on a stage at the Blackfriars talking about Shakespeare's travelling troupe. The claim honours the ASC's origins as a travelling company – and the ASC maintains a touring troupe whose beat is primarily the American campus. The size of 'Shakespeare's travelling troupe' is invoked, in this instance, to justify the small size of the ASC's resident company, a tension elided in the *non sequitur* between the first sentence and the second. The claim that 'Shakespeare's travelling troupe may have had fewer than fifteen actors' is not substantiated with any evidence. Indeed, no hard evidence exists about the precise size of early English playing companies when they travelled and estimates of the acting company to which Shakespeare belonged range as high as the mid-twenties.[9] Finally, it is worth pointing out, or not, that Shakespeare did not 'have' a touring company in the sense that the possessive apostrophe implies. These quibbles are merely 'academic' in all senses, of course, since the programme is after an *idea* – even an abstraction – of Renaissance theatre rather than an authenticated precis of 'the basic principles of Renaissance theatrical production' as the programme claims. 'Basic principles' are not, it turns out, a synonym for 'original practices'.

Following the entry on doubling that ends up suggesting that ASC 'doubles' without duplicating early modern playing practice, the programme turns to 'gender'.

> Because women didn't take to the English stage until after the Restoration (1660), all the women in Shakespeare's plays were originally played by young boys or men. Shakespeare had a great deal of fun with this convention. In a production of *As You Like It* in 1600, a boy would have played Rosalind, who disguises herself as a boy, then pretends to be a woman. Let's review: that's a boy playing a woman disguised as a boy pretending to be a woman. Because we are committed to the idea that Shakespeare is about everyone – male and female – the ASC is not an all-male company, but we try to re-create some of the fun of gender confusions by casting women as men and men as women.

The 'fun of gender confusion' probably depends on whom you ask. As often as not in Shakespeare's plays women dress as men so that they won't be raped. But consider the oddity of the programme's logic – the English Renaissance stage was all male, so we cast women as men. As long ago as 1993, a reviewer pointed out the:

> many misleading programme notes, including the fact that the SSE boasts that like Shakespeare they practice 'gender-blind casting', which in practice translates into putting women in some men's roles. Equal Opportunity casting is explained on the grounds that in Shakespeare's all-male casts, boys played women ... so here women can play men ... and women, but the men can only play men. [Ellipses in the original][10]

The reviewer notices the incoherence of the logic, but mistakes a truth claim for an historical one. Like the avowal that Shakespeare's touring company had fifteen actors so they employ eleven, the company calls upon history to justify a departure from it, inoculating themselves from the charge of 'museum' theatrics by injecting just a dose of history.

The programme covers other aspects of staging ('Sets', 'Costumes' and, most importantly, 'Universal Lighting'; discussed further in Chapter 3), but the final entry on 'Music' distills the ASC's historiography:

> Shakespeare had a soundtrack. Above the stage, musicians played an assortment of string, wind, and percussion instruments before, during, and after the play. The plays are sprinkled with songs for which lyrics, but not much of the music, survive. The ASC sets many of these songs in contemporary style. The result is emblematic of our approach – a commitment to Shakespeare's text and to the mission of connecting that text to modern audiences.

This entry on music is the most historically sound of the ones that precede it, and the historical note that this entry strikes harmonizes the past with the present by invoking the modern. Buried in the smooth elision from 'Shakespeare's text' to 'modern audience' lies the true complexity of the negotiation, a negotiation that the ASC works hard to make look easy, something also emblematic of their approach. The entry does not address the fact that the ASC ignores the rich tradition of Renaissance music, which is well archived and readily available (see the Globe's treatment of early music for comparison). The company is deeply interested in history and deeply interested in music (see Chapter 4) – just not at the same time. Again, the company is not interested in accuracy; they are interested in emblems. A commitment to history ultimately cedes to a commitment to the modern audience.

The point of this harvest of low-hanging fruit is to note that these citations of sameness insist on difference. True to its promise, the pre-show talk – and the material it guides us to – ends up emphasizing difference, though possibly not the difference it imagines. The general gist is that the ASC does Shakespeare a little bit differently that most folks today by doing it a little bit like Shakespeare did. Though just a little bit. For the articulation of ASC practices ends up emphasizing the ways in which the company differs from the 'principles of Renaissance theatrical production' as much as they adhere to them. The pre-show talk is as good as its word, then, though just possibly not in the way it first seems. The company performs an inaugural ceremony before every performance to position themselves in a seam between past and present, with loyalty to both but fidelity to neither.

Why cite history just to pick a fight with it? Why, that is, does the ASC build error into the apparatus of their claim to authenticity? Why does the ASC claim to double but also differ from the precedent it cites? Error is not failure. What can look like a historical rift is really an historical riff. The point – whether pointed or not – is not to get it exactly right but to get it productively wrong, to produce cognate history in which what the ASC puts on the stage is meant to reflect the past without mirroring it. The ASC holds the mirror up to history not to show us its own feature but our own. To 'do Shakespeare a little bit differently' both from the present *and* from the past and, by so doing, do it the same as no one else. And by saying so in the same words before every performance. The aim is to invoke history to inoculate against it, to shake off history by quoting from it since history can be a drag.

The pre-show talk is not trying to tell history, then, it's trying to make it. The ASC leverages an imaginary idea about the theatre historical past, and so objecting to the facticity of such claims is like bringing a knife to a pillow fight. Once we recognize that accuracy is not the goal, we can focus upon what the company is *actually* trying to communicate about its project, and the ASC's project is worth our attention because the last twenty-five years have witnessed a global expansion of historically inspired theatres and practices, most obviously

London's Globe, Staunton's Blackfriars, but other similarly constituted theatres like Atlanta's Shakespeare Tavern and other revivalist projects currently underway. In short, the last twenty-five years have witnessed the greatest building boom of Elizabethan playhouses since the building boom of Elizabethan playhouses and this book pursues the historical retail that frames performances and constitutes the audience at the American Shakespeare Center's Blackfriars Playhouse, the most successful American iteration of the most recent Elizabethan revival.

*

Thus far, this introduction has focused on the way the ASC finesses the syncopated times in which their performances move. To keep time with the past and make time for the present, the company toggles between difference and sameness with an ease that assuages the complexity of the gesture. Lost in the fog of art – which is at its most artful when it seems most artless – an audience may never notice how ably they negotiate the multiple temporalities that jostle to keep time with one another. But the throat-clearing gesture on the threshold of performance actually opens with an invocation not about time but place. 'Here at the Blackfriars ...' the actor begins, not here 'in Virginia', or here 'in Staunton', or here 'on Market Street', but with a reminder of where we are through a proprietary claim to the name. 'The Blackfriars' is the definite article.

Of course, Staunton's Blackfriars is nowhere near the building it mimics – which isn't there anyway – and so reminds us of theatre's unique ability to be two places at once. It is 3,780 miles as the crow flies from Staunton to London, and so the ASC cannot claim the power of proximity that Shakespeare's Globe on the Southbank enjoys. To be fair, the current Bankside Globe is not on the same spot as the original either, standing a few hundred yards from its sixteenth-century prototype. Whether 4,000 miles or 400 feet, proximity is not precisely the same as building in the first place. Still, it would be sophistical to claim there's no difference in aura at the Southbank Globe and at Staunton's Blackfriars. Part of the charm of Staunton's Blackfriars, after all, is the incongruity of its existence. What's a reconstruction of an English Renaissance playhouse retrofitted from out of a medieval monastic refectory doing in a small town in Virginia lodged in a rift between the Alleghany and Appalachian mountains?

If the history with which the ASC keeps time is always syncopated, then so is the place, which is itself a palimpsest of periods. Staunton is often called 'picturesque', for instance, largely because it looks like the past. Whether rendered by camera or brush, pictures are always in the past tense. To call Staunton 'pretty as a picture' or 'pretty as a postcard' is to acknowledge the nostalgic nimbus that hovers over the town. Yet Staunton is not a 'town that time forgot' but one that remembers it. Whether ostentatiously – through its 'Frontier Culture Museum' or 'Woodrow Wilson Birthplace' or, indeed, 'The Blackfriars' – or obliquely – the 'Clocktower' restaurant and 'Once Upon a Time' clock shop, which tick side-by-side in the heart of town – Staunton's past is proudly on display, even when that pride is peculiar ('Robert E. Lee' High School, and countless other sites and streets named after American traitors). Heritage, tourism and the memory industry meet on main street in Staunton, VA, nowhere more so than in a playhouse that's proudly out of place in a Virginia mountain town.

To pursue a more precise coordinate, the Blackfriars in Staunton stands on South Market Street, wedged between the 'Stonewall Jackson Hotel' and the 'Dixie Movie Theatre'. (This wedge is taken up in Chapter 2, 'The Virginia Company', which locates the Blackfriars not in the theatre historical past but within its local histories.) Even a coffeehouse around the corner gestures to the folds of time in its name 'By and By', and the audience enters the Blackfriars as though through a geological cut, encountering strata of time and place as they approach the playhouse. To walk to the Blackfriars from a local restaurant – say 'Zynodoa', named 'in homage to a Native American legend that gave the valley its name'[11] – is to pass through narrow streets lined with well-preserved examples of nineteenth-century American architecture. The architecture cannot be more precisely called 'southern' or 'eastern' since the best-preserved buildings downtown were designed by the renowned nineteenth-century architect T. J. Collins, who used the town as a template to try out various styles. Downtown Staunton includes architectural variations on Italianate, Eastlake, Chateauesque, Shingle Style and Queen Anne styles, as well as churches that range from Gothic and Romanesque revival to the Temple House of Israel modelled after a dream of the Middle East. Thus, a brief stroll down Beverley Street – the town's main thoroughfare – discovers a mock-Tudor cinema, a Federalist office building, a Beaux Arts bank, a Spanish Colonial train station and so on. Proud of its Virginia heritage, Staunton, nonetheless, isn't quite sure where it stands.

The Blackfriars itself, from the exterior, blends in well with its surroundings. Indeed, among the principal architect Tom McLaughlin's principal achievement was to essay a building in dialogue with its surroundings but with its own distinctive voice.

> The primary form of the Playhouse is a large, simple gable with overhanging, bracketed eaves reminiscent of many of the historical structures in downtown Staunton [...] My objective was to create a building profile that closely echoes the rich and varied roofscapes created by Staunton's many historical structures.[12]

The Blackfriars has been wittily described as having 'an upscale Alpine look, like a fire station in Telluride', but its profile harmonizes features of the past and present, of here and there, in a remarkably congruent manner.[13] It was imperative to McLaughlin that the playhouse be a 'good architectural neighbour',[14] and it is. The playhouse's exterior fabric announces its engagement with local history – its brick cladding echoes Staunton's ubiquitous brick sidewalks and ubiquitously bricked homes – while a garland of oak beams over its glass doors hints at the treasure in the playhouse itself. If it has a style, it's Southern Tudor.

Once inside the front doors, the audience finds a lobby that looks blandly corporate. Black slate floor, brightly painted drywall, recessed lighting. It could be the lobby of a Holiday Inn Express or the atrium of a low-fi medical practice. This, too, was the architect's intent: to wrap a replica of a seventeenth-century playhouse in a contemporary shell. From the street, to the lobby, to the playhouse itself, the audience passes through thresholds of history. Of course, the lobby has features that distinguish it from a budget hotel. The first thing an audience faces when they enter is a placard that offers a potted history of the original Blackfriars. It would be pedantic, if it weren't thematically useful for this introduction, to point out that the 'history' gets a few things wrong.

In 1599, eight members of Shakespeare's acting company, the Lord Chamberlain's Men, formed a corporation and became 'sharers' in the Globe and in the Blackfriars Playhouse, England's first indoor theatre. In 1999, Shenandoah Shakespeare's eight Principal Sharers joined to assure the re-creation of the Blackfriars in Staunton.

As Chapter 1 takes up below, this is a romantic version of James Burbage's chancy real estate venture in the late 1590s (it is also inaccurate: the 'eight members of Shakespeare's acting company' did not buy into the Blackfriars in 1599). The lobby-placard suggest an act of collective will on the part of Shakespeare and his fellows – an Elizabethan version of Mickey Rooney's 'Let's get together and put on a show' – rather than a canny real estate move bound up in the intricacies of Elizabethan litigation and reflective of James Burbage's proto-venture-capitalism. Surely unintentionally, this 'history of the Blackfriars' echoes the programme in producing an errant version of the past, one that takes aim at it but misses the mark. Again, however, the ASC's historiography is not particularly interested in history in fact. A theatre company might be forgiven for investing in imagination rather than in verifiability. Indeed, yet another part of the pre-show pitch – the alms asking bit that, itself, faintly remembers monastic origins – points the patron to the ASC's 'invest in imagination' fund, which keeps the operation viable. It is fair to say that the ASC itself has invested heavily in imagination, and so leads the way so that others might follow.

From the lobby, the audience enters the playhouse itself, through solid wooden doors which have a distinctive portal effect. As Jeremy Lopez writes, 'when you walk into the Blackfriars, you feel transported – not really into "another time," which is the obvious intention of a theatre like the Globe, but rather and more simply into another place […] You don't quite notice that it's happening, but you suddenly notice that it *has* happened.'[15] Inside the visitor finds a fabric of Virginia white oak, except for the *frons* that has been covered in paint to look vaguely neo-classical, a hieroglyph for the lacquered effect of the Blackfriars' authenticities: beneath the antiquing patina is real Virginia oak, which is, a tour-script instructs the guide to tell the tourist, 'the closest thing we have in America to English oak'. Virginia oak signifies the oak of the English original, but then the paint that obscures it is meant to represent the Jacobean efforts to disguise English oak as Italian marble. As mentioned above, the *frons* is flanked by electric 'Exit' signs (since fire codes presumably precluded ones that say '*Exeunt*'). Thus the only apparent text in the playhouse proper orders the visitor to leave, in case they get the spins from the vertigoes of history.

The two-tiered playhouse is illuminated by nine heavy, hanging chandeliers, crowned with 248 flame-shaped 'candle-bulbs'. High above, just below the ceiling, the playhouse is ringed with a coronet of ten spotlights, which bounce their light off the ceiling to illuminate the playing space below. The chandeliers – and wall sconces – thus provide a pleasing but ineffectual light, and the spotlights above illuminate their inadequacy. An audience in the orchestra thus gazes up at the roof – the best-lit part of the house – and spies a cluster of modern spotlights through the branches of wrought-iron but electric chandeliers. The spotlights were not exactly part of the original plan. No attempt has been made to obscure them, however, and the spotlights abet other practices to ameliorate the idea that this is a strict reconstruction and/or that the play is a simulation. (Shakespeare didn't sleep here, the spotlights announce.) The trick is to keep re-enactment at bay, to hold off the world of Living History museums – the kind at work just a few miles from the Blackfriars at the American Frontier Culture museum, which is first-stop shopping if you run out of candles or flax.

The spotlights were added to illuminate the actors – whose features didn't show well under the 'original' light – since actors are among the things the audience is there to see. The performers first appear in the balcony above, usually a handful of actors in various stages of artful disarray (since they're not *acting* just yet). The actors' *déshabillé* once more finesses the temporalities at play on the threshold. What one then *hears* are songs from bands with contemporary cred like the Decemberists, Okkervill River, Magnetic Fields, Black Keys and so on, songs easily adapted to acoustic instruments that do not require electric amplification that might counter the 'we do it with the lights on' ethos (lights powered by the same electricity it might take to run amplifiers. You haven't *really* lived until you've seen a group of actors in doublet-and-hose play an acoustic cover of a song by Radiohead). It would be easy to conclude that the modern music ironizes the operations of what's to come, gives the actors plausible deniability against the charge that *they really think they're in the past*. Easy to put the music down to irony – a cheap transistor that connects two nodes of being without making a spark. Easy, but inaccurate. For the blend of pre- and postmodern performance idioms is of a piece with the company's loose way with history, its confusing but winning translation of antique performance practices into a contemporary vernacular ('the Elizabethans had an all-male acting company, so we cast women as men ...', etc.) Along with 'Blackfriars Historicity', then, this book attempts in its second half to develop a 'Blackfriars Performativity', an explanation of the performance practices that modulate past and present. The actors demonstrate a real delicacy, however roughly handled, in the treatment of authenticity and authority – which dress out of one trunk – a way of gesturing towards history without becoming beholden to it. Again, the elision between past and present – from a commitment to Shakespeare's text and its connection to a modern audience – is smoothly, charmingly, easily handled. If there's any anxiety about the complex spatio-temporal negotiation at work here, it's worn lightly on the actor's puffy sleeves.

This walk through various thresholds leads up to the pre-show talk, which gives over directly into the play proper. Of course the play has begun as soon as the audience enters the playhouse, if not before. Even or especially when the ASC is not presenting a history play, the play of history is always on at the Blackfriars. At best, this toggling between the past and present can destabilize an audience, productively destabilize them, that is. At its worst, the pre-show talk and all it represents can erode the very ontology of performance, turning presentation into simulation (or *simulacrum* since the origin of imitation here is imperfectly understood). It seems to go down easy, however, since it is administered so casually. At best it charms the audience into an alertness to the oddity of the experience. A performer could do far worse than play to an oddly alert audience, or an alertly odd one. The ASC purposefully produces this audience, as they make time and place for them as well as for the play.

*

The ASC's threshold events ably coordinate time and place then – the multiple times of past and present, the multiple places of here and there. The company is simply, or complexly, 'making history', the gerund signalling the process by which a theatre company forges history by remembering but also productively forgetting it. As detailed later, this forged history is an inevitable starting over, a return to first principles (even if it often forgets what's come after). Chapter 1 takes up that question at more length, but it remains in this introduction to set the stage for that chapter with a brief sketch of the origins of the American Shakespeare Center, in particular the way in which the 'Shenandoah Shakespeare Express' – a local movement – stabilized into an ambitious claim for national dominance signalled by the name 'American Shakespeare Center'.

As noted above, Shenandoah Shakespeare Express was formed in a college classroom at James Madison University in Harrisonburg, Virginia in 1988. In 2013, under the name 'The American Shakespeare Center', the company celebrated the twenty-fifth anniversary of its founding. In those intervening twenty-five years, the company has performed in forty-seven states, five foreign countries, and one US Territory. They have produced fifty-three different titles, having completed the Shakespeare canon just in time for their quarter-century celebration. Over those years, the company estimates that they've delivered over 4,200 total performances to over an estimated 250,000 audience members. They also, in the late 1990s, convinced a town and a lot of donors to fund a $3.78 million reconstruction of an Elizabethan indoor playhouse. By any number of measures, not least by the numbers, the company's reach, growth and success is extraordinary and warrants critical attention.

The story of those twenty-five years – from a company that 'expressed' Shakespeare across the United States to one that 'centered' him in a reimagined English playhouse in central Virginia – is a story of a journey from transience to stability, from a company that made its home on the road to one with its own playhouse. That journey is also a story of retrograde progress, of a company's successful negotiations with the theatrical past and its own place within the 400 year history of Shakespeare and performance. The ASC's evolving names – from 'Shenandoah Shakespeare Express', to 'Shenandoah Shakespeare', to the 'American Shakespeare Center' (ASC) – therefore frame its relationship with theatre history and modern performance culture. On the surface, that relation manifests itself most obviously in spatial terms. A company formed exclusively to tour ultimately succeeds to a playhouse of its own. In so doing, the ASC roughly recapitulates the most successful of the early English playing companies who inspired the ASC's formation. At the same time, while allegiant to the theatrical culture of early modern England, the ASC has simultaneously courted an outsider aesthetic familiar from a range of DIY incarnations in music, film and art. Particularly in its early years, the company positioned itself against 'establishment' Shakespeare, from which it productively differed. An early company logo featured a crude sketch of Converse hi-tops – the sneakers the company members wore in early years – circled by a crown. The SSE had stuck its foot in it, thrust its trainers into the ambit of royalty, perhaps an unwitting jab at the Royal Shakespeare Company (RSC). Talk about sneakers.

All revolutions ultimately capitulate to the terms they once resisted. The 'SSE' once positioned itself against companies like the 'RSC' but now mirrors that company's well-known acronym with 'ASC' democratically replacing the 'Royal' with 'American' and the 'Company' with 'Center'. In early interviews, Ralph Alan Cohen speaks the SSE's origin story as one that grew out of a frustration with the performances at the RSC: 'I took them [students] to productions in London in the mid-1980s', Cohen says, 'but even the Royal Shakespeare Company was pretentious and overproduced at the time'.[16] In other words, the SSE was founded out of antipathy to the RSC – or at least they provided a company of straw men – but now enjoys a more emulative relationship, which cuts both ways. The RSC's theatre spaces now all cite to various degrees the architecture of early modern performance. If the RSC's past was framed by a proscenium, its present thrusts itself into the past along with Staunton's Blackfriars and Shakespeare's Globe. To be strictly accurate, the RSC's Swan and Royal Shakespeare Theatre outdo even the Blackfriars and the Globe in intrusive staging, since their peninsular stages penetrate deeply into the orchestra while the Globe and Blackfriars keep a more demure distance. In any event, the RSC that the SSE was formed to counter-point no long really exists – if ever it did – but then the ASC has also come a long way from its own origins, largely by standing still.

As Chapter 2 explores at more length, the challenge for a successful revolution is to find something else revolting. The ASC began on the margins – always on the run – but has now 'centred' itself in a lavish playhouse, one that reconstructs not a suburban London playhouse – whose neighbourhoods, 'Shoreditch', 'Bankside', inscribed their marginality – but one comfortably ensconced in an early modern version of a gated community. How do you leverage an outsider image when your name announces your centrality? How do you continue to fire the imagination once the straw men have all been burned? How do you wage revolution once you've won? If this book tells a history – or histories – of the ASC, it also offers its founders in Chapter 5 the opportunity to predict the future, or what the history of the ASC will look like at their fiftieth anniversary.

While all theatre companies must reckon with the past, then, the ASC has never been coy about the ways it processes and produces history. As suggested here, the ASC's engagement with Shakespeare's performance history forms an explicit part of its identity. This book focuses in what follows on the ways that the ASC has capitalized on theatre history while forging some of its own. It begins in Chapter 1 by locating the coordinates of the Blackfriars playhouse, in particular the meanings a reconstructed Elizabethan playhouse register within the geographical and symbolic terrain of the American south, with particular attention to Virginia's colonial status and its Civil War heritage. It then moves, in Chapter 2, to an exploration of the permanent revolutions by which the Shakespeare industry invents and reinvents itself. As a company with a complex relationship to 'original practices', the ASC participates within a tradition of revivalism that repeatedly punctuates the more than 400-year performance history of Shakespeare.

After this opening focus on the time and place of the ASC enterprise – on 'Blackfriars Historicity' – the book investigates 'Blackfriars Performativity' (and in doing so switches methodology from archival work to impressionism). From its inception, the company's core commitment has been to playing in universal lighting and, more recently, to the 'Actors' Renaissance Season', which dispenses with directors and the usual weeks of rehearsal time to produce a collaborative, actor-led mini-season within each year's calendar. The book trains particular attention on the ways that these conventions dispose the audience, which shares the spotlight with the company's actors and therefore plays a central role in its operations. Chapter 3 – 'The History of Light' – and Chapter 4 – 'Time Bomb' – move from architecture to artistry, therefore, from time and place to practice and process to explore the work of the ASC where it most matters, on the stage. Finally, the book finishes with a transcription of an interview with the company's founders, giving them the chance to quarrel or query, annotate or emend the conclusions reached herein.

*

This book is not about the original Blackfriars and the company that played there from 1609 through 1642. But it is not *not* about that Blackfriars, or that company. For the concern in Staunton is to do deliberately what more often happens only by chance. To see to it that history repeats itself. This introduction closes, then, with just one more phrase spoken in pre-show addresses at the Blackfriars – though, I will argue, it operates implicitly at more theatres than just one. Because the *first* thing an audience hears at the Blackfriars – before cell phones are hushed, fires invoked, history cited, alms asked – is a welcome to the world's 'only recreation of Shakespeare's indoor playhouse'. At the phrase 'only recreation' the soil probably shifts just slightly over a grave on the Spanish-French border in which the body of Walter Benjamin lies quietly revolving. For the Blackfriars' claim to be the world's only recreation – a unique copy – proudly articulates the impossibility of its position, strung out between a desire to leverage authority upon history's ledge and an ambition to produce an original event. In doing so, the Blackfriars takes a cue from the 1623 folio, whose first editors claimed in the preface to have based their text upon the 'true original copies'. This paradox has a pedigree, then. But the Blackfriars' claim to be simultaneously unique and a copy only makes overt and explicit what's occluded and implied in most theatrical performances, which, regardless of venue or auspices, present original copies (but no less 'true' for that).

In his seminal essay 'The Work of Art in the Age of Mechanical Reproduction', Walter Benjamin points out that the Greeks had only one art form that required mechanical reproduction: the minting of coins. We might conclude from this that money ceased to be art at precisely the point at which all art became money. Thomas Paine was after the same idea when, in his 'Dissertations ... on Paper Money', he called it 'alchemy by another name', since '[t]he alchemist may cease his labors, and the hunter after the philosopher's stone go to rest, if paper can be metamorphosed into gold and silver, or made to answer the same purpose in all cases. Gold and silver are the emissions of nature: paper is the emission of art.'[17] Art, in other words, derives its reproductive strategies from coining, a strategy we honour and obscure by using the metaphor of 'coining' to connote creativity. To 'coin a phrase' implies that you've invented a locution. You haven't; you've quoted one. To coin is to quote; to 'create' is to 're-create'. Thus, to 'coin a phrase' both discloses and obscures its meaning, connoting something by stating the opposite. Proverbial language often works this way. We use the phrase 'high and dry' to denote abandonment. But consider the alternative.

Speaking of coined phrases, the recently modish term 're-performance' is itself an oxymoron and seems both born out of and to bear out Benjamin's essay. Oscar Wilde once suggested that the words 'All bad poetry springs from genuine feeling', or all bad poetry is sincerely bad, be inscribed above the entrances to all universities. To paraphrase this remark, the following words of Benjamin might be inscribed above the entrance to the Globe and Blackfriars. 'The presence of the original is the prerequisite to the concept of authenticity.'[18] The extent to which the original inheres throughout multiple acts of iteration over a duration of time is the extent to which authenticity gets mobilized. Live performance tends to oppose this idea. The liveness of live theatre often depends, that is, upon the liquidation of the original *work* to mobilize the authenticity of the current *event*. We could adapt Benjamin and say of most theatre that the *absence* of the original is the prerequisite to the concept of authenticity. Therefore, the extent to which a theatre can erase its exemplars is the degree to which it can become, itself, ever original, always authentic. This is merely to point up the scandal of performance, to recognize, at the Blackfriars, that imitation is the sincerest form. The Blackfriars and Globe do not attempt to erase their exemplars. They proudly paraphrase them.

In Giles Deleuze's work on repetition – a positive model of difference and repetition – a repeated word may look the same, but, as he writes, 'it is not sameness that produces repetition so much as difference. Each repetition of a word is always a different inauguration of that word, transforming the word's history and any context.'[19] (Henri Bergson develops this idea through the image of a repeating bell. Each chime of the bell is singular; it is we who are the same or, making a fetish of sequence, it is we who insist that the bell repeats.[20]) To invert Deleuze's formulation, repetition does not produce sameness but difference. And therefore, paradoxically, the more detailed, the more painstaking the attempt to reproduce or even repeat a theatrical event the greater the implications of an evident difference. 'True history', a Deleuzian commentator points out, 'is anachronism', like a spotlight that illuminates an electric chandelier. If you attend a re-enactment of the battle of Gettysburg, what you notice is not verisimilitude but anachronism, the chief of which is that the corpses are not dead. You'll notice the same thing straight off at the Blackfriars. Theatrical reperformance produces a paradoxical effect – liveness here is not a function of difference but sameness. Writing of the Wooster Group's re-enactment of Grotowski's *Akropolis*, Rebecca Schneider aptly writes, 'the more they get the re-enactment exactly right, the more uncannily *wrong* it begins to feel'.[21] What makes an event at the Blackfriars 'live' is not its commitment to being a one-off, different-every-night phenomenon; what makes a performance at the Blackfriars live is its commitment to re-enactment – which, I'm suggesting, magnifies magnificently its anachronistic liveness.

The Blackfriars experience of history – the way that it processes and produces it – may sound like a textbook case of Baudrillard's simulacrum or Butler's performative drag: of copies without an original referent. Yes, there was an original Blackfriars playhouse, but it is long gone, vanished almost without a trace, and it was never in Staunton in the first place. And yet this isn't *quite* right. The ASC *does* posit an original, though as I've argued here it also attenuates its authenticity by wilfully neglecting historical accuracy. The ASC articulates an historical idea – even ideal, even idyll – and then brings its product into alignment with that ideal as capably as possible. The ASC has a story, and they are sticking to it. As they have done nearly every night for twenty-five years.

The doctrinaire ledger of theatrical principles by which the ASC lives is, then, 'historical' not because of its reference but because of its repetition. That is what this book means by suggesting that the ASC is 'making history', since the ASC's history is makeshift, make do, but always under reconstruction. Every performance at the Blackfriars is a duplication, even a double, if only of itself. A 1999 review unwittingly linked duplication with the ASC's special knack for finessing time and space, writing that the 'company [...] manages to duplicate Elizabethan drama with minimal lights, scenery, and props and are most convincing at establishing time and place'.[22] Ultimately, the ASC's historical practices begin as hypothesis but are made – even forged – each night on the stage. The ASC's relationship to early English practice can seem at times tendentious, always insisting upon itself, but the real work at the ASC is in the announcing of a set of practices and then reproducing them like clockwork.

What looks like duplication is therefore difference. Doubling will emerge as a theme of this book, from the obvious – the ASC's small cast of actors often double roles – to the less so – the ASC 'doubles' history in a variety of ways: they double the past in an attempt to reproduce 'Shakespeare's indoor playhouse' and the practices of playing that went on there, but the ASC's history is also a double one. Tucked into their two names – Shenandoah Shakespeare Express and the American Shakespeare Center – is a two-fold history. Furthermore – as Chapter 4 details – the Blackfriars hosts a divided repertory, Shakespeare's plays, of course, but also a portfolio of Renaissance ones. The larger project of the ASC, at the level of institutional identity, is to prevent doubleness from becoming divisive, duality as fission not fusion. The various doubled histories of the ASC should always, ideally, resolve into one.

The ASC occupies one more seam, then, not just the one between the here and there, between the now and then, but between the original and the copy, the precedent and the citation, between the first and the next. One way to close the gap, as Chapter 2 argues, is to pretend that you're the 'first next', the first ones to get back to where it all began. In that way, the ASC works out, or in, the gap between 'nothing new to see here' and the 'something else'. First, however, this book returns to 'where it all began', on the banks of the Thames circa 1606, where a Virginia company set their sights to the west and their caps for profit.

1

The Virginia Company

Staunton, Virginia, is called the 'Queen City of the Shenandoah Valley'. The reason it is called the 'Queen City' is a bit mysterious, but then Staunton also features a full-scale replica of Anne Hathaway's cottage – a must-miss attraction – as well as a recreation of a seventeenth-century English playhouse and an annual celebration called a 'Victorian Festival' – held, confusingly, on Shakespeare's birthday. It is worth mentioning that Queen Victoria never technically held sway over Virginia. A friend of the author once referred to this event as Staunton's 'celebration of being white', which is possibly unjust. It is at least fair, however, to suggest that when William Shakespeare and Queen Victoria compete for the April headlines, you're in the middle of some pretty hardcore Anglophilia. But then Staunton, Virginia, is in Staunton, *Virginia*; English, at least on its mother's side. Its name 'honours' the hymeneal status of England's first Queen Elizabeth. Jamestown – its first English settlement – her successor. The mascot of the state's flagship university is 'The Cavalier'. The state bird is the monocle.

Therefore, it seems altogether natural – or, at least, not altogether *un*natural – that the world's 'only recreation of Shakespeare's indoor playhouse' should be in Virginia. Of course, one could also argue that the Blackfriars is in Virginia because a graduate student named Ralph Alan Cohen from Montgomery, Alabama, working under the great Shakespearean scholar George Walton Williams at Duke

University in the 1970s, landed a job teaching Shakespeare in the English department at James Madison University in Harrisonburg, Virginia, where he met a student named Jim Warren. And the rest, as they say, is history. In these terms, though, the building of a Blackfriars in Staunton, Virginia, is mere happenstance, sheer coincidence. As Catherine Belsey writes, there are 'very few coincidences in cultural history'.[1] While it can seem coincidental that the new Blackfriars is in Virginia – an accident possibly of biography and geography – when viewed from a broader historical perspective, the Virginia Blackfriars seems right at home.

This first chapter considers the primary location in which the ASC plays: Staunton, Virginia. It traces the connections between the early modern and the modern Blackfriars and finds resonance in the presence of a Blackfriars reconstruction in the geographical heart of Jacobean adventurism – a relationship neatly telegraphed by the new Blackfriars' address: 'South Market Street'. This focus locates the Blackfriars on a geo-political map of colonial relations, one played out over four centuries on a circum-Atlantic scale, a map perforated by Jacobean adventurers and their dark cargo.

Chapter 1 also considers matters closer to home, for the Staunton Blackfriars gathers immediate meaning from the two institutions it sits between: The 'Stonewall Jackson Hotel' and the 'Dixie Movie Theater' (closed in 2014, the name's still on the marquee, as it would be even if someone agreed to take it down). The two names remind the visitor not of global but of local history, not of the remote but of the recent past, of the forces and farces that have shaped the American South. These two local landmarks inevitably condition the audience in certain ways when they attend a play at the Blackfriars. Invariably, inescapably, though perhaps only unconsciously, the audience is immersed in the immediate, physical location of the playhouse, one that registers its 'Market' presence, while also reminding the visitor of the peculiar institutions that haunt the American South. This chapter explores the various ways in which the Blackfriars mutes or harmonizes the histories and authenticities of the architecture that surrounds it, both near and far, not least the toxic local history memorialized by the two buildings in whose shadows it sits.

'1642 London, England … 2001 Staunton, Virginia', so a promotional ad for the opening of the new Blackfriars proclaimed in September 2001. The ellipsis is in the original, which serves as both an editorial remark and an historical one. That ellipsis covers a lot of ground and elides a lot of time. It's a long way from London to Staunton and a long time from the seventeenth century to the twenty-first. One way to connect the dots is to fold history in on itself, obscuring a number of points in between. Still, an awful lot of history hides down in the folds. Some of those histories are amusing, some of them intriguing, some of them banal, and many of them horrific – it can get dark down in the creases. This chapter cannot claim to offer a comprehensive history of Shakespeare in Virginia, but it does unfold it – discovering a few stories hidden in the seams – to connect the dots between London, England, and Staunton, Virginia, between 1606 and 2016.

Virginia richly valued

On or around Shakespeare's 44th birthday, the Virginia Company made landfall on the southern edge of Chesapeake Bay. Within a month, they'd established the Jamestown settlement forty miles upstream on the James River, named for the king who chartered the company in 1606 to establish a commercial foothold in North America[2] (as well as to find a passage to China, which only seems retrospectively insane). Within a few years, another of the King's companies secured a foothold of their own on the Thames River, in the liberty of Blackfriars in the City of London. Both companies sported a royal warrant for their joint-stock ventures and, therefore, combined proto-capitalist lateral integration with a neo-conservative patronage model. Both companies were all-male enterprises. Both their primary products – tobacco and plays – extinguished themselves in the act of their own expression and left their consumers with a head full of fumes and a taste for more.

This form of Fluellenism – there is a river in London, and there is also moreover a river in Virginia and there are companies on both – is obviously facile, but just as obviously highlights the latticed networks of patronage, real estate, exploration, exploitation, adventurism, colonialism, slavery and commerce which link the new Blackfriars in Staunton, Virginia, back to the old one on the banks of the Thames. That network features some familiar names – familiar to Shakespeareans at least – but casts them in surprising roles. The network also runs through some familiar places, from London, England, to Staunton, Virginia, but with some surprising way stations in between. A river runs by both Blackfriars; Staunton's is just a long way downstream.

*

Shakespeareans know William Henry Herbert, Earl of Pembroke, and Philip Herbert, Earl of Montgomery, primarily because their names dominate signature A2 in the Shakespeare folio of 1623, for which they served as principal dedicatees. Members of the most important literary coterie of the day, the powerful brothers patronized, according to Alan Stewart, '250 writers […] including such luminaries as Spenser, Jonson, Thomas Nashe, playwrights Philip Massinger, John Ford and George Chapman and Sir Thomas Browne'.[3] Shakespeare is not on that list since it was Heminges and Condell who – out of their 'feare, and rashnesse' – dedicated their enterprise to 'your LL' ('LL' stands for 'Lordships' not, as today in the US, 'limited liability', although that seems to have been one thing H. and C. had in mind). The dedication reminds the Herberts that they favoured Shakespeare during his lifetime and asks that they adopt his orphans. This language is familiar, even formulaic. Patronage and parenthood are nearly cognate terms. The 'office to the dead', which Heminges and Condell perform, is cast in conventional tropes that delineate the links between an author's corpse and his corpus.

But Heminges and Condell close their dedication with something far weirder. They offer up Shakespeare's plays as a kind of burnt offering: 'we most humble consecrate [...] these remaines of your servant Shakespeare.' In so doing, they cite those 'many Nations' that '(we have heard) had not gummes & incense [and so] obtained their requests with a leavened Cake. It was no fault to approach their Gods, by what meanes they could'.

What had Heminges and Condell heard of those many nations who appeased their Gods with cake not gummes? Or, for that matter, how had they heard of them? Had they been reading tales of foreign travel – like, say, Thomas Strachey's reports of wrack and redemption in the Bermudas or his *Histoire of Traveaile into Virginia Britannia* (1610)? Had they read much earlier reports like Thomas Hariot's *True Report of Virginia* (1588) or Hakluyt's translations of De Soto's expedition, published in April 1609 as *Virginia Richly Valued*? Had they cocked an ear to the buzz of news out of Virginia in 1609, including *Nova Britannia: Offering Most Excellent Fruites by Planting in Virginia*? What did they make of the broadsides and sermons advertising a world of opportunities across the wide Atlantic, including Robert Gray's sermon *Good Speed to Virginia*?[4] While we ask what they had been reading, we might also ask what they'd been smoking, since chief among the 'Excellent Fruites' offered to planters in Virginia was the tobacco leaf, one of the few lastingly profitable returns from speculation in the American market, and which, as we will see below, is intricately tied to the drama of the new world. Tobacco is just one burnt offering the new world offered the old.

How Heminges and Condell heard of the 'many nations' is a mystery, but that they did is virtually certain. Reports both true and false, of Virginia and elsewhere, filled the air and the bookstalls of London in the 1600s. This may explain why their dedication to the Herberts opens with a topos of native humility, but closes with a citation of strange lands and stranger practices. For the Herberts' part, when they read the folio's dedication – *if* they read the folio's dedication – one of the many nations to which their thoughts may have turned might have been North America, where their money was currently circling the drain. For the Herberts were among the 650 principal investors in the Virginia Company, first incorporated in 1606 and goosed with multiple infusions of cash across the coming years. From the start, the Virginia Company 'attracted many of the greatest Jacobean patrons of learning', and Philip himself sat on the council of the company from 1612, helping to steer its stubbornly optimistic course through setback after setback.[5] (Incidentally, Henry Condell was also a member of the Virginia Company, as well as the King's, though he might not have known it. For in addition to the 650 'adventurers' named in the company charters, over fifty London livery companies invested as well, including the Grocers, of which Condell was free.[6]) Shakespeare's first folio opens then with a cryptic gesture towards Jacobean adventurism, and Jacobean adventurers. Heminges and Condell went 'native', coming before the adventuring Herberts like the benighted pagans of foreign lands who offer leavened cake instead of more profitable returns.

Their timing may not have been great, however, since by the publication of the Shakespeare folio, the news out of Virginia was decidedly dire. During that spring came reports of an Indian massacre that left over 350 dead, the latest head count of colonists who perished on the banks of the James. The optimism of the early adventurers had guttered, and Virginia looked increasingly like good money after bad. The timing doesn't *quite* work out, but Heminges and Condell could even have taken in *A Tragedy of the Plantation of Virginia* up at the Curtain in August 1623, a lost play that Henry Herbert found to be a bit too long and a tad profane.[7] (In keeping with the run of Virginia's bad luck, the play may have finally brought down the Curtain, for it was the last entry that Henry

Herbert, Master of Revels, made for the playhouse before it finally closed.) On 17 April of that year, the case of the Virginia Company came before the Privy Council, who wished to look into 'the carriage of the whole business'.[8] On 24 May 1624, the court recalled the Virginia charter and nailed the coffin on the Virginia Company. Heminges and Condell had reason, that is, to glance but elliptically at foreign adventures, if they intended to glance at them at all. The Herberts were out at least 12 pounds, 10 shillings a piece, the cost that entitled those who subscribed – no doubt with a combination of fear and rashness – to what profits might arise from the Virginia Company, profits that seemed to have gone up in smoke.

If 1623/24 was a bad one for the Virginia Company, it was a good one for Shakespeare, possibly his best. In that year, he pivoted for once and for all from patronage into posterity. And if 1624 *was* a bad year for Shakespeare's last patrons, it was an even worse one for his first. Henry Wriothesley – dedicatee of Shakespeare's *Venus and Adonis* (1592/93) – died that year, leaving a literary legacy not just to Shakespeareans, but also to Virginians. The story is a complicated one but bears abbreviation since it lays some unlikely tracks between Shakespeare and Virginia. It reminds us as well, if we need to be reminded, that Shakespeare's literary patrons had far more on their minds than narrative poetry and verse drama. The fruits of the English Renaissance that they wished to cultivate offered more immediately profitable returns than Shakespeare's ultimate and unlikely fame, or at least so was their hope.

Wriothesley had been even more involved in the Virginia Company than the Herberts, and he was far more implicated in its disillusion than they. Southampton became a member in 1609 and its treasurer nine years later. However, by the 1620s the company was going under, sucked into a factional whirlpool as well as dismal conditions in swampy Virginia. In 1622, Nathaniel Butler published *The Unmasked Face of Our Colony in Virginia*, a grim rebuke to the heady publications of the century's first decade. For a complex of reasons, James wanted the Virginia Company put down, and it was finally and formally dissolved on 24 May 1624, as mentioned above. Never the king's first choice to lead the Company, Southampton was implicated in its mismanagement.[9] Thus, according to an early biographer, King James 'crushed Southampton out of the Colony' in the final year of both of their lives.[10] Southampton died in the Netherlands, not England, perhaps a fitting end for an earl whose name and aims frequently went south.

James' attempt to 'crush' Southampton from the colonies was not altogether successful. About a year before the Company dissolved, Southampton's ally Nicholas Ferrar (or Sir John Danvers, it is unclear) had surreptitious copies made of the Company's records, which he passed on to Wriothesley, who was glad to have them since they were, 'testimonials of all our upright dealings in the business of the Company and the [Virginia] Plantation'.[11] It is unclear who inherited the papers upon Southampton's death. Some accounts say Sir Edward Sackville, others Southampton's son, who became Lord High Treasurer and lived until 1667. Accounts agree, at least, that the papers passed into the colonies after his son's death, ended up in the hands of Thomas Jefferson and, ultimately, the Library of Congress, where they still reside.

The Company's records map a familiar route by which literary legacies made their way from London to Washington. Shortly before the death of Southampton's son, William Byrd, auditor and receiver general of the colony of Virginia, purchased the manuscript records from the Earl for sixty guineas. They then passed into the hands of the Reverend William Stith, who was living at his glebe on the James River. He used the material to produce his *History of Virginia* in 1746. The books *then* fell into the hands of his brother in law, Peyton Randolph, first president of the Continental Congress. When *he* died unexpectedly in Philadelphia in 1775, his library was purchased by Thomas Jefferson, who always had a keen eye for a bibliographical bargain. When the US government purchased Jefferson's library in 1815 the papers were included in the lot. They are 'bound in two volumes, folio, and contain the Company's transactions from 28th April 1619, until 7th June, 1624', roughly the term of Southampton's tenure. The first folio concludes with these words:

> Memorand re, that wee, Edward Waterhouse and Edward Collingwood, secretaries of the Companies for Virginia and Sumer Islands [Bermuda] have examined and compared the booke going before ... with the originall booke of courts itself. And doe find this booke to be a true and p'fect copie of the said originall courte booke.[12]

The statement concludes that 'this copie doth truly agree with the originall itself', and so the testimonial not only resonates for Shakespeareans who hear an echo of another folio that claims to present 'perfect copies' but for theatrical revivalists who build copies of playhouses that agree with the original itself.

The story of how Thomas Jefferson got his hands on Southampton's records is contested as well – not least by Jefferson, who claimed in a letter to have purchased them from a 'zealous antiquarian' who had lifted them from William Byrd's library.[13] The fact remains that Southampton's records of his final colonial adventure – an unhappy one – made their way, appropriately enough, to Virginia, though Southampton never did. (The 'Hampton River' and 'Hampton Roads' of Virginia mark, if not exactly honour, his involvement there.) Shakespeareans may usually associate Southampton with Shakespeare's early years, as a dedicatee of *Venus and Adonis* in the early 1590s. Roughly thirty years later, however, Southampton staked his claim in the colonies of Virginia, solidifying a different kind of literary heritage since the two folios live at the Library of Congress, in 'a steel safe in the manuscript room, with other priceless manuscripts',[14] just across the street from the Folger Shakespeare Library, where a 1593 quarto of *Venus and Adonis* also resides. Borne on the currents of speculation, colonialism, exoneration, bibliographical zeal, and literary fortune hunting, these documents – prepared thirty years apart and in a city thousands of miles away – came to rest in the capitol of the new world, separated by just a few hundred yards and under lock and key on East Capitol Street.

At the very least, then, in the network that runs from Heminges and Condell through Philip and Henry Herbert, from the Earl of Southampton to Jefferson of Monticello, and from London to Jamestown we can trace just a few lay lines that connect the London Blackfriars on the banks of the Thames with the Staunton Blackfriars, not far from the James which flows into the sea that separates England and America. Shakespeare's first and last literary patrons were primary stakeholders in the Virginia Company and so important links in the chain of events that eventually led, in 2001, to the building of the new Blackfriars in Staunton. Shakespeare's most important patrons are also among Virginia's.

This arcane history may seem to involve Shakespeare but obliquely and Staunton even more so. Southampton's involvement with Shakespeare's career – and colonial careering – is hardly the stuff of headline news for modern residents of Staunton, Virginia. Except that it was. On 29 April 1904, the *Staunton Spectator and Vindicator* ran a front-page story about the folios under the headline 'Early Days in Virginia'. The lede ran,

> Henry Wriothesley, Earl of Southampton and Baron of Titchfield, to whom Shakespeare dedicated his 'Venus and Adonis,' was once the owner of two big manuscript folios, now in the Library of Congress, which are soon to be copied by order of Congress. The manuscript is a record of the transactions of the Virginia Company of London, and throws a flood of light on the early history of that colony.[15]

The *Staunton Spectator* made the connection that this chapter has charted, tracing Southampton through Shakespeare to Virginia to Thomas Jefferson and finally to Washington, DC. It is unclear why Congress chose 1904 to order that the manuscripts be printed. Perhaps the coming tercentenary of the founding of Jamestown prompted the Library to take timely action. Had a Staunton burgher sat down with the *Spectator* in late April, 1904, he might have paused over the astonishing leaps of time and place in the opening two sentences, including the fact that the Earl of Southampton had patronized a frankly erotic poem as well as a coldly colonial adventure that led to the settlement of the state in which he lived. And while we are summoning spectral readers, had Southampton read the account he may have been pleased to learn that he lived into posterity, but surely he would have started at learning that the first thing that history mentioned about him, after his titles, was that he was the dedicatee of some erotic juvenilia. The manuscript, according to the *Spectator*, throws a 'flood of light' on Virginia's early history, but the *history* of the manuscripts themselves – from seventeenth-century London to twentieth-century Washington, from the hands of Southampton to the hands of Thomas Jefferson – throws a flood of light as well, in which is illuminated a living link between William Shakespeare and Jamestown, Virginia.

The Pocahontas exception

Like his patron, Shakespeare also never made it to Virginia – probably, he may have a taken a gap year during his 'lost' ones – but he showed up at the 300th anniversary of the Jamestown settlement in a pageant by George Frederic Viett called, *Pocahontas, the Virginia Nonpareil*. This also made headline news in Staunton. In 1906, the *Spectator* recorded the theatrical event in all its glory, if 'glory' is precisely the word for a play that enlists Shakespeare as a champion of racial purity – as well as colonial adventuring, forced marriage and the repatriation of native Americans. Right next to a feature called 'The Language of Umbrellas', the *Spectator* describes one arresting feature of the show:

The playwright has made a daring innovation in the introduction of the character of Shakespeare on the stage. The
Bard of Avon appears in the first act where, in a fine oration
he wishes God speed to the Colonists as they depart from
Blackwall, England to plant the first permanent English
speaking colony on American soil.[16]

It is tempting simply to reproduce the ghastly play in its
entirety since it adumbrates the latticework of colonialism,
racism, genocide, tobacco, and Anglo-Saxon triumphalism
that underwrites Virginia's English settlement – and gives it
a Shakespearean benediction to boot. But then you'd have to
read it.

Shakespeare's cameo is only the most surprising feature in
a play that advertises its own accuracy. In the preface, Viett
boasts that the play is 'historically correct in every essential
detail' before excusing Shakespeare's farewell address as
a 'piece of dramatic license, but one for which may be
advanced the double claim of probability and consistency
backed by authentic historical suggestion'. Viett found that
suggestion in John Esten Cooke's *The Virginia Comedians:
or, Old Days in the Old Dominion* (1854), which conjec-
tures a friendship between William Shakespeare and John
Smith and upon which Viett 'hung our cloak of fancy'.[17]
The purpose of this 'fancy' is all too plain: in the opening
scene, at the Mermaid Tavern on the eve of departure,
Shakespeare orates over the company and foresees their
success in Virginia, calling them the vanguard of that 'Saxon
genius and Saxon speech […] / that great Saxon tide whose
flood / Shall fertilize and bless the earth'.[18] Talk about ferti-
lizer. Shakespeare's final words to the Virginia Company
– met by '*Tremendous applause from company*' – are 'Fare
you, then, forth upon your destined way, / "Until no wind
can sweep the earth / That bears not [*sic*] echo of our English
tongue"'.[19] If Shakespeare's appearance is surprising, all
the more so is that he comes across as an early modern
Brownshirt with a fondness for blank verse.[20]

George Frederic Viett was a minor poet of Norfolk, Virginia, who, deep in thrall to Robert Browning, published several books of poetry in the early twentieth century, including *The Deeper Harmonies, and other poems*, in 1905. Among Viett's deepest harmonies was Victorian racialism, what historian Stuart Anderson calls 'Anglo-Saxonism', the notion of 'the innate racial superiority of the people who were descended from the ancient Anglo-Saxon invaders of Britain'.[21] The heyday of 'Anglo-Saxonism' came in the late nineteenth century and was a 'vital ingredient in English and American thought' of the time.[22] This context explains why Viett has Shakespeare laud the Virginia adventurers as 'of the tribe whence Vikings came',[23] a description that otherwise baffles. Viett's investment in this fake genealogy – from the halls of Asgard to the shores of Virginia – comes together at the play's conclusion when the 'allegorical figures of Columbia and Britannia, Uncle Sam and John Bull' harmonize in the singing of the 'Star-Spangled Banner' and 'God Save the King', a true English-speaking union that whitewashes any Anglo-American dissent. What's a few armed skirmishes over taxation when Uncle Sam and John Bull are both Vikings at heart?

Victorian racialism also explains the play's deeper racial harmonies. As Uncle Sam and John Bull shake hands, the '*Curtain falls upon [a] grand tableau of Indians, colonists and their wives, and allegorical figures grouped appropriately*'.[24] Grouping figures appropriately preoccupied Viett but also troubled him since he had to explain what makes Pocahontas just so 'nonpareil'. Viett suggests that she had 'perceptions and feelings entirely apart from her race'. Despite the Pocahontas exception, his feelings for 'her race' are fraught. He simultaneously both recoils from and celebrates her tribe. They are 'blood thirsty and cruel', but they treasure 'their freedom and [prefer] death to the least link of bondage'.[25] Sort of like Vikings. Indeed, Viett struggles to find the pitch while eulogizing the 'red children of Virginia' who have, faded away. They 'did give the English a little land,' and from that little land came forth a swarm of black and white, that drove them from their hunting grounds, over the hills, and over the hills again. And there was no place of sanctuary, for wherever they halted, the cunning, well-armed stranger came, and there they left more of their dead and the dead of the enemy – and again to the mountains! But the rising tide was ever rising, and it washed them away, and so it was, and so it will ever be with those who in dumb freedom stand 'to stem the march of the majestic world'.[26]

The white tide rises, the red recedes, which Viett celebrates but with some poignancy (though the next paragraph opens with 'But, now to happier memories'). He concludes of the native Americans that when the 'balance is struck by the great Accountant, the American Indian will be found more sinned against than sinning'.[27] Inappositely quoting Lear, Viett imagines the American Indian as abject other, vanished on a blood tide. One meaning of 'nonpareil' is unmatched, which it is easy to be if you're the only one left.

Inconveniently for Viett's poetry though not for his pageant, the American Indian had not been entirely washed away. Viett supposes that there was 'no place of sanctuary' for the indians, but the US established Indian reservations toward that end, although mainly to group them appropriately. This worked out in Viett's favour, for in a cruel irony the pageant was, according to the *Staunton Spectator and Vindicator*, 'supposed to introduce real Indians into the play for the group parts and the war dances and for this purpose the Secretary of the Interior will be appealed to in order to secure the red men from a government reservation'.[28] At the end of *Pocahontas*, while white actors playing John Bull and Uncle Sam shake hands, 'real Indians' stand by, mute witnesses to their own annihilation. Perhaps Viett was right after all. A reservation is not a sanctuary if you can be forcibly secured to perform in a play about your own annihilation.

Viett's ambivalence about the fate of the American Indian is in stark contrast with his view of black Americans. Viett's Indians are honoured in their absence, ennobled by their extinction. By contrast, it is the 'remarkable fecundity of the negro race' which is a 'matter which no real statesman can view with tranquility'. And that fecundity begins in Jamestown, for Viett describes the arrival in Virginia of 'twenty negroes' in 1619 as a 'dark and monstrous' birth.[29] These were the 'first negro slaves introduced upon the North American Continent, and thus it was that in its infancy, this land of America became the meeting-place of the races – for some the better, and for some the worse'. Viett keeps the 'negroes' off the stage. They are not among the appropriate groups who silently consent to the play's ending pageant. There were some notes that even Viett could not harmonize since they, unlike the Indian, are not part of happier memories but of a troubling present.

The Blackfriars only comes up once in the play, the Globe, never – except when Shakespeare is rhapsodizing about global Saxon domination. In the Mermaid Tavern, an Irish adventurer named 'O'Trigger' hears that Shakespeare is on his way and exclaims, 'Holy smoke! I kin hindorse the gintleman. Hav'nt I attinded at Blackfriar's whin he raised me in me seat with hinthusiasm'.[30] (Viett's historical accuracy does not extend to theatre history, since the Blackfriars was still hosting boy companies at the time of the play's setting.) 'Holy smoke' would make a fine epitaph for the Virginia Company since it marries sanctity with profit. In fact, 'Holy Smoke' would make a good name for a pageant to celebrate the 500th anniversary of the Jamestown settlement in 2106 – perhaps a twenty-first century Viett could stage a closing tableau featuring the marriage of the allegorical figures of Shakespeare and Pocahontas, two nonpareils whose union produces Virginia.

Viett's play does feature one marriage, a group one since the colonists realize that the Saxon tide is likely to ebb without women. Thus, in the Staunton newspaper's frank synopsis, 'The play ends with the arrival of the cargo of maids who came from England to be the wives of the colonists, the price for each maid being set at 120 pounds of tobacco'.[31] If there is anything discordant about a group of colonists trading a packet of smokes for some English wives, those strains dissolve beneath a '*General dance*' to '*Mendellsohn's* [sic] *wedding march ... Indians doing native dances around and between others*'.[32] Thus genocide, forced marriage and the trade in humans – 'cargo of maids' is nicely judged – all keep time with Felix Mendelssohn's 1842 'Wedding March', written to accompany Shakespeare's *A Midsummer Night's Dream*. Holy smoke.

It is tempting to revel in smug superiority at the play's clumsy conscription of Shakespeare in the cause of all that is white and right and end up – in Stephen Booth's terms – 'accusing the past of being the past'. The play, however, is intricately tied up with all-too recent history since Viett's Anglo-Saxonism blistered into a series of horrific actions taken by the Virginia General Assembly. In the 1920s, the Anglo-Saxon Club of America persuaded the Virginia Assembly to pass the 'Racial Integrity Act' and what came to be known as 'The Sterilization Act'. The 'Racial Integrity Act' decreed that the racial composition of every Virginian be recorded at birth, which produced the infamous 'one-drop rule', defining as 'colored' any individual with African ancestry. There was, however, the 'Pocahontas exception', which allowed a person to be considered white if he or she had one-sixteenth or less Native American blood. The exception was made since many of the 'First Families of Virginia' could trace their ancestry to the marriage of Pocahontas and John Rolfe at Jamestown in 1614 (Rolfe grew to prominence and wealth through exporting tobacco). Viett probably would have sympathized since 'The Pocahontas Exception' would have served as a fitting title for his play.

For those who did not enjoy the Pocahontas exception, the law criminalized marriage between white and non-white persons and this was not overturned until the 1967 Supreme Court case of *Loving vs Virginia* (history is a clumsy ironist). Along with the miscegenation laws, the act 'to provide for the sexual sterilization of inmates of State institutions in certain cases' gave hospitals, asylums, and prisons statutory authority to sterilize the 'feeble minded', a statute that predominantly targeted 'non-whites' as defined by the 'Racial Integrity Act'. The infamous Dr Joseph DeJarnette directed the Western State Asylum in Staunton, Virginia; he championed both eugenics and sterilization. In 1938, DeJarnette complained that 'Germany in six years has sterilized about 80,000 of her unfit while the United States – with approximately twice the population – has only sterilized 27,869 in the past 20 years […] The Germans are beating us at our own game.'[33] Obviously, DeJarnette was on the wrong side of history – complaining that you're trailing the Nazis in forced sterilization is hardly a winning argument – but the Western State Asylum still stands, another peculiar institution that's just a stone's throw from the new Blackfriars. It's no longer called that, of course. It's now named 'The Villages'. It's been converted into condos. That's how we do things on Market Street, America.[34]

Shakespeare didn't sterilize anybody nor impede any marriages. That was the work of ardent fantasists with appalling access to power. In early twentieth-century Virginia, however, at the celebration of the 300th anniversary of the Jamestown settlement, Shakespeare was enlisted in the cause of British essentialism and exceptionalism by a young American poet who could barely reckon with the forces he tried to harmonize. It would be hilarious if it weren't so horrifying: vikings breasting the Atlantic rime to found Virginia in Shakespeare's name. Indeed, if the implications were not so awful, Viett's efforts to create a Shakespearean genealogy for Virginia – and himself – would be pathetic. In an 'Afterthought' to his 1900 collection *'Thou Beside me Singing' and other poems*, Viett describes himself as a 'shorn scribbler' who has 'labored handicapped in environments where conditions have been not only unhelpful but distinctively hostile to artistic ambitions'.[35] He also celebrates Shakespeare for his hindsight and foresight, since 'not only did he absorb the past, but he anticipated the future'. Viett had not absorbed much of either, unfortunately. His *Pocahontas* helped produce distinctively hostile conditions for untold others, conditions that Viett probably could not foresee but which he helped abet.

The printed playtext of *Pocahontas, the Virginia Nonpareil* features a colourful profile portrait of the 'Nonpareil' herself, above the words 'Souvenir/Jamestown/Ter-Centennial'. The word 'souvenir' derives from the French for 'remember' and what the play remembers is a fantastic history – I mean that only literally – that supplants the real one and thus encapsulates the way that false memories overwrite real ones in the palimpsestual history of Shakespeare in Virginia. At any celebration of the settlement of Jamestown, its history remains profoundly unsettling.

The African company presents *Richard III*

It is possible to align names, dates and locations and connect the dots of the ellipsis between London's Blackfriars ... and the Staunton one. But Staunton is a long way up the James, much farther than the early adventurers made it, who got about to Richmond, now Virginia's capital. There were, in fact, early efforts – early in the history of the ASC, that is – to reconstruct a Globe in Richmond. (Inverting the history of the Lord Chamberlain's servants, the ASC wanted a Globe but settled for a Blackfriars.) Shakespeare was almost 'centred' in Richmond, then, which would have made for a good history too since the site was named by William Byrd – the temporary warden of Southampton's folios – who was reminded of the view from 'Richmond Hill'. 'Staunton', however, has no apparent connection with Shakespeare – neither Imelda Staunton of the film *Shakespeare in Love* nor Howard Staunton, nineteenth-century chess master, polymath and Shakespeare editor, have any connection to the city. What, then, is the history of Shakespeare in Staunton, the actual history, that is, before the ASC showed up to make some of their own?

According to the local paper in 1896, Staunton didn't much care for 'light tragedy, such as Shakespeare's for instance … but when there comes along a classical work like a "Cake Walk" […] then Staunton's cultivated taste shows at its best and "standing room only" is placarded at the doors early in the evening'.[36] The paper is writing with its tongue in its cheek. A 'Cake Walk' was originally plantation entertainment, a sportive dance, the winner of which 'took the cake', so the *Staunton Spectator* is sharpening its wit on Staunton's dull taste. A 'Cake Walk' is one of those singular phenomena that have a thousand origins. One version claims the cake walks began when slaves hyperbolized the stately waltzes of their white owners, who then turned it into spectator sport before co-opting it themselves. When white men and women participated in a cake walk, then, they were literally making a mockery of themselves. In any event, the paper reminds us to preface any history of Shakespeare in Staunton with the caveat that his success has always been relative. Even today, the Blackfriars is routinely outdrawn by mediocre rock bands playing Foghat covers at the city's outdoor market.

The paper goes on to offer a trenchant analysis of the place of Shakespeare – and the tradition of respectable drama he represents – in Staunton while anticipating some of the founding principles of the ASC over 100 years later:

The real reason why there was an audience at the Cake Walk was because the actors did not look with contempt on the audience. Usually when a bright light in the theatrical world condesends [*sic*] to visit our 'village,' he plays with such contemptuousness for his audience and general surroundings that the audiences invariably swear they will not be duped into wasting time and money on such people. The play is railroaded through as soon after the money is safely in the manager's hands as possible, it is also cut into unrecognizable shape, and the support generally chosen from the loafers on street corners, after the star arrives in town. If the *News* will study this question half as deeply as it has the monetary system, it will find readily why people prefer a Cake Walk to any of Shakesepares plays ever brought to this city.[37]

The ASC, as Chapter 3 details, works overtime to avoid any hint of condescension. Here, however, at the close of the nineteenth century, the *Staunton Spectator* offers a shrewd precis of the history of Shakespeare in Staunton, a history of small-town, chip-on-the-cold-shoulder towards outside agitators, including actors. This wariness persists into the present day. Staunton initially met Ralph Alan Cohen's appeal to build a Blackfriars with coiled eybrows. As he tells it, he was greeted as a northern carpet bagger. He was from Harrisonburg, after all, thirty miles up the road. Even the odd pronunciation of 'Staunton' – 'St*an*ton' – is alleged to derive from a suspicion of outsiders. Local legend suggests the pronunciation developed during the civil war, a linguistic code to ferret out Union spies. The story is implausible, but the fact that it persists speaks some local truth. Even today, if you try to book a train to Staunton, Amtrak's voice-recognition software will not acknowledge the correct pronunciation so that one has to mispronounce the city's name to book a ticket there. Insisting on a pronunciation that differs from how its name is quite evidently spelled would not be the first move of a town eager to court outsiders. In any event, to pronounce 'Staunton' correctly is to participate in a history of ambivalence towards outsiders.

Nineteenth-century Shakespeareans did not have this booking problem. Once the Virginia Central Railroad pushed through the Blue Ridge Mountains in 1854, opening up the route from Richmond to Staunton, the city was transformed. Despite the city's wariness, Staunton was a convenient stop for touring theatre companies, a way-station between Washington to the north-east and Richmond to the south-west, and thespians had no problem finding it. An 1886 map, 'Showing the Railways Leading to the Staunton Opera House', is just one of a mass of nineteenth-century maps and guides designed for touring amusements, many of which prominently feature Staunton's multiple theatres.[38] In fact, Staunton boomed in the nineteenth century in large part due to its location at the nexus of two major north-south, east-west railroad corridors (Staunton has always gathered its energy from being a place where north and south, east and west meet[39]). It formed then an important junction and once boasted several trains a day, at least of few of them carrying Shakespeareans to town. The history of Shakespeare in Staunton is a history of transience. Shenandoah Shakespeare Express (SSE) was only the latest in a long line of touring companies which brought Shakespeare to Staunton. The only difference is that it stayed.

Though a small town, Staunton hosted some big stars during its boom years. When Julia Marlowe disembarked in Staunton in early October 1891, she was a young actor and still on her first husband, Robert Taber, who ran the company.[40] And while 'Shakespeare's traveling troupe may have had fewer than fifteen actors', Marlowe was accompanied on tour with 'a carefully selected company, numbering thirty-three persons'. No street-corner loafers for her. She was there to make her first appearance at the Staunton Opera House for a performance of '"The Twelfth Night", one of the charming plays of Shakespeare, the greatest dramatist the world has ever known'.[41] Marlowe went down a storm, apparently, for 'The audience enjoyed the play very much, particularly those who were familiar with its intricate plot, and curtain calls were frequent'.[42] The curtain calls were also loud since the audience – if the house was full – would have numbered over a thousand. The Opera House advertised its capacity at 1,085 in 1881. (The house was available for rent, orchestra and 'seven sets of scenery with wings' inclusive, at 'one night, \$25; two nights, \$42; three nights, \$55'.[43]) Whatever resentment Staunton felt at being railroaded by marauding thespians melted in the face of Marlowe, who, according to the review, 'is destined to be a bright star in the galaxy of dramatic performers'. The reviewer was prescient since Marlowe became one of the premier Shakespearean interpreters of her day.

Staunton's citizens were lucky to see Marlowe at the beginning of her career, but they were just as fortunate to see Helena Modjeska at the end of hers. During Modjeska's farewell tour she made a stop in Staunton, where she appeared 'at the Beverly' in '"Mary Stuart" or "Macbeth"'. No reviews survive, but 'a crowded house' was 'predicted'.[44] How Modjeska made it from Kraków to Staunton deserves a book of its own, but the fact that such a luminary would stop in a town of, at that point, under 7,500 speaks to its geographical convenience, if nothing else.

Staunton hosted other companies across the years as well. In 1867, Harry Langdon presented 'An entirely new programme consisting of / The 5th Act of Richard III! / *The Ghost Scene and Battle of Bosworth Field!!* / To be followed by the beautiful play of / "The Swiss Cottage," / and to conclude with the highly amusing / Irish Farce of / "Paddy Miles' Boy!"'.[45] Just possibly this is the sort of dramatic excerpting that prompted the *Spectator* to complain of plays 'cut into unrecognizable shape', though the recognizable shape of Richard III probably made its fifth act fairly legible to Staunton.

Later companies seem to heed the paper's warning about how not to treat an audience. In 1908 the *Virginia-Pilot* reported that, 'Mr. Charles B. Hanford [...] and a good company, presented "The Winter's Tale," at the Academy of Music last night, and it may be said that no better presentation of the same play has ever been given in that playhouse or any other, for the production was perfect'.[46] Not ones to quit while they were ahead, the company,

> scored another big triumph here last night in the presentation of Shakespeare's great comedy, *The Merchant of Venice* [...] Mr. Hanford made a little curtain speech in which he complimented the people of Staunton on turning

out so well to such plays. And said that the most beautiful audience he ever spoke to was at Staunton two years ago.[47]

The name 'Charles B. Hanford' does not rank with Marlowe and Modjeska, but the man clearly knew how to give a curtain speech. Perhaps he read the review of Staunton's 'Cake Walk' and decided that if he might be accused of flattery, he could not be accused of 'contemptuousness for his audience'. It worked. According to the *Virginia Pilot*, his *Winter's Tale* took the cake.

Hansford's compliment to Staunton for turning out 'to such plays' betrays a sense that *The Winter's Tale* and *Merchant* were not perennial Staunton favourites. The records bear him out, for while Shakespeare did have some success in Staunton, that success was always relative. In August 1872, *The Staunton Spectator and General Advertiser* announced that, 'Shakespeare's "Hamlet" will be rendered at New Hope [...] in connection with an interesting comedy'. *Hamlet* and the unnamed – and therefore tantalizing – 'interesting comedy' merits only a tiny entry, however, alongside an enormous front-page spread advertising 'The Old Reliable John Robinson' the 'Greatest Favorite and Most Successful Showman of America' who was 'Coming to Staunton with the Best and Biggest Show in the World!!'[48] John Robinson was one of America's 'Circus Kings' of the nineteenth century, whose circus later became the property of Ringling Bros.[49] The advertisement for Robinson dwarfs that for *Hamlet*, but then, at the Jamestown exhibition in 1906, *Pocahontas* was second on the bill to 'The Great Feature Attraction/The Miller Brothers' Famous 101 Ranch Wild West Show' from Bliss, Oklahoma, that featured '500 Indians, Cowboys, Cowgirls, and Mexicans' – grouped appropriately we imagine – along with 'Buffalos, Bucking Bronchos, and Long Horn Steers in a Stupendous Reproduction of Western Life. Unrivalled in its Immensity', which played in a venue with 'Seating Capacity for 15,000 Under Cover.' No reports on how many turned out for Viett's reproduction of Western life. Apparently the patrons in Jamestown preferred the Miller Brothers' fantastic visions of the American West to Viett's Anglo-Saxon fantasy. In any case, the relative prominence of John Robinson over William Shakespeare speaks to the preferences of early Staunton, who, like the Virginia Company, looked to the West for both profit and pleasure.

Staunton's taste for cake walks and frontier fantasias may account for an emphasis on Shakespeare's literary prestige – rather than his theatrical power – evident from chronicles of Staunton's past. In newspapers, advertisements and pamphlets, Shakespeare features prominently as part of the late nineteenth century's cultural emphasis upon 'improvement'. While Shakespeare may have been in short supply on the stage, you could buy his works in a wide range of formats at 'Olivier's Bookshop' (there may be *some* coincidences in cultural history). An 1887 advertisement for Olivier's – right next to an ad for 'Mexican Mustang Liniment', which promises to cure everything from 'Spavin Cracks' to 'Saddle Galls', fit 'For Man and Beast!' – offers Shakespeare's works 'in sets of 13, 6, 4 and 1 vol',[50] among a redoubt of Anglo authors including Thackeray, Dickens, Scott and Eliot. The papers are full of students who took the cake at penmanship or elocution and who went home with an armful of Shakespeare. In 1873, 'Prof. J. A. Richardson gave public readings from Shakespeare, Byron and others, in the City Hall'.[51] A decade later, there were also 'Shakespearian Readings [...] by Miss Alice Margueritte King, the celebrated Dramatic reader' at the Masonic Hall.[52] Shakespeare appears more often in the context of cultural improvement than of light (or heavy) entertainment, a Victorian emphasis that, as we will see, provided some later grist for Shenandoah Shakespeare's mill.

Furthermore, long before the ASC built their new Blackfriars, Shakespeare was alive and well on market street, and not just at Olivier's Bookshop. Staunton's nineteenth-century newspapers feature ads for dubious cures that open with a little Shakespeare before hawking the latest 'nerve' remedy. Under the heading 'Black Vesper's Pageants', for instance, an 1894 ad warns, 'So speaks Shakespeare of those dark sombre clouds that we often see toward night. They foretell a storm. Just as surely do functional irregularities and "female derangements" foretell a life of suffering or an early grave'.[53] That same year another writes that Shakespeare says, '"When sorrows come, they come not single spies but in battalions." How true this is of disease [...] You must stop this complaint at once if you value your life. The way to do it is to take Dr. Greene's Nervura blood and nerve remedy.'[54] Whether for physical or moral improvement, Shakespeare was a prominent pitch man, more credible as a sage than on the stage.

The history of Shakespeare in Staunton, then, is occasionally piquant, but not terribly surprising. The historical record of Shakespeare in Staunton will startle no one familiar with Shakespeare in America. Appropriated by hucksters and hack writers, the star vehicle for touring actors, a literary must-have for the respectable home, Shakespeare's place in Staunton was Shakespeare's place in America. Except for one thing. The *Staunton Spectator* made one exception when they claimed that Stauntonians preferred a 'Cake Walk' to Shakespeare. Their full assessment reads 'Staunton doesn't care much for light tragedy, such as Shakespeare's for instance (unless played by our own colored star)'. Hidden in the parenthesis is the extraordinary story of 'the colored amateur actors of this city' who performed *Richard III* in 1894 to raise funds for a library for Staunton's black community. The play prompted two stories by the local paper; the first reads in full:

'Richard III by Colored Amateurs.'/While this issue is being worked off, the colored amateur actors of this city, are playing Richard III to a large audience of both races in the Opera-house – the whites below and the colored above. This is a bold undertaking and has elicited much interest, and attracted a good audience. Costumes for this occasion were obtained from New York. This performance presents a unique spectacle such as has never been witnessed before.

It is given for the benefit of the Eureka Library for the colored people.[55]

Probably because there is so little of it, Staunton tends to make exclusive claims about its Shakespeare. However exceptional, the 'coloured' *Richard III* wasn't exactly 'unique'. (A theatre is a place where nothing ever happens for the first time.) The 1820's saw an 'all black company of *RIII*', in New York City, in which

> a little dapper woolly-headed waiter at the City Hotel personated the royal Plantagenet [...] how delighted would the bard of Avon have been to see his *Richard* performed by a fellow as black as the ace of spades [...] Several fashionable songs, sung with no mean taste, concluded the evening's amusement, and the sable audience retired peaceably to their homes. Richard and Catesby were unfortunately taken up by the watch.[56]

Plus ça change. (The company inspired the 1989 Carlyle Brown play *The African Company Presents Richard III*.) If it was not entirely a unique spectacle, Staunton's 'Colored Amateurs' introduced one innovation. The New York performance seems to have drawn an entirely 'sable audience' (except, presumably, the reporter). Staunton's *Richard III* played to whites and black alike, however; and while the audience may have been racially unmixed, so was the reaction. Staunton took enthusiastic interest in the event and, a week later, the *Spectator* details a repeat performance.

> 'Richard III Repeated'/The colored amature [*sic*] actors of this city who gave such a successful performance of Richard III in the Opera-House to a very large audience on Tuesday night of last week, gave a repetition of it last night. The manner in which they acted this difficult play was a surprise to all who witnessed their rendition of it. Nearly all did very well, and the acting of Jas. W. Woods, who acted

the part of Richard III, was most remarkable. He plays that
character as well as many professional tragic actors do.
He has fine talent, and is a young man – a servant at the
Virginia Hotel.[57]

In the same issue of the paper is an ad for the hotel at which
Woods worked. It promises that the hotel is 'Refurnished
and Refitted Throughout' with the 'Finest Cafe in the City'
featuring 'Steam Oysters and Chafing Dish Stews'. The ad gives
a flavour of the kind of work Woods did when not dishing out
Richard to whites below and blacks above. The newspaper also
reminds us that, however popular this *Richard* was, its success
was still relative. A huge ad touts the 'Adam Forepaugh Show /
America's Oldest, Largest, Greatest and Best Exhibition'. The
ad's header is, within quotations, 'The Circus is the Thing', lest
Shakespeare get too big for his breeches.

One of the myths of the Shenandoah Valley is that – as an
historian puts it – 'slavery never took root here'. Apparently
nineteenth-century historians were eager to promote the
concept that the 'Scotch–Irish were averse to bondage'. While
it is the case that larger plantations never developed in the
area, small farms and merchant concerns might own one to
five slaves and lease them out to others when they were not
being used. In fact, the first Federal census in 1790 reports
that Augusta County – of which Staunton is the seat – was
14.4 per cent black and that 96 per cent of these were slaves.
The black population outgrew the white population, and by
the Civil War, Staunton hosted a robust population of African
Americans, both slave and free. Not far from the reconstructed Anne Hathaway cottage stands the Allen Chapel,
the oldest African American church west of the Blue Ridge
Mountain.[58] Woods' efforts to fund the Eureka Library can be
understood as part of a larger effort by the African American
community to establish churches, schools, and libraries in the
era of Reconstruction. That both Hathaway's cottage and the
Allen Chapel are products of 'Reconstruction' initiatives only
serves to signal how cross-hatched is the history of Staunton.

Although he was a servant, James Woods was no one's slave. He was born free. The same cannot be guaranteed of his fellow cast or his black audience. The Civil War was still living memory. It still is – in the sense that more than 150 years later, people continue to keep its memory alive. When James Woods faced his troops – comprised of a 'handful of colored youths jogging around in hopeless defiance of a military appearance'[59] – and said 'You sleeping safe, they bring to you unrest; / You having lands, and blest with beauteous wives, / They would restrain the one, distain the other [...] / Shall these enjoy our lands? lie with our wives? / Ravish our daughters?' (5.3.294), a shudder ran through half the house, a thrill through half the other. No prizes for guessing which was which. The *Spectator*'s 'our colored star' has therefore a double valence, a proprietary ownership of Woods' work that could still cut both ways. It still can. The African American company's *Richard III* was museum theatre at its most sophisticated.

Still, perhaps because we've come to expect so little from the past, the *Staunton Spectator*'s coverage of *Richard* sounds large hearted and open minded. The paper seems to recognize that 'amateur' performances come from the heart since that is what the word means. Against its wariness towards the condescending 'bright light' of the theatrical world, the paper takes pride in the company, or at least the light thrown off by its 'colored star'. The paper further notes, without prejudice, that the performance is tied to local efforts at educational up-lift, an investment in the literacy of the city's black population. Discovering this event – and its local coverage – over a century later produces at least a mild 'Eureka'.

Truer to form – and falser to our hopes – is a long review by Mary Shattuck that subsequently ran in *Kate Field's Washington*. Field was a former actress, friend of Anthony Trollope and all-American weirdo who founded a short-lived eponymous periodical in *fin-de-siècle* DC. Unlike the *Spectator*, Shattuck's view of the spectacle is not open hearted but close minded. The *Spectator*'s headline 'Richard III Repeated' simply means the company did *Richard* twice, but the review in *Kate Field's Washington* views Staunton's 'coloured' *Richard III* as a form of mimicry.

> It was with some amusement that I read the announcement, several weeks ago, that on a certain evening, 'Shakspere's Greatest Tragedy, "Richard III,"' would be presented at the Opera House by 'colored amateur talent.' Negroes rendering Shakspere; this was something new! The evening came, and I went to the opera house, to find it crowded with people, while many were unable to gain entrance. The floor of the house had been reserved for white spectators, who certainly showed their interest in the advancement of the colored race along dramatic lines by their attendance that evening. Every household in town had turned out to see its butlers, coachmen or maids act Shakspere. The gallery was densely packed with the colored friends of the performers–an enthusiastic crowd, who laughed vociferously in the most tragic parts of the play [...] When James S. Woods entered in the title-role, we understood where he had obtained his cue, and why the colored amateurs were playing this particular play. Early in the winter, Thomas W. Keene, with his company, came to Staunton and played 'Richard III.' James S. Woods evidently saw them in that performance, and being an intelligent mulatto, endowed with the powers of mimicry, often found among the negroes, he began his work of imitating Keene.[60]

You want to hit her with a brick. Thomas W. Keene had toured with the Charles B. Hanford company, he of the 'perfect' *Winter's Tale* who was so smitten with Staunton's beautiful audience, an audience which – if Shattuck is correct – included some 'colored amateurs,' among them James S. Woods. Thomas Keene was accounted the successor to Edwin Booth, not least by Thomas Keene, and he found acclaim in a number of Shakespeareans roles, including Richard, Hamlet, and Othello. The latter role he played in blackface, of course, and Shattuck's impression of James S. Woods is that he was essentially playing Thomas Keene's Richard, only just in blackface that he could not remove. A coloured *Richard III* is a kind of Cake Walk for her, a black parody of a white performance that even in her most positive estimate can only be a hilariously negative spectacle. 'Throughout the play our amazement grew – and it is still increasing – over the fact that such an intelligent rendering of a Shakespearean tragedy had been given by a few negroes entirely without dramatic training'. It isn't the lack of dramatic training that amazes her.

Shattuck is also amazed at the range of black on offer at the Opera House. The cast showed, 'all grades of color, from the blackest possible *Buckingham* to the light and pretty mulatto girl who played *Queen Elizabeth*, and evidently enjoyed to the full extent sitting on a throne in queenly robes of silk and ermine'. There were also the priests between whom Richard prayed, 'as black negroes as ever were created' as well as the ghosts who appeared to Richard before Bosworth, 'each draped in a white sheet from which the black face peeped out'. Despite her attention to the varieties of skin, Shattuck had trouble with shades of grey. For her, at least, and possibly for others in the audience, all she could see were white sheets and black skin.

George Frederic Viett of Norfolk could have made it to the show in Staunton, although he probably did not. It's too bad. A man interested in Virginia nonpareils might have appreciated Staunton's 'unique spectacle'. On the other hand, as much as Viett lionized Shakespeare, he may not have appreciated what the 'remarkable fecundity of the negro race' produced in Staunton in 1894. As for the sight of a mulatto queen playing Virginia's namesake – an offspring of the 'dark and monstrous birth' which he describes in 1619 – we can only guess that it would have made his face go white.

A peculiar institution

This chapter closes with a further meditation on blackface and the Blackfriars, a theatre right around the corner from the Opera House in which James S. Woods either gave an original Richard or a second-hand Keene depending on whom you ask. A framing question is what it means to perform *Othello*, today, in a small town in central Virginia in a reconstructed Blackfriars between the Stonewall Jackson Hotel and a theatre called the Dixie. As suggested at the outset, these two local landmarks cue the audience in peculiar ways when they visit the Blackfriars and, in particular, when the play is *Othello*. The Blackfriars playhouse explicitly recalls its English original. It's in the memory business after all. It does not go out of its way to remember local history but local history does that for them. The Blackfriars literally cannot get out of its shadow. The close of this chapter, therefore, briefly stirs the ghost of Stonewall Jackson and the Dixie to unfold some more history pleated into the fabric of the new Blackfriars.

One salient, though silent, fact of the Blackfriar's interior architecture is that it is a best-guess recreation of a playhouse in which the role of Othello would have been performed by a white man in blackface. Today, performances of *Othello* at Blackfriars, as elsewhere, are not performed in blackface. If not actually, Laurence Olivier's 1968 blackface Othello proved the figurative end to that peculiar tradition. The ASC flirts with historical practices, then, but draws the line at blackface. It's easy to forget this element of early modern theatrical practice when watching *Othello* at the Blackfriars. There is no mention of blackface in the programme's review of 'Shakespeare's staging practices'. That's one original practice that was practiced long enough.

Among those institutions which didn't draw the line at blackface – other than the English Renaissance of course – is the Dixie Theatre, just a couple of doors down from the old Opera House. Right around the corner from the

Blackfriars then – a playhouse that replicates a playhouse that hosted blackface performers – is an actual theatre that hosted blackface performers, or at least films of them. The Dixie, named the 'New Theatre' when it opened in 1912, was built to host silent films and vaudeville shows, which included popular blackface sketches. This is central Virginia, after all, in the early twentieth-century. The theatre was converted to a cinema when Warner Brothers leased the Dixie during the mid-1920s, and it became one of the first theatres in Virginia to be wired for sound. This was specifically done to showcase Warner's revolutionary new talking picture, 'The Jazz Singer', in 1927, featuring the blackface performer Al Jolson, whose first song in the film is 'Dirty Hands, Dirty Face'. As noted in the introduction, the ASC performs pre-show and interlude music, often thematically linked to the play they're about to do. You will not be hearing 'Dirty Hands, Dirty Face' before any performance of *Othello* at Staunton's new Blackfriars.[61]

Given the popularity of vaudeville in the period and the popularity of Shakespearean adaptations within the American vaudeville vernacular, it is unsurprising to learn of several blackface, vaudeville adaptations of *Othello*. In fact, *Othello* parodies were extremely popular on American stages. These blackface performances capitalized on stage 'black English' and usually transformed the murder scene into slapstick farce. There is not space here to belabour them in all their gruesome variety, but in one pertinent burlesque Desdemona and Othello sing a duet to the tune of 'Dixie' that concludes 'I'll love dearly all my life, / Although you are a nigger'. Entering the final scene with a black eye, Desdemona vows, 'I really think Othello must be mad; / That was the hardest thump I ever had / Just one day married, and to cut this figure – / But I'll have satisfaction on that nigger ... .'[62] These are the sorts of deeper harmonies whistled at the Dixie just around the corner from the new Blackfriars.

The most familiar harmony hummed at the Dixie was the song of the same name, the unofficial anthem of the confederacy. The song 'Dixie' – also known by the names 'Dixie

Land' or 'I Wish I Was in Dixie' – originated in the blackface minstrel shows in the 1850s. (In 1860, it showed up in a John Brougham burlesque called *Po-ca-hon-tas, or The Gentle Slave*.) Endlessly parodied and repurposed by north and south alike, its origin and meaning hotly contested, the refrain remained relatively stable:

> I wish I was in the land of cotton, old times there are not forgotten,
> Look away, look away, look away, Dixie Land.
> In Dixie Land where I was born in, early on a frosty mornin',
> Look away, look away, look away, Dixie Land.
>
> Then I wish I was in Dixie, hooray! hooray!
> In Dixie Land I'll take my stand to live and die in Dixie,
> Away, away, away down South in Dixie,
> Away, away, away down South in Dixie.[63]

The song was a favourite of Lincoln, who had it played at the news of Robert E. Lee's surrender. It had also played after each southern state voted for secession in Charleston, South Carolina as well as at Jefferson Davis' inauguration. If Lincoln could harmonize nostalgia for the antebellum American South with his joy at its post-bellum surrender, a modern theatregoer probably has little trouble reconciling the presence of a Dixie Theatre around the corner from a Blackfriars Playhouse. To 'whistle Dixie', after all, means to engage in 'unrealistically rosy fantasizing' according to the *American Heritage Dictionary*.[64]

You do not need a working familiarity with American vaudeville to take the register of 'Dixie' from the theatre's marquee. The name says it all, although it did not say so at first. The 'New Theatre' suffered a fire in 1936 and was extensively refurbished. Warner Brothers sponsored a contest to rename the theatre. Fourteen-year-old Mildred Klotz took the $50 prize with the name 'Dixie Theatre'. It is lost to time what Klotz had in mind, but 'Dixie' is a complicated word since, like 'Hollywood', it refers both to a physical place and a perceptual space – and one of rosy fantasizing. Literally, 'Dixie' is a toponym for those southern states that seceded from the Union in the 1860s. The most common etymology proposes it derives from the name 'Dixon' of the 'Mason-Dixon line'; those states to the south of the line became known as 'Dixie'. The perceptual coordinates of 'Dixie' are harder to map. The name conjures aspects of the antebellum south, however. Some of the aspects of the Dixie 'heritage' (not hate, the sons of the confederacy will tell you) include minstrelsy, blackface, and of course slavery, into which Othello tells us he was once sold. In sum, even when it is a black man playing Othello at the Blackfriars, he does so under a film of blackface. Old times there are not forgotten.

On the other side of the Blackfriars is 'The Stonewall Jackson Hotel', whose name outdoes the Dixie's in being larger, higher, and cast in red neon. Ralph Alan Cohen fought hard to have the name changed when the hotel was refurbished and refitted throughout in 2005, largely due to the success of the Blackfriars it sits beside. (It is perhaps just as well he failed, since it might well have been renamed for Staunton's most famous son, Woodrow Wilson, who had his own peculiar thoughts on race and eugenics.) The 'Stonewall Jackson' literally overshadows the Blackfriars and takes its name from Thomas Jonathan 'Stonewall' Jackson, the best-known general of the south after Robert E. Lee. Jackson was accidentally shot by his own pickets at the battle of Chancellorsville on 2 May 1863 – like Othello, an insider mistaken for an outsider, or the other way around. Stonewall Jackson survived the shooting, though lost an arm to amputation. However, he died of complications of pneumonia eight days later. Historical sources report that his death was a severe setback for the Confederacy, as well as for himself we might imagine.

Stonewall Jackson was not from Staunton. Before the war, Jackson lived in Lexington, VA, about half-an-hour south, where he taught at the Virginia Military Academy before being called to active service. According to historians, Jackson was revered by many of the African Americans in Lexington, both slaves and free blacks. In 1855, Jackson organized Sunday school classes for blacks at the Presbyterian Church. His second wife, Mary Anna Jackson, taught with Stonewall, as 'he preferred that my labors should be given to the colored children, believing that it was important and useful to put the strong hand of the Gospel under the ignorant African race, to lift them up'.[65] The pastor, Dr William Spottswood White, described the relationship between Jackson and his Sunday afternoon students: 'He was emphatically the black man's friend. He addressed his students by name and they in turn referred to him affectionately as "Marse Major."'[66] This all sounds relatively benevolent – *relatively* – until you learn that among other things Jackson wished taught was the Biblical warrant for slavery. Unsurprisingly, Jackson's family itself owned six slaves in the late 1850s, three of whom he received as a wedding present.

Quite literally then, it's this other general who has his name in lights on Market Street and overshadows any and every Othello at the Blackfriars. For, ultimately, the meanings of Staunton's *Othello* coalesce in the body of the man playing him. As is not unusual for regional and smaller professional theatres, the actor playing Othello at the Blackfriars is often either the only African American in the cast or one of just two. The racial composition of the cast of *Othello* mirrors, therefore, the racial composition of the community being portrayed. Not for want of effort by the ASC, there are rarely any African Americans in the audience either. Unlike the Opera House in which James Woods played Richard, the Blackfriars is of course not segregated, but what that means is that it's whites below *and* whites above. There's a good chance that on many nights the actor playing Othello is the only African American man or woman in the building. But then, the play is not called *Othello, a Moor of Venice*, it is called *Othello, the Moor of Venice*. Othello is no longer performed in blackface by a white man at the Blackfriars or elsewhere. There, Othello's the definite article, but he's also the only one, a Virginia nonpareil.

One way to connect the dots is to fold history in on itself, then, which bypasses a number of points in between. One final point is that circum-Atlantic human traffic has often been performed in the name of Shakespeare. On Christmas Eve, 1855, the ship *Shakespeare* left New Orleans for Liverpool, with 6,507 bales of cotton – 2,922,652 pounds – the heaviest load ever to have left that port.[67] The shipbuilders presumably did not mean to make 'Shakespeare' carry the fruits of new world slavery to the ports of the old one. But this accident of nomenclature makes Shakespeare the link between the land of cotton and the green and pleasant one. Over 200 years after Shakespeare's patrons put their money down to help open up trade between the new world and old, their investment returned in the form of some of the '*Most Excellent Fruites*' to be reaped '*by Planting in Virginia*'. Shakespeare has no very explicit part in this adventure, and it takes some straining to make him so. And yet, one very great, very erratic Shakespearean actor saw clearly the link between new world and old and the bloodline that connected them. In the early eighteenth century, George Frederick Cooke once had a bad night in Liverpool, but turned the tables on an ugly audience: 'Acting once at Liverpool, he was hissed for being so far drunk as to render his declamation unintelligible. He turned savagely upon the people. "What! Do you hiss me! – hiss George Frederick Cooke! You contemptible money-getters! You shall never again have the honor of hissing me! Farewell! *I* banish *you*." After a moment's pause, he added, in his deepest tones: "*There is not a brick in your dirty town but what is cemented by the blood of a negro!*"' Cooke parrots the pariah Coriolanus to impose a self-exile from his country men, whose practices he finds contemptible. But as Coriolanus discovers, there's no escaping history.

*

In an early grant proposal, circa 1990, under a subheading 'Who is the Shenandoah Shakespeare Express?', the author writes 'Say "Shakespeare" and most Americans think of tights and posturing, of British accents and three and a half hour productions'.[68] It's a broad indictment, but its target is specific: England, with its accents, posturing, long plays, and tight tights. This was nearly a decade before the company decided to rebuild a Blackfriars, a project that required the Virginia company to recast its relationship with England from resistance to recapitulation. The transition from the SSE to ASC isn't quite one from Anglophobia to Anglophilia, but the company at the new Blackfriars now don their tights without grudging. The early antagonism of the SSE sounds adolescent in retrospect, a blurt of protest against an inevitable truth: Shakespeare *did* speak in an anglo accent, though presumably not a Saxon one. The ASC has made its peace with England, at least Shakespeare's England – a formula that, like 'Shakespeare's Globe', would have surprised more than a few of Shakespeare's contemporaries. One of the harmonies the company now strikes, and strikes effortlessly as the introduction discusses, is the relationship between past and present and between England and Virginia. The Staunton Blackfriars advertises itself as a reconstruction of an early English playhouse, and does so proudly, but the state of the Blackfriars is always Virginian. Named after Shakespeare only queen, settled in the name of his only king, patronized by his patrons, and settled by his peers, Virginia had Shakespearean properties without him investing a cent.

Even in this early document, the SSE does acknowledge one lineal link to England: 'Even now the reconstructed Globe is rising on the banks of the Thames and with it a revival of Shakespeare in precisely the style that we are pioneering here in America.' The tension in the claim to be pioneering a revival, one that is simultaneously going on elsewhere, is taken up in the following chapter, 'Revolutionary Nostalgia', but here it only remains to consider how hard the ellipsis between '1642 London, England … 2001 Staunton, Virginia' is working and how many periods it elides in the dot, dot, dot of history.

2

Revolutionary Nostalgia

*The relentless search for a purity of origin is a voyage
not of discovery but erasure.*

JOSEPH ROACH, *CITIES OF THE DEAD*[1]

The first step in any revolution is to convince others that the
best way forward is to go back. The next step is to convince
your followers that you're the first to think of it. Santayana
famously said that those who forget the past are condemned
to repeat it (though no one seems able to remember precisely
how he put it). This is usually meant as a cautionary note, not
a revolutionary one, but forgetting the past – at least part of
it – has been a prerequisite in the perpetual revolutions that
shape the history of Shakespeare and performance.

This chapter examines the emergence of the American
Shakespeare Center and the Blackfriars Playhouse both
against and within the history of permanent revolution by
which the Shakespeare Industrial Complex constantly renews
itself. Those 'revolutions' – a hyperbolic term for minor
adjustments within a minority enterprise – generate their
torque by advocating for a return to something that we've
collectively forgotten – usually a purity of textual or theatrical
origins that modern practice has corrupted or from which it
has fallen. This revolutionary rhetoric is predictable, and just
as predictably effective. Considered as recursion, then, the

emergence of the American Shakespeare Center seems inevitable and functions as a form of manifest prophecy by which we can predict the future of Shakespeare and performance. That future can be found in the spasms of wilful amnesia that produce Elizabethan revivals across Shakespeare's stage history and produce them over and over again, each time for the first time.

A 'deep history' of Elizabethan revivalism would require a book of its own, a lengthy survey of academic, amateur and professional efforts that leverage authority on history's edge.[2] Here, I construct a genealogy of revolutions for the ASC which begins in 1576 and ends 400 years later in 1976, with a way station in Victorian London. The torch passes from James Burbage to William Poel to J. L. Styan to Ralph Alan Cohen – advocates, entrepreneurs, enthusiasts all. This genealogy demonstrates certain common threads of memory and forgetfulness, feigned naiveté, ambition and disappointment, but, above all, fracture and transformation. These revolutions all insist upon a purity of origin that require, in Joseph Roach's words, discovery by way of erasure.

*

We should have seen it coming. The Elizabethan revival is one of those phenomena always heralded as an innovation but that happens at least once a century – like the rise of the middle class. For that matter, the antiquarian impulse in the Shakespeare industry seems to be a more-or-less *fin-de-siècle* affair. The forms of its expression will differ, however. At the turn of the seventeenth century its outlet was editorial, as Nicholas Rowe memorialized Shakespeare through a monument in print, repeating the 'office to the dead' that Heminges and Condell had performed at the other end of the century. As the eighteenth century drew to a close, theatremakers grew suspicious of Shakespeare's early adapters – like Cibber, Garrick and Tate – and began to return to the 'original' texts, while Nicholas Rowe pursued authenticity on the other side of the table.[3] At the end of the nineteenth century, it was William Poel's Elizabethan Society that flew the standard for Elizabethan practice as a reaction against the scenic wonders – or excesses depending upon your perspective – of Irving and Beerbohm-Tree. It is not hard to see in the late twentieth-century interest in 'original practices (OP)' a reaction against the 'director's theatre' of the 1960s and 1970s, shifting focus from auteur to architecture, the most obvious examples of which are the Globe and the Blackfriars' reconstructions. (It is not hard to see that since that is the tradition the Globe and Blackfriars projects originally positioned themselves *against* even while positioning themselves *towards* the past.) At the turn of each century, Shakespeareans also pivot, refreshing current practice with reflections of the past. But then, revolutions always turn backwards to go forwards. That is, after all, what the word means.

Pervading these various revolutions is a style of 'revolutionary nostalgia', Terry Eagleton's term for Walter Benjamin's inclination towards an avant-gardist longing for return which always accompanies the desire to progress. Eagleton defines revolutionary nostalgia as 'the power of active remembrance as a ritual summoning and invocation of the traditions of the oppressed in violent constellation with the political present'.[4] Eagleton is describing Benjamin's approach to political, not theatrical, revolutions, but he helps us understand the constant return to Elizabethan origins among Shakespeareans, particularly when they're calling for something new. (He is also contrasting Benjamin's style with Nietzsche's 'active forgetting', 'the healthy spontaneous amnesia of the animal who has willfully repressed its own sordid determinations and so is free'.) Within the dialectic of nostalgia and revolution, origins are invoked to sanitize modern decadence, so that innovation is always simultaneously a form of antiquarianism, and vice versa. (As we'll see below, we find in both William Poel's and Ralph Alan Cohen's calls for revival an insistence that antiquated practice is just what's needed to bring forth the new.) There is nothing 'oppressed' about Shakespeare's stage craft, of course, but calls for a revolution in Shakespearean staging begin by suggesting that we have forgotten past practices, repressed if not oppressed them. Forgetfulness may not be the worst form of oppression, but it is one form. By these means, a deeply conservative return can be designed as radical progression, and of course the opposite is true. Back, as the familiar 1980's formulation has it, to the future.

Renaissance drama was a backwards affair from the very start, however. The turn of the sixteenth century had its own tribe of Elizabethan revivalists. They were called 'the Elizabethans'. For what Burbage, Brayne, Henslowe et al. were after was not so much innovation as resuscitation. This is most evident in the signal name that Burbage and Brayne chose for their Shoreditch playhouse, 'The Theatre'. For what might seem to us like the *least* imaginative name possible for a playhouse was an act of incredible ambition. While the name 'The Theatre' may strike us as unimaginative, it was, in fact, an audacious act of the imagination and a form of deep nostalgia, even of the revolutionary kind. This was because what James Burbage and John Brayne must have hoped to conjure was not the image of a corner pub – like 'The Globe', 'The Rose' or 'The Hope' – but rather that of classical antiquity, and the Latinate name they assigned to their playhouse broadcast their ambitions (or pretensions). While other theatrical entrepreneurs may have wished to make their seemingly weird-looking buildings seem as commonplace as an inn – as ordinary as an ordinary – by giving them comfortably familiar names, Burbage and Brayne had their eyes fixed on a future for The Theatre – and the *theatre* – by fixing them firmly in the past.

As is well known, the word 'theatre' means a place 'to view'; thus, what James Burbage may have seen in the past was a place for himself in the English Renaissance. To make a more modest, and supportable, claim, Burbage had a rare vision for his 'Theatre' which spoke powerfully for the ambition of

a theatre industry that wasn't yet an industry.[5] 'The Theatre'
signaled a re-nascent interest in classical antiquity and an
attempt to revive its spirit in a London suburb. Clergyman
John Stockwood knew what was up when he sermonized
against 'The Theatre' at Paul's Cross, in 1579, inveighing
against the 'gorgeous playing place erected in the fieldes [...]
as they please to have it called, a Theatre, that is, even after
the maner of the olde heathnish Theatre at Rome'.[6] You
get the sense that if Stockwood did not find The Theatre so
threatening, he would find risible the idea of a 'Theatre' in
the middle of a field. Stockwood could not have been the
only one, however, who recognized that The Theatre was a
playhouse with an historical consciousness, an historical self-
awareness, which its name conveyed in a way that 'The Rose',
'The Swan' or 'The Globe' did not.

Burbage's and Brayne's big idea did not catch on. It might
seem like an upgrade when 'The Theatre' became 'The Globe'
– a mere theatrical venue come up in the world – but it was
a conservative return to standard naming practice. The name
'Globe' would likely have struck its early patrons as more
modest than 'The Theatre'. After all, early modern London
featured a number of Globes, including inns, bookstalls and
shops. The Bankside 'Globe' was just one more possible
world, though the name was so anodyne that it likely struck
no one as exceptional, ambitious, or unlikely. As it turned out,
'The Theatre' would be the only purpose-built playhouse in
the period explicitly to market its aim at theatrical revivalism.
But like the middle class, which is seemingly always emerging,
but never quite arrives, Elizabethan revivalism always ends in
a form of disappointment. We should see it coming.

In any number of ways, the outburst of English theatrical
energy in the late sixteenth century can be seen as a proto-
original practices movement that was, itself, part of a larger
pan-European theatrical revival. Prompted, in large part, by
the editions of Terence, Seneca, Plautus and the illustrated
editions of Vitruvius that began to come out in the first
decade of the sixteenth century, theatrical revivalists across

Europe were attempting to recreate ancient performance on stages in academies, universities and at royal courts.[7] When Andrea Palladio and Vincenzo Scamozzi built the Teatro Olimpico in Vincenza in the 1580s, they relied upon Sebastian Serlio's *Architettura* (1545), along with Vitruvius. Scholar dramatists, like those at the court of Tudor King Henry VIII, who attempted to create reconstructions of the ancient theatre throughout the sixteenth century were primarily drawing upon printed texts that circulated antique ideals. This search for theatrical origins – and its practical renascence – will sound familiar to Shakespeareans who have followed the rise of the Globe and Blackfriars. There is, however, one big difference: the European theatrical revivalists had *much better* evidence than we do. Ironically, that is, theatremakers of the fifteenth and sixteenth centuries had far more solid evidence in their attempt to revive classical drama than we do in reviving theirs, and not just because the ancients built their subsidized theatres out of stone instead of timber and lath like the privately financed playhouses of Elizabethan London. They also had much better printed sources to rely upon since the ancients left more systematic and searching writing upon the making of drama than the English ever did. The point is, that *our* – or any – Elizabethan revival is a revival of a revival. It's all revival, all the way back to the very first one.

Ironically, while 'The Theatre' looked back to classical antiquity – a search for a purity of origin as Joseph Roach's epigraph calls it – it had simultaneously to forget its own history, not least the centuries of native English drama. For it was not 'the first' theatre in early modern England, or even London, though history has been happy to call it so. Indeed, one of the more enduring myths of theatre history is that English playing as a commercial enterprise sprung fully formed from the head of James Burbage in 1576. In the introductory chapter to *A New History of Early English Drama*, having cited such transformative events as Luther's theses and Guttenberg's press, Margreta de Grazia writes that:

if there is any event in the history of the early English stage comparable to the epochal ones listed above, it would have to be the building of the first public theater in London in 1576. The event is singled out in the annals of English stage craft as the beginning of commercial theater.[8]

To quote is not to condemn, for the notion persists everywhere. The introduction to the *Arden Shakespeare Complete Works* tells us flatly that: 'The Theatre, built in 1576 for James Burbage, was the first building to be erected in the suburbs of London expressly for the presentation of plays.'[9] Indeed, as de Grazia asserts, Glynne Wickham used 1576 as the break point of his three-volume *Early English Stages: 1300–1660*, calling it 'a point toward which everything seems inexorably to move and after which those same things are never quite the same again'.[10] Occasionally a scholar will amend the assertion that The Theatre was the first playhouse in London with the caveat that it wasn't. Such scholars will cite John Brayne's 1567 Red Lion playhouse, but dismiss its existence as a mere fact. The discovery of the Theatre's Shoreditch remains probably means this myth is unlikely to subside soon, and we are left to contemplate the paradox that James Burbage's Theatre was the first such building in England even though it was not. As the late Douglas Brooks wrote, 'The presence of paradox generally exhibits the force of an underlying desire'.[11] The desire in this case is for a purity of origins. If it is not strictly the 'truth' that James Burbage built the first playhouse in England, then it ought to be, but then, to paraphrase David Byrne, facts don't do what we want them to.

There are historically traceable reasons for the tenacity of Burbage's Theatre myth. Namely, it got off to a quick start. James's son, Cuthbert Burbage, put an early spin on the narrative in the so-called 'Sharers Papers' of 1635. Despite the name, Cuthbert's account credits one man and one building as the birthplace of commercial English theatre.

The father of us, Cutbert and Richard Burbage, was
the first builder of playehowses, and was himselfe in his
younger yeeres a player. The Theater hee built with many
hundred poundes taken up at interest. The players that
lived in those first times had onely the profits arising from
the dores, but now the players receave all the comings in
at the dores to themselves and halfe the galleries from the
housekeepers. Hee built this house upon leased grounds, by
which meanes the landlord and hee had a great suite in law,
and, by his death, the like troubles fell on us, his sonnes;
wee then bethought us of altering from thence, and at like
expence built the Globe.[12]

Talk about a 'purity of origins' – butter wouldn't melt in
Cuthbert's mouth. The account's paternal pride ('the father of
us [...] was the first builder of playehowses'), its nostalgia for
an edenic past ('the players that lived in those first times'), its
tale of inherited woe ('by his death, the like troubles fell on us,
his sonnes'), its strong Biblical cadences ('Hee built this house
upon leased ground'), its hyperbolic grandeur ('many hundred
poundes [...] a great suite in law') and the redemptive ending
in which the two figures take a journey and inherit the world
('wee then bethought us of altering from thence, and [...] built
the Globe') all gather to grant the testimony a providential
force that has clearly influenced the making of theatre history
in centuries hence. Above all, Cuthbert's emphasis on the
priority of 'those first times' creates a genesis for English
playhouses right out of Genesis.

Seduced, perhaps, by Cuthbert's powerful account, E. K.
Chambers confirmed that the 'accuracy of this [testimony] is
fully borne out by the records',[13] but like the biblical story it
seems to echo, if Burbage's story is true it is only allegorically
so. Burbage neatly, and pointedly, elides his father's early
business partner, John Brayne, and erases from the record
Brayne's big idea, the 1567 Red Lion (which could plausibly
be considered the first English playhouse, although in all
probability it is not, either). In other words, the Red Lion

was ignored from an early stage. James Burbage might not have been the 'first builder' of theatres, but his son, Cuthbert, was certainly one of the first makers of theatre history and his testimony has clearly shaped the way Shakespeareans make history. Of course, just because something is not true, it does not mean we won't believe it. Myths, we know, are good to think with, and Burbage's story organizes the mess of theatre history, which has no beginning, into a tidy tale that collapses Shakespeare and the origins of English theatre into a convenient and vendible package.

There is nothing inevitable, therefore, about the year 1576 being the watermark of early English drama. Yet, there is no reason to nominate 1567 instead to be 'singled out in the annals of English stage craft as the beginning of commercial theater' any more than to choose 1520, the year in which Henry VIII raised a polygonal timber theatre in Calais, a less than fitting site, to be sure, for the first 'English' playhouse. Simply because these dates mark literally groundbreaking events, it does not follow that they must also prove figuratively so. To read Burbage one would never know that early English theatre was a largely itinerant phenomenon both before and after 1576. Despite the notion that theatre became 'real estate' in 1576, there was no totalizing conversion of transient playing into a static enterprise during the 1570s.

If we need significant dates to make theatre history, and we do, we might as well nominate the edict of 1572, which brought playing companies under the control of aristocratic patrons, or, for that matter, 1582, when the organization of the Queen's Men occurred, or 1594, which marks the formation of the Lord Chamberlain's Men – and so on. These events arguably provided the auspices that stabilized the formation and endurance of playing as a commercial enterprise. These latter dates point towards the organization of personnel, however, not property and are, therefore, less legible within the language of late capitalism. The years 1567 or 1576, or any date which locates the origins of playing in the building of a playhouse, bring early modern theatre within the alluring purview of bourgeois scholarship's dominating concern: property (the near erotic pursuit of which Marjorie Garber has wittily diagnosed as bourgeois culture's 'primary object of affection and desire'[14]). Above all, 1576 signals for modern scholarship the date when the transient ephemerality of occasional playing reifies as timber, lath, leases and lawsuits, *traces* that enable scholars to translate early English playing from a language of 'being' into a language of 'having'. This translation – as we'll see below – is in itself a recurrent feature of revivalism, as the impulse towards recapturing a 'spirit' of performance always converts itself into a desire for property.

James Burbage seems to have had a specific idea about theatre history, then, and about how the theatrical past might be reawakened through the medium of architectural homage. Furthermore, there seems to have been an early sense among Burbage and sons, Richard and Cuthbert, that the spirit of classical revivalism inscribed in their playhouse's name also required a claim to be the first revivalist structure, the world's only reconstruction. In these terms, the Shoreditch 'Theatre' was the first original practices playhouse, and James Burbage the first Elizabethan revivalist – the spiritual ancestor of Sam Wanamaker and Ralph Alan Cohen, the primary driver of the Blackfriars reconstruction. It is James's legacy (not his sons) that the twentieth-century Globe and Blackfriars truly honours, for these buildings also suffer or enjoy an acute case of historical self-consciousness that requires that they claim to be the first reconstruction while acknowledging that they are a distant second.

All of this might just be merely a matter of theatre history were it not for the 'Spirit of '76' haunting the late twentieth-century building boom in the Shakespeare industry, as well. Cohen suggests that 'Shakespeareans looking back at the present century will note that it began with the recreation of two theatres for which Shakespeare wrote his plays'.[15] Cohen's proleptic nostalgia – the ability to imagine fondly remembering something that has just happened – is the inverse of the revolutionary kind, the ability to remember something new as always already old. Cohen is probably prophetic (for the same reasons that Cuthbert was prophetic) because theatres provide a place to see, not just where we've been, but also where we might be going. At the same time, the imperative to build, to rebuild, is most often leveraged upon a vision for the future that is also a vision of the past, though a partial vision that always leaves a lot out by design.

Just as the 'Renaissance' had to ignore hundreds of years of artistry, enterprise and imagination during the *med oevum*, so twenty-first century theatrical revivalists often forget – perhaps purposefully so – the intervening years of Shakespearean regression, a wilful forgetting so that certain verities can be reasserted. But, to circle back to where this chapter began, making a regression look like a revolution means actively forgetting that you're not the first. Thoroughly, ostentatiously, even programmatically committed to remembering and honouring theatrical origins, the Blackfriars engages in a systematic forgetfulness of all the revivalists that have come before, not least the patron saint of the forgotten man, William Poel.

Poel and the forgotten

Why is there not a statue of William Poel in the lobby of the Blackfriars? Or of Nugent Monck in the courtyard at the Globe? Or photographs of various World Fair Globes at the Oregon Shakespeare Festival's 'Elizabethan Theatre', outside of which stands a sign that calls it 'America's First Elizabethan Theatre', a claim that grows ever more opaque the closer you get to it? Why does revivalism always forget its actual history while making its own? Perhaps those who forget the past get to repeat it. For the late twentieth-century Shakespeare revolution that means forgetting William Poel, Nugent Monck, the various Globe reconstructions that came

before and any number of other revivals. For that matter, the
Blackfriars might – next to the placard about the original
Blackfriars – post a genealogical stemma running from Poel
to Granville-Barker and Tyrone Guthrie to Sam Wanamaker,
advocates all of the open stage.[16]

This systematic process of willed forgetfulness is nowhere
more obvious than with William Poel, a representative figure
for the active erasure of actual history in the creation of a new
one. Yet the ASC owes him an enormous debt – although it
shows no sign of paying it. Possibly nagged by a sense of this
debt, a grant proposal from the early years of the Shenandoah
Shakespeare Express goes out of its way to repudiate Victorian
tradition: 'the Shenandoah Shakespeare Express does not
strive to promote William Shakespeare as the cultural icon
our public schools received from the Victorians'.[17] And yet,
today's Elizabethan revival is also a Victorian one, since it
received from the Victorians – or rather from Poel, a Victorian
– the return to Shakespeare's staging conditions. Poel was also
not the first person to think of it, however, and was equally as
eager as his inheritors to forget where he came from. Revivals
always practice the art of artful amnesia.

There are many ways of understanding what Poel was up
to in the late nineteenth and early twentieth centuries, and
just as many ways of misunderstanding it. For if the modern
Shakespeare theatre tries to forget about Poel, theatre history
has not.[18] Indeed, as Robert Speaight explains in his book on
Poel and the Elizabethan revival, 'in 1948 the first long-term
project which the newly-founded Society for Theatre Research
proposed to itself was the commemoration in 1952 of the
centenary of the birth of William Poel'.[19] Thus, Poel is not
just an influential, but also an inspirational figure, even an
inaugural one, for students of theatre history. Nevertheless,
Speaight knowingly embarked upon a reclamation project,
even a revivalist one. While he was writing the book on Poel,
he was, as he explains, often faced with the question: 'Who
was William Poel?' This spurred Speaight on with his project
since it reminded him 'how largely he had been forgotten, and

of how little he had ever been known'. This is rhetorically useful for his project, of course, but it suggests that there's something self-erasing about the programmes of revivals and the profiles of revivalists.[20] Those who remember the past are condemned to be forgotten.

On balance, Speaight was largely successful, since he introduced, or re-introduced, Poel to posterity. Today, Poel figures in any number of academic studies of Shakespeare and performance. Indeed, he's even taken on an outsized importance according to Robert Shaughnessy, given that Poel's 'Elizabethan' staging of the first quarto of *Hamlet* at St. George's Hall in 1881 was 'in most contemporary accounts [...] judged to be a misguided venture bungled by its amateur performers'.[21] Poel will always merit at least a footnote in accounts of the transition from Beerbohm-Tree to Granville-Barker, who was a wayward acolyte of Poel. In these terms, Poel plays an odd role as midwife to the modern, his antiquarianism a spur to the avant-garde. Cary Mazer argues, for instance, that Poel's influence may be traced through the 'new stagecraft' of the early twentieth century.[22] It is, in fact, Poel's architecturally determined brand of revivalism that lives on today, though often in attenuated forms. As Peter Thomson points out, 'what made Poel so influential' was that his 'determined pursuit of forgotten styles of performance necessitated a reassessment of the nature and function of performance space'.[23] In these terms, Poel's legacy looms large over the late twentieth-century's preoccupation with theatrical space, not least in the Shakespeare industry where the Globe, the Blackfriars and the RSC's renovations consumed so much attention at the turn of the twentieth century.

Another way of understanding Poel is as an embarrassment, for giving Poel his due often means giving him grief. (Speaight writes that Poel 'was his own worst enemy', but history suggests that it was a close contest.[24]) Peter Thomson roughs up Poel in *The Routledge Companion to Directors' Shakespeare*, suggesting that 'The uncomfortable fact is that, faced with the exigencies of performance, Poel's practice was always more half-hearted than his theories'.[25] Thomson also calls Poel's one-off effort to costume his audience in Elizabethan garb his 'daftest inspiration' (Andrew Gurr suggested the same thing for the Globe and escaped the rhetorical tar and feather),[26] but Thomson is just a late entry in a long line of deriders. After Poel's first 'experiment' Basil Dean described his 'peculiarities of speech and manner', which were 'mercilessly burlesqued in the dressing room by us youngsters'.[27] Max Beerbohm paid Poel a backhanded compliment – or a forehanded insult – when he credited him with 'teaching us to pity the poor Elizabethans and be thankful for the realism of the modern theatre'.[28] Paul Prescott has written that Poel's critics – Beerbohm and also William Archer and A. B. Walkley – were 'merciless about his eccentricities'.[29] Even supporters acknowledged that Poel was fighting an uphill battle. Harcourt Williams notes in his memoir of his years at the Old Vic that Poel enjoyed but 'meagre support from the public' during the years of his work.[30] And the sympathetic Granville Barker noted that Poel often worked in the 'the teeth of ridicule', which continues to gnaw at him even to this day.[31]

Recalling Thomson's characterization of Poel's work, we might ask 'uncomfortable' for whom? What was – and what *is* – so embarrassing about Poel, so 'uncomfortable' about him? Max Beerbohm probably put his finger on it when he took exception to Poel's exceptionalism:

> It seems absurd that we should have to make a stand in the matter. Yet it is a fact that the mode of the Elizabethan Stage Society is by some authoritative persons pretended to be the one and only dignified mode of presenting Shakespeare's plays – to be a mode in comparison with which ours is tawdry and Philistine and wicked.[32]

This is a characteristic of revivalism (and of revolutions). It insists upon singularity. Revivalism is never just one way, it is the only way, the one true faith. Poel and his followers had a smack of the scourge about them, as though they'd showed up at the temple of Shakespeare to overturn a table or two. Beerbohm's comic characterization of 'our' way of presenting Shakespeare as 'Philistine and wicked' lampoons the extent to which revivalism is always just a step from evangelism.

Poel's place in the history of Shakespeare and performance is relatively well known, therefore – at least to theatre historians – so it may seem a waste of time to give him this much attention. Better just to skip him and move on. To do so, however, would be to mimic the process by which modern revivalists erase his work. For while Poel often gets a cameo in histories of twentieth-century Shakespeare and performance – that of a cranky uncle – his name is absent from the manifestoes and rationales of the ASC (and Shakespeare's Globe for that matter). The argument here is not that the ASC should honour Poel – 'Here at the Blackfriars we do Shakespeare a little differently, just like William Poel did before us'. The purpose here is to examine Poel's absence from modern revivals. Indeed, forgetting him is among the first moves of those that he inspired but who can never credit his inspiration. The reason is not too hard to find: reproducing the staging practices of William Shakespeare looks like a revolutionary act. Reproducing those of Poel looks like a reactionary one. Poel embarrasses modern revivalists because he reminds them that they're not the first ones to think of it. Nevertheless, the late twentieth-century revival of Elizabethan practice owes as much to the nineteenth century as to the sixteenth.

From an historical perspective, the genealogy of the ASC must include William Poel, though Poel's name is nowhere to be found in the ASC archives. The parallelism of Poel's project with the SSE/ASC's is uncanny, however, which no doubt accounts for his erasure. Consider as a signal instance how similar the rhetoric of Poel and modern revivalism is. In July 1896, William Poel's Elizabethan Stage Society (founded 1894–7) produced a pamphlet that reads like a prototype for modern revivalists:

THE ELIZABETHAN STAGE SOCIETY is founded to illustrate and advance the principle that Shakspere's Plays should be accorded the build of stage for which they were designed [...] A theatre specially built on the plan of the sixteenth century could be erected at a moderate cost, and could be used as a schoolhouse for instruction in the poetic drama as well as for performance of Shakspere's plays in accordance with his original design. With little or no scenery, and with no necessity for costumes of different periods for every play, the bill could be changed at comparatively small cost [...] The original subscription to the Society has been one guinea per annum, the season being from the 1st of October to the 30th September in the following year. This subscription has not proved sufficient to cover the cost of more than one performance and the deficiency has been met by the Director, Mr. William Poel.

The language is familiar to anyone who has ever been on either side of a fundraising appeal for a revivalist project: the 'advancement' of a lofty principle based on architectural determinism ('the stage for which they were designed'); the focus on pedagogy ('a schoolhouse for instruction'); the invocation of thrift ('at comparatively small cost'); followed by an appeal for money. Indeed, it is often alleged – with Poel – that staging plays the Shakespeare way will chasten the excessive costs of huge companies and lavish sets. Theatrical revivalists quickly learn the true costs of such thrift.

Perhaps Poel's bill would have been 'comparatively small', but revivalist ambitions – if successful – always move towards reconstruction, which carries a hefty price tag. After all, the ambition of the pamphlet is that Shakspere's [*sic*] plays need the 'build of stage' for which they were 'designed'. For all his attention to language and dramaturgy, Poel dreamed of building a permanent stage. He never achieved that ambition, and shifted ground frequently between venues with his Fortune 'fit-up', a scaled down reproduction based on the Fortune contract that he eventually sold off in 1905.

The impulse to architecture is considered at length below, but Poel's reputation would be very different had the Elizabethan Stage Society fulfilled its founding principle, which was to erect the kind of playhouse for which Shakespeare's plays were designed. Something very like the new Globe or new Blackfriars. Poel was not crazy; he was under-capitalized and his reputation has paid for it ever since.

For all Poel's adherence to the stage and the principles of the Elizabethan theatre, he took a surprisingly progressive stand on the issue of gender equity. This may have arisen from necessity. A publication of the Elizabethan Stage Society in 1896 lists the 'Original Members' of the Society, of which seventy-one are women and just fifty-two men.[33] Perforce, Poel's productions regularly featured women in men's roles. His biographer puts it down to an 'eccentricity', not an exigency, but he 'at least never claimed that it was Elizabethan' in practice.[34] As in so many instances, the ASC inadvertently apes Poel's practices in casting women in men's roles, though, unlike Poel, they claim *some* inspiration from the gender-play of the Shakespearean stage.

This no doubt reads like an attempt to give credit where it is due, to tip the hat to William Poel whenever a revivalist project gets around to reinventing the wheel. But that is to repeat the process by which history came to identify The Theatre as the point of origin for early modern theatre – to replace one 'purity of origin' with another. William Poel's zeal can erase the fact that Poel himself had predecessors and that Poel had a case of forgetfulness himself. To be fair, it is unclear if Poel knew of the Benjamin Webster and J. R. Planche *Taming of the Shrew* in the 1846–7 season at the Haymarket. The Haymarket manager Webster and antiquarian playwright Planche collaborated on a quasi-Elizabethan production that was played without scenery in Elizabethan costume. As is so often the case with revivalism, Planche was prompted by a dissatisfaction with contemporary treatments of Shakespeare, in his case with Garrick's 'miserable, mutilated' version of *Shrew*, 'Katherine and Petruchio'.[35] It occurred to Planche, he recollects, 'to try the experiment of producing the piece with only two scenes' – he means sets – 'as they would have done in Shakespere's own time under similar circumstances – viz., without scenery'. Planche concludes that the 'revival was eminently successful, incontestably proving that a good play, well acted, will carry the audience along with it, unassisted by scenery'.[36] The production was a one-off, a 'revival' not reviv-al*ism* (Planche more often turned his attention to Christmas extravaganzas like 1845's 'The Bee and the Orange Tree'). Nevertheless, when Poel pronounced his Q1 *Hamlet* in 1881 to be 'the first revival of the draped stage in this country or elsewhere'[37] he made up for in audacity what he lacked in accuracy. His was not even the first revival that century. Nevertheless, Speaight calls it 'the birth of a new idea', since it is characteristic of the born again to forget their real birthday.

J. R. Planche and Ben Webster weren't the first either, of course, and it would surely be possible to find yet earlier incar-nations of the spirit of revival in the annals of early drama, earlier incarnations that nevertheless strike the world as novel. ('It was thought an extraordinary thing when Garrick first put on a pair of Elizabethan trunks for *Richard III*,[38] as Lester Wallack put it in the late nineteenth century). Even as Poel pursued his project, the Mermaid Society under the direction of Philip Carr were reviving Ben Jonson's masques and Poel had been much influenced by Frank Benson's travelling company, who lived outdoors while on tour, recreating the conditions of early travelling troupes. It would be possible to push a study of revivals on past Poel to other twentieth-century attempts to capture the spirit of Shakespeare in the revival of his staging practices. In the *New York Times* of 2 April 1916 – under the broad heading 'Shakespeare Tercentenary; 1616–1916' – Ashley H. Thorndike's essay 'The English Theatre in Shakespeare's Time' features two photographs from the Irving Place Theatre of 'an effort to reproduce the Shakespeare stage'.[39] Around the same time, on the other side of the country, a production of *The Knight of the Burning Pestle* was played on an 'Elizabethan Stage' at

Stanford University.[40] And on and on, through Ben Greet's quasi-Elizabethan outdoor productions to Nugent Monck's Maddermarket playhouse to the Earl's Court 1930's replica of an Elizabethan stage.[41] There is a deep genealogy for the American Shakespeare Center, particularly for its reproduction of a physical space for which Shakespeare's plays 'were designed'. The focus here, however, is not – or not just – on remembering where the ASC actually came from but on the history of forgetfulness that tesselates across the history of Shakespeare and performance. The watchword for these spasms of revival is not, that is, all shall be remembered, but rather all shall be forgotten.

*

The point of pointed forgetfulness is so that certain verities can be discovered as though for the very first time. J. R. Planche sounds, for instance, as though he were the first one to think of the 'experiment' of reviving a play under original conditions. These experiments pretend not to know what they will discover. For however novel Planche finds his attempt, his conclusion sounds familiar: the discovery, announced breathlessly, that a good play needs no help. Poel made the same claim of his *Hamlet*, an 'experiment' that proved that 'the absence of scenery did not lessen the interest, and that with undivided attention being given to the play and to the acting, a fuller appreciation and keener enjoyment of Shakespeare's tragedy became possible'.[42] A review of his first experiment, *Measure for Measure* in 1893, reported that it 'proved at least that scenic accessories are by no means as indispensable to the enjoyment of the play as the manager supposes'.[43] Richard Flecknoe had made a similar point nearly 200 years before Planche and Poel, writing that,

> that which makes our Stage the better, makes our Playes the worse perhaps, they striving now to make them more for sight, then hearing; whence that solid joy of the interior

is lost, and that benefit which men formerly receiv'd from Playes from which they seldom or never went away, but far better and wiser than they came.[44]

Part of the logic that underscores this old saw is that audiences are incapable of looking at scenery and listening to blank verse *at the same time*. (This particular form of condescension to audiences courses through theatre history, from the Renaissance debate over the preeminence of the eye or ear to modern reviews of Shakespeare that can praise a production for scenic beauty or the aural kind, but rarely both.) Whether Planche, Poel or Flecknoe, the theatre is always discovering that it does not need scenery.[45] The permanent revolutions by which theatre renews itself means repeating verities it constantly forgets … so it can discover them all over again.

These discoveries always serve as a corrective, usually to the scholarly types – the whipping boys and straw men – who have forgotten that Shakespeare was a 'man of the theatre'. Lecturing to the Royal Society for the Arts in 1916, Poel quoted George Brandes to remind his audience of what they had forgotten due to the ignorance of 'educationalists':

George Brandes, when lecturing in this country, said: 'It is forgotten, here, that Shakespeare wrote plays to be acted'. Surely this forgetfulness is in great measure due to the persistent way in which our educationalists ignore the stage on every occasion when reference is made to the dramatist.[46]

Dover Wilson echoes the sentiment in 1936. He was giving his inaugural lecture as Regius Professor of Rhetoric and English Literature at the University of Edinburgh, but there was nothing new to his claim that it is 'one of the most important literary discoveries of our age that Shakespeare wrote, not to be read, but to be acted; that his plays are not books, but as it were libretti for stage performance. It is amazing that so obvious a fact should so late have come to recognition'.[47] How many times, and in how many accents, has it been alleged that we have forgotten that Shakespeare wrote his plays to be acted? Each critic or scholar reacting to this 'fact' like 'stout Cortez' encountering the Pacific.[48] Has anyone ever *actually* forgotten this? In 'Introduction to the Study of the Old English Dramatists' (1840), an anonymous critic – while reminding us, helpfully, that: 'We must also never lose sight of the rakehelly, wild, adventurous life led by these dramatists' – adds that 'they wrote *for the theatres*, not for posterity or closet criticism – a fact self-evident, but strangely overlooked.'[49] With Lucky Jim, we might reply, this what overlooked fact? This strangely what fact? There's a near compulsion to point out that Shakespeare's theatricality is overlooked even though everyone knows it and says it. It is far more often alleged that it is overlooked that Shakespeare and his contemporaries wrote '*for the theatres*' than it is ever actually overlooked.

The twin moves of revivalism are, then, to blame the academy for forgetting that Shakespeare was a man of the theatre and then claim to have rediscovered a theatrical energy immanent in the practices that Shakespeare himself employed, and then to be the first one to have rediscovered it. (A reviewer in 1994 praised Cohen's *Much Ado About Nothing* and gave: 'Much credit to director and "inventor" of this back-to-the-time-of-Shakespeare-style, Ralph Alan Cohen.'[50]) A related move – certainly for Poel, but for his followers as well – is to distance the impulse for revival from the work of antiquarianism. J. R. Planche, for instance, was an avowed and successful antiquarian – his voluminous history of British costume still influences costumers today, not to mention his heraldry research. But William Poel had his eye fixed firmly on the now. In the same lecture in which he reminded the fellows of the Royal Society of Arts that Shakespeare was a man of the theatre, Poel stressed that: 'It is vital to the best interests of the stage that Shakespeares name [*sic*] shall be immediately connected with the *modern* English theatre of which he himself, actor and part theatre manager, as well as dramatic poet is the founder, inspirer and highest ornament [emphasis added].'[51] As Peter Thomson writes, 'Poel had his eye on the future'.[52] Poel's revivals and those that followed were not 'the past for the past's sake' but the past for the sake of the present and the future.

Ben Greet once levied the antiquarian ideal when he billed his production of *As You Like It* at Wilton House in Wiltshire – fancifully thought to be site of its composition and first performance – as 'the *second* performance of this play at Wilton'.[53] But Poel imagined his 1881 *Hamlet* to be the start of something big that required that he claim to have staged 'the first revival', which is something like the 'world's only recreation'. There's a big difference between the first revival and the second performance. Poel not only claimed that the 'draped stage' was new (again) but that 'here, then, probably for the first time since Shakespeare's day, was reality given to Shakespeare's words: "The two hours' traffic of the stage".'[54] Whether he was discussing scenery or pacing, Poel's point is that he is the 'first' to revive these practices. (The first since Shakespeare, at least.) And this revival was meant revitalize the modern stage. Poel was just one among other theatrical revivalists to ignore history in the interest of making a new one (Cuthbert Burbage was another, as described above). It would be an odd kind of criticism, however, that accused a theatremaker of fabrication. In fact it is a compliment.

Perhaps the price that Poel paid for his forgetfulness was to be himself forgotten, at least by those who emulated him. Perhaps one thing he pioneered was a mode of forgetfulness. It is fitting then that Poel doesn't show up if you search for him in the archives or on the website of the ASC, but he does merit a brief mention by an actor in the digital archives of the Globe and there *is* a 'William Poel Studio' in the Globe's educational facilities. Poel played a part in early attempts to rebuild the Globe on the Southbank, something that took many years to materialize and which slowly morphed into the National Theatre. You will not find that effort mentioned in the Globe's archive but you will find Poel in a transcription of a podcast by Alex Hassell: he mentions that the Globe stage 'seemed smaller than I remember from the William Poel Festival'.[55] The Globe's website provides no further information on the festival, but the 'Poel Festival' dates back to the 1950s and was under the auspices of the newly formed Society for Theatre Research. The Poel Festival developed over the years into a contest in verse speaking and – like Poel himself – often changed venues, moving from the Old Vic to the Olivier, then to the Globe and the Theatre Royal Haymarket. The Poel Festival finally settled back at the Globe as a separate 'Poel Event' developed at the National. Still, you won't find a mention of the 'Poel Festival' at the Globe today as it was renamed 'The Sam Wanamaker Festival', as though Wanamaker was the first one to think of it. As Poel wrote in the programme to his production of Samuel Rowley's *When you see me, you know me*, 'History repeats itself', if only in forgetting itself.[56]

The spirit of '76

Poel's scale model of the Fortune Playhouse – liquidated to pay his debts – and his dream of a permanent stage locates one of the prevailing curiosities of Elizabethan revivals: a desire for a return to Shakespearean staging turns into a desire for a Shakespearean stage. For all Poel's interest in versification – the natural Shakespearean music he longed to rediscover – his interests bent towards architecture. He made do over the years with various approximations, while dreaming of a platform-stage, 'around it a tiered semi-circular auditorium, the seats rising a few inches for each row and topped by a tier of private boxes'.[57] A desire for a return to a kind of theatre becomes a desire for a theatre, even The Theatre, of which the Globe was a kind of revival. Similarly, while later 'revolutionaries' like J. L. Styan and John Russell Brown often speak of the 'spirit' of the Shakespearean stage, they are also irresistibly drawn to the matter as well. For instance, Styan writes in *The Shakespeare Revolution* that 'the superficial placing of tapestries or pillars or audience on the stage, the mechanical retracing of the original stagecraft, the most elaborate of Elizabethan costumes, would not do it; the task was to recreate the spirit and intention of the original to the best effect'.[58] Nevertheless, while Styan seems to eschew fussy historical precision he, too, called for a reconstructed stage and served, early on, as part of the team responsible for the Bankside Globe. Revivals often begin with a desire to 'express' the spirit of Shakespeare but move towards a wish for a 'centre' in which to house that spirit. In the evangelical terms with which revivalists always flirt, the original altar call turns into an ambition to rebuild the true church.

The peculiar arc of the ASC grows most immediately out of the revival sparked in the 1970s by a group of pioneering Shakespeareans who collectively called for a return to Shakespearean staging as the avenue towards a rediscovery of Shakespeare's spirit. And a neat coincidence of history found Shakespeareans – exactly 400 years after Burbage opened the Theatre – with revolution on the mind. In 1976, Washington, DC, hosted the 'International Shakespeare Association Congress: a Bicentennial Congress', though, as Stephen Booth wrote at the time, one 'insurmountable problem' with the occasion was that 'Shakespeare doesn't really have anything to do with the American Bicentennial'.[59] Nevertheless, the American Bicentennial had something to do with Shakespeare. Inspired, perhaps, by the memorializing events of 1976, the stage-centred scholarship of the period revolved to the events not just of 200, but of 400-years previously. The era's 'Shakespeare Revolution' – launched by J. L. Styan's 1977 book of the same name – brought together Shakespeare, revolution, nostalgia, and real estate in a manner that provides what Booth found wanting in the Bicentennial Congress, 'the missing link between Shakespeare and American history'.[60]

Intentionally or not, Styan's 'Shakespeare Revolution' created the academic impetus behind the greater theatrical reconstruction effort in the years since his book was published. The claim that a 'revolution' helped engender an antiquarian movement may seem initially perverse, but, as argued here, the link between revolution and nostalgia is not all that odd. All revolution begins with and includes an impulse to revolve, or return to the 'first times' to recover something lost. A longing for the past infuses every utopic dream. There may, then, be more than coincidental concord between 1576 and 1976 since the seeds of the most recent 'Elizabethan Revival' were sown in the mid-1970s, when Shakespeareans like Styan were thinking about a revolution. In these terms, the recent development of theatrical reconstructions and the original practices movement might seem not just explicable but also inevitable. The peculiarly American preoccupation with rebuilding early English theatres may owe something to our own 'Spirit of '76' which prompts us to revolve to the 'first times' of English theatre before centuries of fire, war and progress razed our theatrical eden. There is, then, a familiar logic behind the American Wanamaker's Globe project or the American Shakespeare Center's attempt to reorient Shakespeare to the colonies, to start again with a utopic return to a Golden Age of Shakespearean performance in, of all places, Virginia, which, in 2007, celebrated the 400th anniversary of the Jamestown settlement.

Bicentennial longings, that is, only accelerated an already existing strain of American nostalgia. Americans have always had a passion for colonial shopping, buying up England's Shakespearean heritage and relocating it to our shores, be it Henry Clay Folger's bibliophilic zeal, P. T. Barnum's attempt to buy Shakespeare's birthplace and bring it to New York or Staunton's own efforts to rebuild English farmhouses in the Shenandoah Valley at its Frontier Culture Museum. Thus, if it cannot be bought (or if the alarmed English scuttle the efforts, as in Barnum's case), it can be rebuilt. America has a long history of Globe reconstructions, for instance, which became a notable feature of World's Fairs during the Great Depression. The 1933–4 'Merry England' exhibition at the Chicago World's Fair, branded as the 'Century of Progress', featured a Globe replica that was then further replicated in San Diego, Dallas and Cleveland. In 1939, Chicago's entire 'Merry England' exhibit was recreated at New York City's World Fair, 'The World of Tomorrow', in an abortive attempt to franchise the project.[61] The polygonal timber-and-lath building supplied a legible glyph that spelled 'Shakespeare', 'the past', 'Merry England' and, oddly, 'progress', all at once. (Why does no one ever attempt to rebuild The Fortune, the only Elizabethan ampthitheatre for which we have something like contractual details? Is it because Poel got there first? Because Shakespeare didn't work there? Or because approximation trumps accuracy within the rebuilding industry?) Appropriating, theming, and commodifying the trademark cultural material of the former colonizer is what we might call 'nostalgia with a vengeance'. As noted, it is mere happenstance, but a loaded one, that Staunton's Blackfriars Playhouse makes its home on 'Market Street'.

Benjamin's notion helps explain the oddly contrapuntal language of retreat and advance that has always informed theatrical revivalism, why a 'Century of Progress' or a 'World of Tomorrow' might feature, or indeed require, a replica of a late sixteenth-century playhouse. Such projects inevitably include some suggestion that to go forward we must first go back. Poel also understood his project as part of the contemporary *avant-garde*: 'some people have called me an archaeologist', he said in 1913, 'but I am not. I am really a modernist'.[62] From Poel to the present, the language of progress inevitably attends upon the language of recovery. The dialectic language of recovery and progress informs not just the commercial but also academic efforts to 'rediscover' Shakespeare's stage. The title of Styan's *Shakespeare Revolution* neatly telegraphs this initiative in which a 'rediscovery of the Elizabethan stage' will lead to 'the biggest single advances' in the project of 'recovering Shakespeare'.

Cohen has also addressed the recovery implied by his project while calling for a conversion of that recovery into future inspiration: 'We're very much about recovering possibly lost joys; and let's recover them and let modern playwrights start writing for an audience that's visible'.[63] The impulse to recover is, in these terms, a twin desire, both nostalgic and revolutionary, conservative and progressive, 'reactionary and radical' as Christie Carson calls the Globe.

Spirited by revolutionary nostalgia, the well-documented 'Shakespeare Revolution' of the mid-1970s found academics attempting to return Shakespeare to his theatrical origins, freeing him, and themselves, from 400 years of oppressive appropriation by literary history and criticism.[64] The simultaneously theatrical and emancipatory tone of the period's scholarly work – most obviously J. L. Styan's *The Shakespeare Revolution,* but also John Russell Brown's *Free Shakespeare*, and even Alan Dessen's more modestly titled *Elizabethan Drama and the Viewer's Eye* – suggests a generation of scholars reckoning with the past and attempting to free the academically oppressed Shakespeare by returning him to his roots. So if the year 1976 may have triggered revolutionary impulses among, in particular, American academics, the nostalgia Benjamin diagnoses drew many scholars to the stages of the past and produced a drive to rebuild them. For all his emphasis on the 'spirit' over matter, Styan advocated for performance – even a particular kind of stage – as a crucible of interpretation: 'we need, first, a Shakespeare Theatre in which a generation of scholars may be as used to seeing as to reading the play'.[65] Styan was quoting Granville-Barker, since, for generations, scholars have been calling for a generation of scholars to get used to seeing plays. It is difficult to know what, precisely, Styan imagined this 'Shakespeare Theatre' to look like, but his support of Wanamaker's Globe (he was Chairman of the effort from 1981 to 1987) is telling. There were in the mid-1970s plenty of theatres doing Shakespeare but apparently no 'Shakespeare Theatres' that fulfilled the function for which Styan called.

John Russell Brown's *Free Shakespeare* (1974) spearheaded the movement to unshackle Shakespeare not just from its appropriation by literary scholars but also from the accretion of theatrical conventions in the 400 years between the Theatre and Brown's book. Robespierre to Styan's Jefferson, his call for 'radical experiment' went beyond Styan's 'Shakespeare Theatre' to specify the particular contours of a new/old performative regime:

> Radical experiment is necessary to achieve a free Shakespeare performance. I would like to see what a company of about a dozen actors could achieve, if they were 'set upon a stage' and closely surrounded by their audience in the same light. The actors would have to be in charge of the whole enterprise, and its continuance should depend on their success. They would have few group rehearsals, sufficient only to arrange for the movement of supernumeraries and the handling of properties in the more elaborate scenes. They would be given their parts only, and not the text of the whole play, and most of the rehearsals would be in private study, or in twos or three with no director to guide them. In group rehearsals and performance they would have the assistance of a book-keeper.[66]

From some thirty years out, the Free Shakespeare Revolution could be judged a success. In projects like the Globe's original practice productions, the ASC's 'Actors' Renaissance Season' (where actors perform from parts and without directors in new perfect accord with Brown's desire), Patrick Tucker's late 'Original Shakespeare Company' and Peter Cockett's 'Shakespeare and the Queen's Men' project, John Russell Brown has seen his call answered, and J. L. Styan has his 'Shakespeare Theatre' in both London and Staunton and still other works-in-regress. Though the fabled cooperation between academics and practitioners of Shakespeare seems always just around the bend but never quite in sight (again, like the ever ascending middle class), it has produced real estate, which, as argued at the opening, is a critical contemporary measure of success. The revolution is over, the insurgents won, and Shakespeare is finally free.

The danger, as the social critic Eric Hoffer has observed, is that every great cause begins as a movement, becomes a business, and eventually degenerates into a racket. 'Racket' would be an ungenerous and inaccurate description of the Globe or Blackfriars, but Hoffer gets at the central irony of revolutionary impulses. If successful, revolutions come to resemble that which they rebelled against and inevitably attract dissent. The Shakespeare Revolution has moved quickly from cause to commodity in which scholarly work of the mid-1970s has been institutionalized in the emergence of hybridized scholarly/theatrical venues like Staunton's Blackfriars that centre their activities around a reconstructed Renaissance-style theatre. There is no downside to these developments and they certainly are not 'rackets'. The question for the institutions remains, however, what to revolt against when you get what you asked for.

In this regard, Cuthbert Burbage's testimony also works as a proleptic paraphrase of the original practices movement in its expanionist phase. In Burbage's account, after all, we find both the hyperbole and the nostalgia that fuels funding efforts to rebuild the Globe, the Blackfriars or the Rose, or whichever reconstruction project looms on the horizon. While Burbage's account seems animated by a desire to memorialize his father, he was also making a financial argument (itself a kind of 'nostalgia with a vengeance'). In 1635, Eliard Swanston, Robert Benfield and Thomas Pollard, sharers but not 'householders' with the King's Men, had petitioned the Lord Chamberlain, the Earl of Pembroke for the right to purchase shares in the Globe and Blackfriars. Pembroke ordered the Burbage family to sell shares to the three actors and Burbage filed a counter claim. Burbage's testimony is not necessarily inaccurate, then, but it is hardly impartial. In fact, it is entirely and self-interestedly partial. The effort to preserve one's family's name *and* financial position are by no means incompatible, of course, and the power and profit of nostalgia drive equally the theatre reconstruction business. Burbage and the OP movement come together most clearly in their attempt to reap the profits of nostalgia – and 'profit' is intended both literally and figuratively here (most theatrical enterprises would glumly report that no one profits, ever, nostalgically or otherwise).

To read Burbage (and the mission statements of some OP projects), one would think early modern playing spaces were venues built solely by and for the profit of players. (We recall here the Blackfriars placard that credits a group of sharers – rather than an individual venture capitalist – as the impetus behind the original project.) Burbage states that his father was 'himselfe in his younger yeeres a player' and mentions prominently – and pointedly – that the players' take has increased over the years. The seemingly more relevant fact that James Burbage was also a carpenter and proto-capitalist has no place in the narrative. Cuthbert Burbage was not a player, of course, he was management and management always romanticizes labour, particularly when it is suing it.

Currently, the most successful concerns operating under the loose remit of original practices are identifiable by the tireless and creative entrepreneurs who had the idea and raised the money, be it Sam Wanamaker's Globe or Ralph Alan Cohen's Blackfriars. In historical terms, these men are the James Burbages and Philip Henslowes, not the actors who inhabited their buildings. It is, indeed, telling that the names of actors that come most readily to mind are those that entered management: Richard Burbage, Edward Alleyn and the original sharers. When we seek for the names of the men and boys who regularly filled their stages, we draw a blank, relatively speaking. As theatre history retails a particular narrative that privileges property and, in so doing, authorizes the greater reconstruction project, it sustains an ongoing history that champions architecture over artistry and management over labour. The ASC has a stable company, but one early modern practice that the company has not explored is giving them a share in the playhouse. Labour is transient; property is forever.

The conversion of revolutionary zeal into institutional status means that history is likely to repeat itself, as future groups of revivalists will push back against architecture's privilege. It's easy to see in found-space and immersive Shakespeare a nascent movement away from reconstruction towards less material, more ephemeral products and processes of playing. If Cohen is right that future Shakespeareans will look back to the beginning of this century as a time of reconstruction – and I suspect they will; in fact I am doing so – they will also locate a more ephemeral insurgency out and away from historical reconstructions. In this respect, the function of the ASC's touring company is vital to an understanding of the way the institution honours its own history as well as the early modern kind. Its touring company tirelessly travels the US, often converting 'found' academic spaces into one-off venues. The touring company is apparently profitable, but the profits of the ASC's road show are more than merely financial. There are more bottom lines than one, and while the touring company is called – not without some tension in their name – the 'Blackfriars on Tour', the travelling troupe nonetheless inoculates the ASC against becoming just a building, ranging some mobile ephemerality against the brick-and-mortar stasis of the Blackfriars. Nevertheless, nearly thirty years down the road, the ASC's travels have led it inexorably towards architecture. This is a recurrent and recurring theme of revivalism. It begins with a spirit but then seeks accommodation. The move from an 'express' to a 'centre' is literally realized in the conversion of the SSE into the ASC. The centre can only hold if it has something to hold it.

US vs Them

Shenandoah Shakespeare Express became well known in the 1990s for fast-paced performances that adhered loosely to some of the performance conditions of travelling companies in early modern England – casts that employed doubling, 'universal lighting', minimal sets and a swift-paced commitment to 'two hours traffic of the stage'. Stephen Booth praised the company in a 1992 *Shakespeare Quarterly* review that singled out the company's pace: 'The speed advertised by the word "express" is of the special aesthetic essence of The Shenandoah Shakespeare Express [...] [T]hese productions move like light.'[67] (They also move *in* it, as the next chapter explores.) Other reviewers frequently noted the breathless pace of the company's performances (almost literally 'breathless' since Ralph Cohen and Jim Warren rigorously policed pauses), with only the occasional carp about what gets lost at high speed: 'sometimes the emphasis on brisk pacing reduces the poetry and emotion to the level of a foot race'.[68] In its nomenclature, marketing, reviews and practices, the 'express' in SSE connoted not just histrionic 'expression', but a company commitment to express-lane Shakespeare. Whichever nuance was sacrificed to speed, or velocity the SSE found, can be incredibly stabilizing.

Though based in the Shenandoah Valley of Virginia, the SSE was, like Federal Express, in the business of delivery. The company toured relentlessly, arriving at high schools and on college campuses with little more than what could fit in a van. The actors were usually recent college graduates themselves, and they might set up in a variety of more or less unpromising performance spaces, stage a lightning-fast show or two, and disappear without a trace. The company employed a dozen wooden boxes upon which the performers sat at the back of the stage and out of which might appear the odd prop or costume piece. The costumes, such as they were, were usually uniform for male and female actors alike: jeans or chinos, a simple shirt or blouse and, perhaps, a sash or hat to indicate rank or status. And, invariably in the early years, the company members wore Converse Chuck Taylor sneakers. Indeed, the company's commitment to swift-footed play was branded by a graphic that showed a crown encircling a pair of the ubiquitous Chucks (the converse star replaced by a sketch of Shakespeare's head). The SSE had no permanent playing space and the sneakers neatly conveyed both the pace and practice of their actors' express delivery.

While the sneakers helped convey the company's scrappy approach to Shakespeare, they also helped to convey its ideological commitments. For while the young actors and the gritty *mise en scène* charmed and disarmed audiences and reviewers, while aggravating some, they also signaled the company's 'outsider' status: with no permanent place to call home, the company attempted to infiltrate and reclaim Shakespeare from the institutions mostly likely to embalm him, institutions of higher education and those of higher artistry. The 'storm-the-barricades' rhetoric showed up in the company's programmes and brochures that spoke of 'blowing the cobwebs' off Shakespeare or – borrowing a then-current MTV locution – offering Shakespeare 'Unplugged'.[69] The company promised to do so, paradoxically, by returning Shakespeare to his theatrical origins. This fantasy of return has been considered above, but in its theatrical approach and ancillary imaging, the company broadcast the message that Shakespeare needed to be reclaimed, saved even. Along with their boxes, the Express packed an agenda.

The 'us-versus-them' language was always clearer about the 'us' than the 'them', though the 'them' seemed at times to be an army of upholsterers. '"We don't do crushed-velvet Shakespeare," is how Mr. Cohen puts it' reports one paper.[70] 'Here they throw away the notions of 'crushed velvet' and regal language' says another.[71] Jim Warren reported in 1997 that 'we're not doing the crushed velvet Shakespeare the way the Victorians did',[72] while Boston's *Patriot-Ledger* called the company a 'welcome antidote to the flabby, overstuffed productions we too often see strutting about the stage'.[73] Washington, DC's *City Paper* allowed that the SSE's lack of upholstery 'doesn't provide much to look at. But frankly, we get more than enough crushed velvet from our resident Shakespeare companies'.[74] The SSE was the perfect antidote, therefore, 'for those who feel like fabric and folderol have overwhelmed the Bard's work in recent years'.[75] Prompted by Cohen and Warren's rhetoric, critics responded as though Henry Irving still had the Shakespeare industry in a stranglehold, along with his Lyceum army of crush velveted soldiers. The idea clearly captivated critics who return to the image again and again in positive reviews. That the tradition of Shakespeare they were dismissing is almost wholly imaginary does nothing to lessen the rhetorical torque, for this is the excoriating language of revolution, which offers lean purity in the face of fat excess. If the idea of Shakespeare the SSE pledged itself upon was largely imaginary, so was the Shakespearean stage they found so revolting.

Underneath the upholstery lurks the real target. Abetted by a willing press, 'them' in these early years had a distinctly English accent. (As noted in the previous chapter, this antagonism would quietly disappear once the SSE rebuilt a quintessentially English theatre.) 'There were no men sporting tights and thick British accents' a newspaper reports of the SSE's *A Midsummer Night's Dream* in 1993. Employing the same tights-and-lights rhetoric, another newspaper asks, 'Wait a minute. Aren't they supposed to be wearing tights and intoning some imposing lines full of "thees" and "thous"'?[76] True to the text, the SSE certainly intoned the odd 'thee' and 'thou', but the reporter couldn't hear them since they were speaking 'American'. And why shouldn't they be? 'Shakespeare was America's bard', one critic pugnaciously pronounces while another asks, tongue in cheek, 'Where were the stuffy British accents?' These light-hearted snarks could turn to heavy-handed sneers: 'There were no boring moments with poncy men in tights' or 'poncy men in tights spouting off endless soliloquies in phony English accents'.[77] With the use of 'poncy' you can hear an uglier adjective through the wall, but the coded homophobia is loud enough. In any event, perhaps one thing lost to the brisk pace was irony, since a critic will find himself relieved at the absence of 'cumbersome British accents'[78] before quoting Jim Warren saying 'We are trying to bring back Shakespeare's original stage and condition'.[79] Only without the tights and accents, presumably.

The upholstered elephant in the room was the Royal Shakespeare Company (RSC). The origin story of the SSE begins with Cohen taking college students to England to see – and hear – what's so great about Shakespeare. The only flaw in this plan is that they were, of course, in England: 'I took them to productions in London in the mid-1980s, but even the RSC was pretentious and overproduced at the time.'[80] By 'even' Cohen might have meant 'especially' – perhaps he was misquoted – since the RSC served as the broadly cushioned target for SSE reviewers, one of whom suggested that the SSE made 'the Royal Shakespeare Company look boring and inept. They bring the work to life'.[81] The paradox of this move – returning to the practices of the early English stage to combat the practices of the modern English stage – is comprehensible under the logic of revolutionary nostalgia, as the SSE purified their product by out-Englishing the English. By doing so, they set up the dialectic under which they emerged and thrived, whether the critic bought it or not. For every ten reviewers relieved to discover that there 'were no British accents, nor were there any men running around in tights', there was at least one who concluded that the 'unhappy fact is that most Americans cannot adequately recreate the beautiful cadences and rhythms of Elizabethan speech'.[82] How the reviewer knows how the Elizabethans spoke is unclear, but his objections simply fuelled the fire. When an anonymous Washington, DC reporter snarked in 1992 that 'The Royal National Theatre of Great Britain [...] have nothing to worry about from the Shenandoah Shakespeare Express', he played right into the SSE's hands,[83] which is where *The Scotsman* liked its Shakespeare, praising the SSE's *Comedy of Errors* when the company took its coals to Edinburgh, as being 'in good American hands where it belongs'.[84] One early rejected name for the SSE – a name chosen to suggest, according to

Cohen, 'wholesome American straightforwardness' – was the 'Un-Royal Shakespeare Company'.[85]

From 1988 to 2000, the company's relentless pace and antic mobility helped it float free of the institutional gravity (and budgetary burdens) that permanent playing places exert, and the company toured with increasing acclaim and financial success, a product of their finesse in pitting the stuck-out stage against the stuck-up one. With success, however, came a cost. Over the decade, the Chuck Taylors and wooden boxes came to look less like choices born of necessity than faux naïf calculation. Less DIY and more like an aging hipster in a pre-distressed Pixies t-shirt. The SSE, accordingly, began to transform their look and approach, with more elaborate costumes – sometimes even made of crushed velvet – and longer residencies. Furthermore, though the SSE's early years were committed to transforming unlikely spaces (cafeteria, classrooms and on one memorable occasion, a cattle auction yard), the attractions of *place* proved irresistible. Finally, while campus touring allowed the SSE to target academic malpractice, the company remained peripheral to the world of institutionalized theatrical Shakespeare. In sum, over the years, a variety of centripetal forces combined to retard the company's mobility and draw it towards the centre.

Fortuitously, the company's early years neatly coincided with robust markets and, by the late 1990s, the funding was sufficient to begin construction on the Blackfriars Playhouse in Staunton, Virginia. It opened in September 2001 and the company dropped the 'Express' from its name. Shortly thereafter, 'Shenandoah Shakespeare' became the 'American Shakespeare Center'. The move to the middle was nearly complete. Today, the ASC uses quite a different graphic than the crudely drawn, crown-encircled Chucks. In its promotional materials, the Center uses a silhouetted chandelier to represent those that illuminate their reconstruction of the Blackfriars Playhouse. From tatty sneakers to Restoration Hardware in just over ten years.

Establishing the 'Center' of American Shakespeare in a small town in Virginia may seem hubristic, but the cheeky (and purposeful?) substitution of 'American' for 'Royal' in the familiar 'RSC' acronym discloses the impulse for a deliberate revolution against an English monarchical Shakespeare. As noted, the RSC figures prominently in the founding narratives of the SSE-*cum*-ASC. Cohen has often linked the origins of the SSE to his students' dissatisfaction with the RSC and therefore his own. A 2007 article in a National Endowment for the Humanities publication entitled *Shakespearetown* (and subtitled 'Ralph Alan Cohen and the American Shakespeare Center want to turn the sweet little town of Staunton, Virginia, into the world capital of Shakespearean theater', with which Cohen would cheerfully agree) sketches the company's origins:

> Starting in 1974, Ralph Alan Cohen, then a young professor of English at James Madison University, began taking groups of students to London to see productions of the Royal Shakespeare Company. A semester-abroad program soon grew out of Cohen's realization that literature students responded better to Shakespeare's plays as theater [...] Over the next ten years, Cohen caught every production the RSC did. He recalls seeing Jeremy Irons as Richard II in February 1986, a highlight one would think, but his students were unimpressed.[86]

Reacting against the conceptual 'director's theatre' of the RSC (and inspired by Cheek by Jowl, itself a company without a permanent home), Cohen and a student, Jim Warren, founded the SSE. In the same article cited above, Cohen is quoted as saying that the 'Royal Shakespeare Company [is] [...] the gold standard as far as everyone's concerned',[87] and the RSC has proved a useful trope for the SSE in their promotional campaigns: The staid, entropic, plummy Shakespeare of the RSC ranged against the plucky guerilla insurgency of the underdog Americans. There is more than a little of the spirit of '76 in the ASC's attempt to recentre Shakespeare in the earliest colonies through the efforts of Ralph Cohen and his 120-minute men.

In fact, the building of the Blackfriars Playhouse and the forming of the ASC echo the opening strategies of the early federalists: the appropriation and repurposing of English forms within the peculiar economies of mid-Atlantic America. The commercial viability of a reconstructed Blackfriars relies upon the heritage conferred by the building's antecedent; the space is a form of 'instant history' and markets itself by offering familiarity and novelty in the same package. Ultimately, the move from 'Express' to 'Center' has consolidated the SSE's founding purposes and intents through the forms and practices of institutional theatre. Moreover, the SSE made it to the middle in theatre historical terms. They did not reconstruct a suburban playhouse but a citified one, not 'public' but 'private' in the legal language of the time. If this move fits uneasily with the company's early rhetoric, it is just one more way that revivalism forgets itself.

To put this another way, the ASC is what it looks like when revolution becomes institution. The ASC now resembles many professional regional theatres in its operational structure, educational outreach, and funding profile. By adopting the procedures, protocols, and rhetoric of regional theatre operations, the ASC now smuggles its 'revolutionary' impulse within the banalities of institutionalized American theatre. The company has, however, innovated various spirited attempts to maintain the clarity and novelty of their original approach. For example, as chapter four details, for three months each year, the 'Actors' Renaissance Season' dispenses with directors altogether and mounts four to five minimally rehearsed plays in repertory. Shows during this brief season demonstrate the vitality of performances in which authority inheres in the performer. The ASC, in short, stages its own revolution each year, only this time against itself. The history of the SSE/ASC/ Blackfriars is, then, a fascinating but familiar study in reaction, revolution, appropriation and consolidation. It remains to be seen whether the sheer entropic force of institutional practice ultimately results in yet another familiar scenario in which a revolution installs a regime indistinguishable from that against which it revolted. Or, rather, whether the ASC can successfully balance mobility and inertia and centre their expression, while maintaining their velocity.

The institutional history of the Virginia company is, therefore, at least two different histories. From 1988 to 2001, Ralph Cohen and Jim Warren shepherded a touring theatrical troupe called 'Shenandoah Shakespeare Express' that featured pace as their 'special aesthetic essence'. Between the years 2001 and 2004, this institution reinvented itself by building the Blackfriars Playhouse and rebranding itself as the 'American Shakespeare Center'. The shift from 'Shenandoah' to 'American' represents more than a simple ambition of scale; it traded the local and specific for the national and generic even while the company pledged allegiance to place by investing in real estate. A columnist in 2003 attempted to 'reconcile' 'the contradictions' of 'an institution traditionally fueled by the raw energy and eagerness of its youngish performers' trying to create a 'Shakespeare destination, a mid-Atlantic theatrical mecca in the mold of Ashland, Ore., or Stratford, Ontario'.[88] The article quotes Cohen as wanting to 'create a kind of community where actors have tenure' – the academic language seeping through – a place where 'performers can settle in, "buy a house if they want to".' In 2001, with the building of a playhouse, the Express had finally come home.

The ASC continues to run a thriving touring company called the 'Blackfriars on Tour' ('The American Shakespeare Express' being, presumably, perilously close to trademark infringement), but the shift from 'Express' to 'Center' signaled an exchange of mobility for stasis as well as outside to in since it is impossible to claim a marginal status when you have claimed the centre. Furthermore, though the ASC's programme mentions brevity as a feature of Shakespeare's stage, performances at the Blackfriars are no longer noticeably shorter than at other theatres. Like the touring companies of early modern England, an investment in real estate shifted the

SSE/ASC's energies from occasional performances in spaces defined by temporal boundaries to daily performances in a place of brick and mortar – the move from an Express to a Centre required a performative space determined not by time but place. In 2003, with the ASC comfortably ensconced in the Blackfriars, a local paper innocently announced the opening of the fall season with the headline, 'Men In Tights on Blackfriars Playhouse Stage'. Crushed velvet, after all, is fabric that can be rubbed both ways.

Coda: The Queen City

All revolution begins with an impulse to revolve, or return, or recover something lost. As noted, Cohen has addressed the recovery implied by his project, while turning that recovery into future inspiration: 'We're very much about recovering possibly lost joys; and let's recover them and let modern playwrights start writing for an audience that's visible'.[89] The impulse to re-enact is, in these terms, nostalgic and revolutionary, conservative and progressive, sentimental and radical. The ASC's reconstruction of the Blackfriars Playhouse is, therefore, the implied and inevitable extension of J. L. Styan's 'Shakespeare Revolution' (itself written in 1976, around the time Cohen was taking students to London to see Shakespeare performed). To some degree, the SSE's founding may be seen as the most literal manifestation of Styan's call-to-arms and all of Ralph Alan Cohen's theatrical work could be read as a direct response to Styan's closing remarks, that 'the [Shakespearean] text will not tell us much until it speaks in its own medium'.[90] There is a comfortable logic and a familiar narrative behind the ASC's efforts to recentre Shakespeare in the colonies, a utopic return to a Golden Age of Shakespearean performance in, of all places, Virginia.

   Like all nostalgia, the revolutionary kind is a longing for something that didn't exist in the first place. The lack of

historical accuracy the ASC exercises explains the tenden-
tiousness of their version of the past. Even when you buy
a ticket online your confirmation reconfirms the ASC's
commitment to a particular version of the theatrical past,
since the company takes every opportunity to tell you what
you are about to see before they show it to you. At the
Blackfriars, performance never fully speaks for itself (this is
another way, considered below, that the ASC is an 'academic'
theatre, in that their rhetoric mimics the academic style of
'tell 'em what they're about to hear, tell 'em, tell 'em what
they heard'). At the close of the confirmation email, we get a
version, even a vision, of the theatrical past the ASC imagines:
'You're about to experience what we think is a wonderful
re-creation of not only Shakespeare's indoor theatre, but
the entire lively, interactive, fun, moving, wonderful, theatrical experience that Shakespeare's audiences enjoyed.' The
assertion about the experience that Shakespeare's audiences
enjoyed is not footnoted (this is at least one way in which
the ASC rhetoric *departs* from academic style). The company
speaks *ex cathedra* even when they're selling a low-church
experience. The emphasis here is that it isn't just the playhouse
but the entire 'theatrical experience' that is being recreated,
howsoever imaginary the original. It takes wit and rigour to
invent a history and stick to it. It also takes repetition, and the
ASC never misses a chance to repeat history.

Queen Victoria never visited, or even reigned over,
Staunton, but, in 2004, the current 'Queen' paid a visit. Not
the current Elizabeth, of course, who has other things to do
with her time – those corgis aren't going to walk themselves
– but rather Queen Elizabeth I or, what's better, Dame Judi
Dench, who came and blessed the Blackfriars. The Queen
City of the Shenandoah Valley finally had its Queen, though,
perhaps fittingly, not a real one but something even better
than the real thing. The event was and is proudly proclaimed
by the ASC and Judi Dench's regal photograph shows up in
the programme, as well as gracing the wall of the ASC offices.
(She provides a silent 'R' before the 'Shakespeare Center'.)

Upon her visit to the Blackfriars, Dame Judi is reported to have said, 'This beautiful theatre should be in England.'[91]

A reviewer in *Shakespeare Bulletin*, in 1993, noted that 'within the hollow crown of the The Shenandoah Shakespeare Express logo sits a high-top sneaker emblazoned with the face of Shakespeare'.[92] It is obviously the case that Shakespeare still wears the crown, or least the laurel, at the American Shakespeare Center, but there – and they – are no longer sneakers. The ASC may have forgotten – or selectively forgotten – their early insurrectionist spirit, but if so they have merely recapitulated the rhythm of their own revolution. The ASC has come a long way from its scrappy origins, but they are prepared to let you forget it.

3

The History of Light

We all know what light is; but it is not easy to tell what it is.

SAMUEL JOHNSON

At the outset of every performance by the ASC, whether at the Blackfriars or on tour, actors tell the audience that the house-lights will stay on throughout the performance. And they will. The lighting is universal, as unvarying as the pre-show recitation. This has been true of the company over the twenty-five years of its existence, a central collect – even *the* central collect – of the pre-performance liturgy diagnosed in the introduction. Whatever other alterations have been made to the ASC's style – and that style has evolved from a minimalist aesthetic to a more sumptuous approach – the invocation of light has been universal across the thousands of performances the company has given. The implication of that invocation is that light is transhistorical: the ASC has left the lights on for twenty-five years, but it's the same light that lit Shakespeare's stage, that pushed its beams through the windows of the original Blackfriars. It is fairly unlikely at this point that an audience member at the Blackfriars will be unaware that the lights will stay on. The pre-show announcement about the lighting scheme can be understood, then, not just as reminder that the lights stayed on – or could not be turned off – during the first performances of Shakespeare's plays but also that the ASC has never knowingly left an audience in the dark. If the pre-show speech at the new Blackfriars is a kind of altar call, the invocation of 'universal lighting' is its central sacrament.

Chapter 3 turns from considerations of time and place (which all drama takes) and explores the performance convention that most distinguishes the ASC from other institutions of Shakespearean performance: its treatment of light. It also marks the book's fulcrum as it pivots from history to practice, though, with the ASC, the two are inseparable since the company both processes and produces history. It is its primary import and export. As the introduction outlined, the company adheres loosely to an array of early English theatrical practices – doubling, touring, pre-show and interval music – but its essential policy is universal lighting, which constitutes not just a material practice but a figural ideology for the communion the ASC forges with its audience past and present. The ASC's commitment to 'original practices' – both the phrase and all it implies – has always been lukewarm, but its commitment to universal lighting is red hot. It's not just a convention; it's a rite.

Tellingly, the company's very identity is figured by universal lighting. This is conveyed in any number of marketing schemes – its standard motto is, 'We do it with the lights on', the Blackfriars' logo is a sketch of a chandelier – but universal lighting also determines its approach to acting and therefore signifies *the* central experience of the audience at an ASC show. For if the ASC has a 'house style', it is a relentless commitment to connect the actor with the visible audience. The Blackfriars company is at home with doubling, music, and touring, that is, but they go about the business of 'audience contact' with a malice. It is universal lighting that sets the terms of performance at the Blackfriars, terms that may be summarized as intimacy, proximity, contact and community. 'Blackfriars Performativity', after W. B. Worthen's work on 'Globe Performativity', is almost wholly constituted by its commitment to sharing a uniform field of light – and a uniform field of social experience – with actor and audience alike.[1]

The ASC's commitment to what it calls 'universal lighting' places them in an odd spot, however, since they also claim that there's nothing to see here. For instance, the 'Blackfriars Playhouse Tour Script' requires guides to tell visitors that, in the Renaissance, the 'audience was more interested in hearing a play, rather than viewing a spectacle'.[2] In doing so, again, the ASC echoes William Poel, who claimed that 'in those days' the real object of going to the theatre 'was not to *see*, but to *hear*'.[3] That Renaissance audiences went to 'hear a play' is one of those theatre historical myths that just won't die (why do minstrels wander, why do players stroll?) According to Gabriel Egan's tabulation, for every use of 'hear a play' in the annals of Renaissance drama, there are twelve references to 'seeing a play'.[4] Again, though, accuracy is not the target the ASC is aiming at. (As the introduction argued, the ASC cites history to indemnify itself against it.) Just to be sure that there's no mistake, the script further instructs guides to tell guests that 'this ideology is proven through Shakespeare's texts and the playhouse construction'. The awkward syntax and questionable claim reveals just how special the pleading is, but the invocation of historical precedent is the surest way to convert an idea into an ideology. As with Worthen's idea of performativity at the Globe, the Blackfriars variety positions itself between the authorizing text and the authenticated experience of an vanished audience who went to 'hear a play' by the trans-historical light of day. The rhetorical appeal to universal lighting that previews every show lingers like light throughout the performance, casting a wan glow of authenticity across the event that follows.

A guest might wonder why the Virginia company went to the trouble – $3.7 million of trouble – to build a Blackfriars reconstruction if what it was after was an auricular drama not a spectacular one. The Blackfriars is a *gorgeous* room, thoughtfully conceived, rigorously executed and deliberately appointed. Why tell guests that they're there to listen, not look? The tension between a rigorous commitment to illuminating everything – universal lighting – and to a theatre of the ear strikes at the enabling paradox, even the galvanizing mystery, at the heart of the ASC enterprise. That paradox is a residue of the fact that the ASC never set out to build a playhouse. It was established in the early 1990s as an 'Express' not a 'Center', and the spaces in which it originally played were immaterial so long as they could be configured as a thrust and universally lit. This flexibility was a point of pride, and remains one for the touring company (called, in another paradox, 'The Blackfriars on Tour'). From inception until 2001, it was *space* not *place* that the company stressed. It is important to distinguish the new Blackfriars from the new Globe, then. The SSE was formed to recreate the *conditions*, not the habitations, of early modern performance. As gracefully executed as the playhouse is, it awkwardly accommodates a company formed to entertain the ear, not eyes. Again, 'the presence of paradox generally exhibits the force of an underlying desire'.[5] Here the desire is to have it both ways, which the theatre is traditionally quite good at, as is the ASC. If the approach to history can seem casually pedantic, or wilfully philistine, its approach to *performance* is brazenly paradoxical: it takes giddy perversity to build a playhouse as beautiful as the Blackfriars and invite people in just to watch each other listen.

If the mission has crept as the company evolved from an Express to a Center, the central strategy has remained constant, to create theatrical community through a quasi-devotional experience of Shakespeare. Upon the opening of the Blackfriars, Ralph Alan Cohen wrote feelingly about the kind of theatre the building was designed to house. Or, to be more precise, the kind of *experience* the building was meant to house, since the Blackfriars is both by name and nature not a theatre – a place 'to see' – but a 'playhouse', a site designed to domesticate festivity. (The building is officially incorporated and licensed as the 'Blackfriars Playhouse', and promotional material assiduously avoids calling it a 'theatre'.) The festivity housed at the Blackfriars is distinguished by a communal act of watchful listening. Threading the eye of the paradox, Cohen writes in a 2000 promotional brochure – the words undershadowed by a sketch of a chandelier – 'When the actors can see us and we can see one another, we hear more clearly the language of the plays [...] When we hear Shakespeare with the lights on, we hear him in the right light.'[6] This is less a truth claim than a wilful truth – we '"make them hear the words," Cohen says'[7] – not an historical claim but a manifesto for the kind of experience the Blackfriars was built to house. Cohen was once quoted to say that he has '"dedicated my life to making students see the importance of language"'.[8] The universally lit experience of Shakespeare is a form of synesthetic theatre, where the ear is enfranchised by the eye's illumination.

Like most sacraments, the way this transformation actually works, the way one might hear Shakespeare 'more clearly' in the light is a mystery – but the mystery is the meaning. Across the twenty-five years of its existence, no position has been more fundamental – even fundamental*ist* – to the company's identity than a belief that a communion with Shakespeare, past and present, is only truly possible with the lights on. The promo material in which Cohen outlined his belief carries the headline 'Light, after 359 years of darkness'. The headline riffs on the idiom of theatre 'going dark'. The original Blackfriars was officially shut in 1642, though playing went intermittently on there, and reopened in Staunton in 2001. The headline smuggles in another sense: the last 359 years of Shakespearean production have been benighted. The quasi-religious, even evangelical tone of bringing light to darkness suggests that everything since 1642 has been a void, dark ages during which audiences could not hear the revealed word of the Bard until a new playhouse opened at the dawn of a new century, a coincident of time – or not – that explains in part the millenarian language that announced the Blackfriars renaissance.

In what follows, an examination of the qualities of light at the Blackfriars, the qualities of acting, and the qualities of experience it affords takes this book into the hot bulb of 'Blackfriars Performativity'. This chapter diagnoses the dynamics of the ASC's performance aesthetic, its house style, with special attention to its most visible performance technology and the way it disposes the audience towards its productions, its actors to its audience, and its audience to Shakespeare. Universal lighting at the Blackfriars is *always* present though also always of the past, a figural and literal presence that defines the heart of the Virginia company's evangelical insistence that what they do, they do with the lights on. Above all, this chapter attempts to define the essential feature of Blackfriars Performativity. What precisely is the 'it' that the ASC does in the universal light, since, it turns out, 'it' isn't precisely Shakespeare?

Canned light

No natural light penetrates the Blackfriars. Everything is illuminated, only artificially. The design of the building – a faux Jacobean hall inside a modern shell – means that while the building has exterior windows the playhouse proper does not. It remains hermetically sealed from the light of day. The lighting sources are therefore all electrically generated. The most apparent sources of light are nine hanging chandeliers, which hold 248 'candle bulbs'.[9] The bulbs look about as much like candles as plastic bottles of Coca-Cola look like the real thing. No one would be fooled into thinking that the chandeliers hold real candles, but then that's not the point. The point is to cite, not simulate, early modern lighting, and, indeed, the chandeliers shadow the tiered ones that hang above the stage in the 1673 sketch of an indoor playhouse on the title page of Francis Kirkman's *The Wits*. The chandeliers are complemented by sconces placed about the galleries, sconces made out of hammered tin that reflect the light of yet more 'candle bulbs'. The light that audiences *see*, therefore, radiates from wrought-iron fixtures with vaguely candle-shaped bulbs – restoration hardware. It is, in short, an historical light, illuminating its own faux-antiquity. But much like the building it illuminates, the light only looks old and doesn't care who knows it.

The light that an audience sees, however, is not the light by which they see. While the lighting is universal, it is not uniform. In fact the playhouse has widely varied pools of light. The most brightly lit part is the ceiling since ten fresnels bounce light off of it to supplement the warm but diffuse glow from the chandeliers. The spotlights were added when the playhouse opened since the chandeliers alone proved incapable of adequately lighting the actors' faces. The spotlights are trained on the ceiling, not the stage, however, not least out of embarrassment since the spotlit actor plays the whipping boy in Blackfriars' promotional material: in an invective against tardy pacing, a brochure argues that, 'An actor in a spotlight knows that the audience has nowhere else to look. He or she can take plenty of time'.[10] As the chandelier serves as a graphic metonym for the Blackfriars project at large, the spotlight serves as synecdoche for the tradition of playing against which the ASC revolts, of self-indulgent actors tyrannizing the audience's eye. However anathema the spotlight to its practices, the Blackfriars is crowned by an ellipse of them. They are the most anachronistic features of the house – other than the neon exit signs and actors over six-feet tall. The above-cited script for Blackfriars tours instructs the guides to point out the chandeliers – 'Ironwork Chandeliers: Metalsmiths of Waynesboro ... 248 candle-bulbs' – but is silent on the matter of the spotlights since they're not what the visitors are there to see. They are instruments that you will see by, not see or hear about, when you visit the Blackfriars as audience or guest.

At the same time, the ASC has made no move to hide the spotlights from the audience at any point over its first decade plus of operation. They are ostentatiously apparent. Something, then, offsets whatever embarrassment might attend on the inveighing against spotlights and the employment of them. Perhaps mere utility. The spotlights are functional, and recessing or disguising them would probably prove expensive or impractical. Nevertheless, the visible spotlights – and the visibility enabled by the spotlights – ironizes the operation of the chandeliers. As William Casey Caldwell puts it, they 're-advertize the context of performance as that of a reconstructed venue, constantly re-citing the location, reminding us where we are, what this location allows to happen, and that the present is still here impinging on this vision of the past'.[11] In these terms, the spotlights do not 'ironize' the operation in the post-modern meaning of irony – the 'ha ha, just kidding' school of modern performance – but actual, dramatic irony in its strictest sense. The only lights the characters recognize, for instance, are the hanging chandeliers (actors will occasionally seek out a chandelier by which to read – in character – a letter). The audience watches actors use 'old' light by the new light, the canned light that bounces off the ceiling that illuminates the chandeliers while compensating for their inadequacy. When characters occasionally bring torches or real candles on stage, the layers simply – or complexly – multiply. Even though you can read by it, the light at the Blackfriars is thick – thick with irony, thick with multiple temporalities, thick with layered meaning. If it is an artificial light, it is also an alluvial one.

One thing the spotlights illuminate, then, is the inefficiency of the chandeliers. But the modern spotlights also verify the chandeliers, which are modern in their making but mystify their modernity by their inadequacy. Sitting in the orchestra, the audience can look up through the chandeliers at the spotlights above. The scene inverts temporality. The light of the present is filtered through that of the past. The wilful anachronism is strategic and cunning. What the spotlights illuminate is the obvious fact that this is all a simulation. And the ASC knows it. And they want us to know they know it. (This is comforting. If the organization really thought it was 1611, it would be cause for concern.) It is another way in

which the Blackfriars differentiates itself along the spectrum
that runs from living history museums to modern theatres.
The Frontier Culture Museum, just down the road, takes
greater pains to disguise the systems that make its operations possible. Harder to render into a reproducible glyph, an
image of a spotlight shining on a chandelier would probably
be the *most* fitting logo for the Blackfriars Playhouse since it
is a place that sheds light on the past, not merely reflects it.
Above all, the Blackfriars is an interpretation of history, not
a recreation of it.

Given how central lighting is to the ASC's enterprise, it is
surprising that it was not more carefully researched before the
playhouse opened. As noted, the chandeliers proved inade-
quate, even at full wattage, and the spotlights compensate for
them. While the spotlights are visibly twenty-first century in
their construction, the ASC added another lighting element to
help illuminate the actors. Above the upper gallery, facing the
stage, the ASC carved a 'Rose Window' into the upper facade
to mimic the clerestories in the original Blackfriars that let in
natural light. This 'Rose Window' does not, however, open
onto the sky. It is a picture window only, lined with frosted
glass (it looks slightly, though unintentionally, like a walk-in
shower) behind which a scoop pours out light. The 'Rose
Window' allows in modern light while disguising it as the
historical variety, simultaneously sustaining the illusion of
historical authenticity while allowing audiences to actually *see*
what they are there to listen to. It is, therefore, not a window
into the past but a window out of it. As Caldwell notes, it is
'only for allowing in, and not for letting out' and therefore
pushes *actual* universal lighting – the variety used in outdoor
playhouses – one step further 'by redoubling rather than
simply framing the sun'.[12] At the Blackfriars even the play
of light is a play, or is always also a representation of light
while being the actual thing itself. What is *actually* behind
the window is not, of course, an early English sky, nor even
a twenty-first century Virginian one. One thing that's behind
the rose window is a lighting board, which controls the level

– though not always the layers – of universal light at the new Blackfriars.

Making contact

For every production of Shakespeare in the dark there's one of Shakespeare in the park that uses the universal light of the sun. Far from 'dark' for over 359 years, Shakespeare is often performed *al fresco*, where lighting distinctions between audience and actor are – as in early modern outdoor playhouses – hard to achieve. When the ASC implies that theatre has 'been dark' for 359 years, however, it is not another case of selective amnesia as explored in the previous chapter, an instance in which history is invoked but as often ignored to rationalize revolutionary change. The materials in which the 'dark' claims are made are promotional, not historical, ones after all. But the argument for universal lighting is not actually about lighting. It's about acting. The explanation of universal lighting that has pride of place in the *precis* of 'Shakespeare's Staging Conditions' in every ASC programme does make an historical claim, but not one about lighting. It reads, in full,

> Shakespeare's actors could see their audiences; ASC actors can see you. When actors can see an audience they can engage with an audience. And audience members can play the roles that Shakespeare wrote for them – Cleopatra's court, Henry V's army, or simply the butt of innumerable jokes. Leaving an audience in the dark can literally obscure a vital part of the drama as Shakespeare designed it.[13]

Universal lighting is not there just so that audiences can watch one another listen. It is there to enable a particular kind of acting that the ASC employs both at home and abroad, a style of acting the ASC claims is baked into the Shakespearean cake as well as the icing upon it. Or a particular kind of engagement, even communion, between actors and audience. Cohen writes of the light that it promotes the 'simultaneous *presence* of artist and audience [...] which asks for an investment by the audience in the show *per se*, and that investment brings ownership, and ownership creates access'.[14] Above all, the ASC's embrace of universal lighting allows actors to look an audience in the eyes. It is not light alone that produces this engagement, however. It is entirely possible to place an audience in the light and leave them in the dark (the opposite is also obviously so). The engagement called for by universal lighting requires and demands a particular kind of performance style. Universal lighting sounds like a technology, but it is actually a practice.

That practice is an urgently intimate one. Actors are on friendly terms with audiences at the Blackfriars, or at least they act like they are. The actors speak to them and with them from the moment the audience sets foot in the door until the time at which they leave. Like the lighting that foments but does not itself enable contact, the scale and shape of the Blackfriars abets but does not alone produce intimacy. As theatres go, the Blackfriars is a small space – the stage is twenty-nine by twenty-two feet but flanked by 'gallant stools' that diminish the space yet further – and feels even smaller when it is full of people. Its official occupancy is 301 and feels especially intimate when crowded with people, particularly since the audience wraps around the actors and shares the stage with them in the form of 'gallant stools' that provide onstage seating. Theatrical intimacy is often, as here, imagined in architecturally determined ways. In Bridget Escolme's fine study of direct address, for instance, she describes the RSC's old Royal Shakespeare Theatre as a place where intimacy might be possible in the first few rows but its 'large proscenium arch theatre will not permit such intimacy any further into the auditorium'.[15] In these terms, intimacy and proximity are imagined as co-terminous (and intimacy is thought to be impossible to extend from behind the arch of a proscenium frame into the body of the house). It is of course possible to be on intimate terms with someone who isn't even in the same room, however, or, more pertinently, with an actor who's acres away from your seat. Blackfriars intimacy is not a result of lighting, thrust staging, or spatial proximity alone, then, but of histrionic practice. The veteran actors at the Blackfriars are comfortable with a style of play that seduces the audiences into a sustained intimacy. They make it look easy, which is obviously hard work.

Where the rubber really meets the road for the ASC, then, even when they aren't on it, is the point of contact between an actor's eyes and the audiences', a moment of social reciprocity that is *the* most characteristic torque to mimesis that ASC actors wrench. In her work upon the neurological effect/affect of eye contact in theatrical venues, Lia Wallace distinguishes between the 'spectatorial' and the 'social' gaze, the latter a reciprocating exchange between – and among – actor and audience eyes at the Blackfriars. To reduce her subtle argument, the 'spectatorial' gaze looks through a window, the 'social' into a mirror, and the latter therefore induces self-consciousness in all its positive and negative valences.[16] Whatever claims to historical uniqueness pervade the boast to be the world's 'only recreation of Shakespeare's indoor playhouse', the truly distinctive event at the new Blackfriars is this reciprocated act of human exchange between actors and audiences. That exchange is made possible by an egalitarian light shared by performer and audience, but it is not the result of light alone. It helps, but it isn't enough. The force of performance at Staunton's Blackfriars is fundamentally constituted by a rage to connect actor and audience and to forge a community for the duration of the event.

What one more often sees at the Blackfriars than the whites of an actor's eyes is an actor making contact with an audience member other than oneself, which has an oddly duplicative effect. Watching another watch the same show one is watching is a lot like watching oneself, attending to one's own attendance, a voyeur to one's own voyeurism. Universal lighting and audience 'contact' allow an audience to make a spectacle of itself. Universally lit performances are therefore suffused with self-consciousness for everyone but the actors, who at least act like they are not self-conscious (an actor is always the least or most self-conscious person in the room). Audience contact, to be precise *eye* contact, can turn every event into a mirror stage.

This engagement, this communion, is meant above all to be 'fun', as Cohen describes it in his paean to hearing by the light: 'when a production acknowledges an audience's place in the play, we in the audience have more fun'.[17] This is a characteristic of the Blackfriars – and of the Globe, for that matter, part of what Caldwell calls the 'comic "mooding"' of the Globe or what W. B. Worthen describes as 'ye olde merriment' that prevails there.[18] Despite the appalling hygiene and a subsistence economy, the past was above all *fun*. The Blackfriars promotes a comic *esprit* as well. Cohen writes that we should go to Shakespeare 'expecting to enjoy ourselves – literally – and that we come away enjoying each other'.[19] Even when they are performing a tragedy, the effect of direct address is generally and generically comic. The ASC takes its fun seriously, then; indeed, 'serious fun' was an early motto. How this commitment to fun registers against or within the drama on offer – what's the 'fun' part of *Titus Andronicus* again? – is considered below, but the Blackfriars is, by design and policy, primarily a comic house, the universal lighting encouraging an experience more concerned with audience enjoyment than with the diegetic concerns of the particular dramatic piece.

The ASC shorthand for the connection that its actors forge is 'audience contact'. The phrase only sounds violent since the company is usually careful to avoid physical contact with audience members. They have in mind something more metaphysical, which is the production of theatrical community, even theatrical communion. In the hands of the ASC's actors the 'audience's place in the play' is, whatever the play, always in play. In these terms, actors are never precisely 'talking to the audience' because they are never precisely *not* talking to the audience. As veteran actor John Harrell put it, 'it's not that we can see the audience so much as that we can never *not* seem them'. Since the actors can never not see the audience, they start talking to them from the moment they step on stage for the pre-show and don't stop until after they've announced the winner of the ticket raffle, which takes place after the final curtain call while the audience is trying to leave. The festivity that the Blackfriars domesticates is, then, marked by a forceful familiarity between actors and audience. The Blackfriars has a location – has a few in fact – but it has no *locus*. It is all *platea*.[20]

Prepositions are the most ideological parts of speech since they configure relations between subject and objects. Bridgett Escolme's work on direct address – *Talking to the Audience* – presupposes a one-sided conversation. Which is to say not a conversation. The ASC might – though interestingly doesn't – use the phrase 'talking *with* the audience'. They prefer 'contact' to 'conversation', which, like Escolme's 'talking *to*', is a one-sided affair. The actors, in fact, are careful to police the borders even while they cross them. In a playhouse that does not mark its territories through lighting schemes, actors often have to put their foot down, to define the rules of engagement that govern playhouse decorum. Harrell describes one of those rules as the right 'to brush them [the audience] back' if they take their prerogative too far: 'It's about pushing them back when you need to push them back [...] These are people who are surrounding you and some of them are hoping that you will fail.'[21] As often, they are hoping that the actors will succeed, or will make 'contact', if only with somebody else. The Blackfriars' lighting and its physical arrangement can encourage a sense that there are no boundaries, that these are actors without borders, so actors work hard to put everybody in their place. Theatre is, whatever the space, an art of proxemics. At the Blackfriars, the light, the space, and the actors collude to define audience relations and the boundaries that govern them, even or especially because there don't seem to be any. The mild violence implied by 'contact' is the point policed by actors at which an audience goes too far.

That contact has been refined by the ASC over the years and so has an actual institutional history along with its alleged historical precedence. In fact, audience contact grew out of but evolved away from the ASC/SSE's historical obligation to the Universal Lighting of the Shakespearean stage. Cohen has confessed that audience contact was not a deliberate part of the SSE's first principles: 'using the audience, referring to the audience, being seen by the audience [...] the more active forms of audience interaction were not a founding principle'.[22] Moreover, Cohen has reservations about the historical authenticity of audience engagement:

> We don't know that Shakespeare – and I'm only going to speak for myself – we do not know that audience members ever were asked to dance, and I doubt very seriously an actor ever sat on anyone's lap, any of those things. So that was not part of the idea behind it [the SSE's founding]. But what is true is that every audience was aware that they were visible, they were aware that actors were talking to them, they were aware of their own kind of agency as audience. So that word's a very important one to start with, because if there's been a shift, it's been towards planning to act with the audience in some way that forces audience members to do something.[23]

Cohen carefully distinguishes between the kinds of historical experiences he imagines early modern audiences to have had, settling on a sense that they were aware of their own agency, that they were being talked to, though probably not sat upon. There is little evidence either way. The ASC education department, as well as the Blackfriars Tour Script, cites instances such as Nerissa's nomination of Portia's suitors in *Merchant*, the Porter's litany of hellish inhabitants in *Macbeth*, Pompey's roll call of brothel dwellers in *Measure for Measure* as evidence that audience members were being singled out by actors for good-natured ridicule. Perhaps, though play scripts make for odd evidence of their own performance (is the rehearsal scene in *Midsummer* evidence of Elizabethan rehearsal practice or just the opposite?) At least one early playgoer scolded an actor for recognizing that he had an audience other than his onstage partner. John Stephens complained in 1615 about a 'common player' who, 'When he doth hold conference upon the stage; and should look directly in his fellows face; hee turnes about his voice into the assembly for applause-sake, like a Trumpeter in the fields, that shifts places to get an eccho'.[24] Stephens is complaining about a show-boating actor, so it is unclear if he's critiquing a particular or a general practice. Either way, the evidence is thin, but the ASC – as has been the argument throughout – makes its own history, one inspired by, but not beholden to the Shakespearean stage.

For the actors of the ASC, in any event, the audience that they are attempting to 'contact' is an audience of the present, not the past. For them, audience contact is a tactical matter not an historical one. When asked to define 'audience contact', Harrell replies that 'it's an interesting question to ask [...] because we talk about it all the time and I don't know what it is'.[25] Like Samuel Johnson's epigraph that opens this chapter, ASC actors know what audience contact is, though sometimes have trouble *saying* what it is. Most of their comments centre on reciprocity, however. Benjamin Reed, after his first season with the company, describes what, for him, is at stake in its success: 'You have to first focus, and then you have to find a way to get in with them, and then you have to actually have that connection, and then you can translate an idea. Which is very different from just throwing your eyeballs at somebody [...] if the connection isn't made, I can't communicate'.[26] Gregory Phelps, an actor of long standing with the ASC, expanded on Reed's reciprocal sense. For him, 'contact' means 'actually having a conversation with them, asking them for information and asking them for information about the information they just gave you and riffing off of that'. For Phelps this means responding – in real time – to the information in the room, not just in the script: 'There's a lot of pressure [...]

in this audience contact, having the lights on, even if you're not going off text there's still a lot of improv, there's a lot of new information coming our way'. That new information can transform the very nature of the theatrical experience from a textualized play to a more free-form variety:

> In regards to changing from a performance to a social interaction, I think when you go off text it also changes because the audience can tell this is something different. You are not just saying Shakespeare's lines or Middleton or whatever, you are not just Hamlet having a conversation with somebody, it's actually like, 'okay everybody, step right up!' It's almost vaudevillian or circus-like. It's like a standup act.

Phelps' points of reference – vaudeville, circus, stand up; he elsewhere mentions professional wrestling – are all relatively modern rather than early modern. The pressure created by audience contact can open up, rather than elide, the space between the two. But then, actors are interested in making theatre, not history.

However 'fun' audience contact might be, sometimes fun requires a little antagonism, as the stilettoed professionals of New York understand. What universal lighting also allows is for the actors to make fun of the audience who have paid to watch them do so. As the programme suggests, the role that Shakespeare 'wrote for them' is as courtiers, soldiers, and butts. They are there to serve at the actor's pleasure. Making use of the audience often turns into making light of them. (Bald men and young couples are frequent targets of actor ridicule.) Harrell notes, 'I like to have that sense of hostility against the audience. I like to push back a little bit, especially in a comic role'. Audience 'contact' may not be physical contact, but there is still an implied antagonism, moments when, in Escolme's terms, 'an inclusive, communal warmth' turns to 'something more aggressive and combative'.[27] If the experience at the Blackfriars is synesthetic, it can also be sadistic. Be it as Portia's hapless suitors or Pompey's brothel dwellers, the audience if far more often embarrassed than ennobled. This antagonism is not designed to alienate the audience, however; the principle at work seems to be 'we only hurt the ones we love'. Perhaps acting is the world's second oldest profession.

There are, however, perils in the power of audience contact. Not those moments where an Iago or Richard attempt to ally the audience in repugnant behaviour. There is rarely any legitimate danger that an audience member will condone the murder of the two princes in the tower, say. More troubling is the tendency for reconstructed playhouses to produce unreconstructed politics. A Petruchio in full communion with the audience is one more likely to solicit – and even receive – audience consent for his wife-taming programme. As Harrell notes, 'When Ben Curns, our Petruchio, took a deep theatrical bow after having shown off his skills at shrew-training, our audience always – always – applauded. Was that the past coming alive? Bringing its zombie hands together for the old boy? Or does performing these old plays somehow reveal contemporary ugliness?'[28] Sarah Werner has similarly described the reaction at the Globe to Albany's put down of Goneril, 'you are not worth the dust the rude wind blows in your face' as having a chillingly misogynist ring to it, in part enabled by the license that the past allows.[29] Universal lighting and audience contact can collaborate with a reconstructed playhouse to suspend not disbelief – in fact quite the opposite – but modern sensibility. The 'fun' of audience contact always comes at *someone's* expense.

There's a fine line between turning on the audience and turning them off, then. Cohen speaks of forcing an 'audience member to do something', but not every member of the audience member wants to be forced to play a part, especially not a fool or a flunkey. Phelps explains what happens when reciprocity breaks down: 'If you take something to someone who's like, "I don't give a shit" or looks immediately down at the programme or is completely blank, that's kind of difficult because you were thinking, "I'm giving 100% and I'm getting zero back."' (The audience member might as well reply 'I gave forty-five bucks. I want to watch you work.') Allison Glenzer echoes Phelps, addressing an audience member who shies from contact: 'it happens and sometimes I still get pissed at them. It still ruffles my feathers'. At other moments, actors are aware when they may be asking too much. Sarah Fallon describes playing Lady Macbeth at the Blackfriars and an intimate moment that was too close for comfort: 'when I take my hand to somebody that's front and center and say, "all the perfumes of Arabia will not sweeten this little hand." And it's me, I'm at the lip of the stage and it is close, [...] a lot of people can't handle that. I have learned how to stay in character and not get thrown by them not being able to be that close with me. It is uncomfortable'. And Cohen worries about, but finally finds worth it, the cost of putting the audience on the spot, one that might obscure the very words they are there to hear:

I have a fear about direct contact and here it is. Unless everybody is used to and expecting it, is that particular audience member hearing the words clearly, or is there an adrenaline rush that obscures the words? [...] What I think is happening is that if one out of 250 people is being spoken to, that one person may actually have a little bit harder time taking it in [...] but the other 249 people, because a person is actually being used, it's not them, are going even more to focus on what the words that were said to this poor person that could have been them but isn't, and therefore there's a little schadenfreude there. And you hear even better.

Cohen and the actors collectively articulate the peculiar tension between a theatre – a place where one goes to see – and a playhouse – a space in which actors and audience alike are meant to be at home with play. The universal light illuminates a delicate equilibrium between communion and coercion – 'a person is actually being used' in Cohen's unsettling phrase. This tension is the enabling force of 'Blackfriars Performativity'.

A universally lit audience in constant contact, sometimes playful, sometimes not, with the actors can sound like a description of a Brechtian event, where theatrical artifice is always in the foreground, illusion kept at bay through self-conscious theatricality. Yet artifice never comes into the foreground at the Blackfriars because it never fades into the background (this is another function of the pre- and post-show rituals). Or, theatricality is not self-conscious at the Blackfriars since it forms the *un*conscious of Blackfriars Performativity. The Blackfriars is in fact a profoundly anti-Brechtian house – a result of artistic principles not architecture – in that audience contact is not meant to estrange and alienate, it is meant to engage and connect. In other words, audience contact is meant to highlight social interaction instead of social processes, though the two are not obviously at odds. Bridget Escolme, for one, has challenged Stanislavski's tendency to 'oppose human feeling and theatricality',[30] and performances at the Blackfriars answer this challenge by naturalizing theatricality into the operations of the enterprise, finding human feeling via unselfconscious artifice (unselfconscious on the actors' part that is). Since Blackfriars actors are never exactly *not* talking to the audience, it is not apparent and certainly not estranging when they more explicitly do so. Whatever the particular play is about, the real drama at the Blackfriars takes place between the audience and actor.

Blackfriars Performativity demystifies the theatrical event, then, as a matter of house policy. Other venues might produce their actors from backstage like rabbits out of hats, but at the Blackfriars they mill casually about both on and above the stage before the show, chatting with audiences, performing pre-show music. At the Blackfriars, the rabbit was never in the hat in the first place since it is a deliberately anti-illusionist enterprise. Cohen has written and spoken often about 'the theatre of the imagination' – what Shakespeare intended, what the Blackfriars offers – versus the 'theatre of illusion' – what everyone else producing Shakespeare does. Variegated lighting is just another form of illusion, in these terms, the illusion that the audience is not in the same room as the actors. If how we hear better by the light remains a mystery – remains productively mystified – everything else about the event is ruthlessly demystified. If there's nothing to see here, there's also nothing to hide. Audiences at the Blackfriars are under no illusion that they're at the actual Blackfriars, which is one more reason that the spotlights stay on.

What this chapter is after, thus far, is some sense of the performance aesthetic at work – or play – on the Blackfriars stage. And it is possible with the ASC to speak of *the* performance aesthetic since it is invariable, as unvarying as the light. The relative stability of the company, the inflexibility of the stage-space, the unchanging light, and the lack of outside directors has produced a remarkable consistency of acting approach across the last decade. This is a matter of policy, not history, since there is good evidence that early modern companies altered the space and its field of light to match the play. Thomas Dekker, for instance, writes of the shutters being closed at the Blackfriars during the performance of a tragedy, others of the house draped in black, or of the arras being changed show-by-show, but the Blackfriars maintains a consistent level of light regardless whether it's *King Lear* or *Comedy of Errors*. (One of the blind spots of original practices is to the idea that playing companies might have varied their style from day to day, play to play, company to company. Original practices foreclose on the idea that a member of the King's Men, say, might have suggested one day that they do 'Shakespeare a little differently'.) For the ASC, however, Shakespeare's staging conditions are a constant.

In fact, the Blackfriars delivers on Shakespeare's staging conditions even when the play is not by Shakespeare. This introduces yet another paradox, the idea that Shakespeare's plays work best under Shakespearean staging conditions, and so do everyone else's. The result is a consistency of approach at the playhouse that makes it difficult to differentiate between play and play, season and season. Whatever the genre, whomever the author, plays at the Blackfriars have a Blackfriars *feeling* that transcends titles, a *gestalt* that traverses times so that even plays from well outside the early modern period get the period treatment. It's another way that the ASC converts sameness into distinctive difference.

There are, depending on your perspective, downsides to stylistic consistency and vice versa. It produces performances that feel less like interpretations of Shakespeare's plays and more like cover versions, though expertly performed ones. ASC performances manifest, in these terms, what Richard Schechner calls 'Realization' as opposed to 'Interpretation' or 'Adaptation' or 'Deconstruction', which he identifies as the 'four possibilities regarding classical texts'. 'Realization [...] says, "I know what the author intended; I know what this play means, and I'm going to realize it, I'm going to do it faithfully"'.[31] There is an obvious way in which materialization and realization work in conjunction. A faithful reproduction of a Jacobean playhouse and a faithful allegiance to Jacobean performance practices faithfully reproduce the plays 'as designed'. Schechner probably intends a value judgement, a prejudicial one, when he sketches a spectrum of approaches to classical texts. But the language of fidelity courses through the ASC's work, from a trust in the text to a faith that an audience wants to see Shakespeare by the same light.

'Realization' is a rhetorical position, not a theatrical effect, however. The ASC no more 'realizes' what Shakespeare intended than Forced Entertainment's 'Table Top Shakespeare', which stages Shakespeare's plays with found objects – a bottle for Lear, an ewer for Cordelia. All theatre is legitimate, all performance is authentic, every manifestation of Shakespeare's plays a realization of 'what the author intended' (as if an author always or even ever knows his or her own intentions). The ASC promulgates a rhetoric of 'realization' through architecture and publicity, then, though not through performance. It is not possible to perform intentions; it is only possible to announce them. Once the performance begins, the sovereign contingency of theatre takes over, whatever the stated intentions. In fact, this book has focused so much attention on the pre-show rituals because performance at the Blackfriars is so heavily annotated, so aggressively framed. Nevertheless, regardless what the actors or the programmes tell you, what the ASC is up to is, of course, an interpretation of history, a play on it that takes history as a starting point and then makes some of its own. Once the performance begins, the present overwrites the past, which is one more effect of audience contact.

This consistency of theatrical approach can also lead to a flattening of style, in which Shakespeare, Marlowe, Wilde and pieces like *A Christmas Carol* and *Return to the Forbidden Planet* are performed with roughly the same approach. (The ASC *does* wander from the Shakespearean songbook at times, though never too far off the reading list, with the exception of the 'Actors' Renaissance Season' considered in the next chapter.) Such consistency can flatten Wilde's archness, straight-iron Goldsmith's curly apercus or level the grandeurs of a Faust or a Lear. But then, as the programme details, universal lighting lets the audience play the roles 'Shakespeare wrote for them'. Wilde, Goldsmith, even Marlowe probably constituted their audiences differently than Shakespeare, and so with some plays the Blackfriars pushes square pegs into round – or thrust-shaped – holes.

Quibbles aside, the ASC has successfully developed what so many other Shakespeare companies have tried to sustain: a stable, working, ensemble-based company with a coherent, legible, and consistent approach to the production of Shakespeare's plays. To risk a form of 'would have' scholarship, the ASC may even have recreated a feature of early modern playgoing, where audience members 'would have' gone to the Globe or Blackfriars, say, to see a company, not a play. The audience knows what to expect when they visit the Blackfriars, and if they have forgotten they will be quickly be reminded. Ultimately, Blackfriars Performativity is characterized by what might be called an 'outwardness of affect', with material consistently given over to the audience with a kind of off-hand aplomb. Again, it would be wrong, decidedly wrong, to think of it as a kind of neo-Brechtian *Verfremdungs effekt,* whereby actors work to make characters – their motivations, moral weaknesses, social embeddedness – transparent to all. What the 'contact' produces, instead, is an *affect effect*, a general recognition that *something* has taken place, been exchanged, in that the actor has for a moment become audience and the audience, actor (or at least such is the illusion). Actor and audience are never both at the same time, however, since the dynamic described here depends, in fact insists, that *someone* perform and others attend. If we're all actors or all audience, it's no longer a playhouse, it's a waiting room.

Neither does the consistency of style mean that the material is ironized – a wised-up 'just having a laugh' diminution of dramatic power and energy. Rather, what comes across is the virtuosity of the performer, the flexibility of the ensemble, an insouciant mastery of material that, at its best, erases any presumption of difficulty or distance between the origins of a piece and its reception at the Blackfriars. The 'house style' domesticates everything in its path, takes in the ridiculous and the sublime, the chronologically foreign and the temporally native, and converts it all into its own idiom. The emphasis on sociability above all supersedes the particulars of the play on offer. Necessary questions of the play can go beg while actors engage their audience. This is by design, however; whatever the name of the play, the name of the game at the ASC is audience contact. The 'play' being performed by the ASC is always a by-play, even an inter-play, among a community of social actors.

Against interpretation

That which makes the audience visible can make it hard for the critics to see. Theatrically productive – even, perhaps, historically justifiable – the consistency of Blackfriars Performativity can baffle reviewers. Disappointed by a 'so-so *Macbeth*', a 2006 critic was prompted to ask 'what makes Shenandoah's productions so consistently accomplished yet so seldom exceptional'.[32] A more successful *Tempest* helped the reviewer answer her own question: 'its *Tempest* was not a definitive interpretation or a brilliant production or any of the descriptions by which we typically measure the sparks generated between actors and audiences at the best performances, but it did engage the audience exceptionally well, and their engagement coaxed even wittier, more exciting, and more intimate work from the players'. Engagement, excitement, intimacy – these are the attributes the ASC courts rather than a 'definitive interpretation'. Reviewers are unused to having to review the audience, of course, but the reviewer in this case shifted her attention to them – she could see them after all – to diagnose the dynamics at work at the Blackfriars. Measures of success at ASC performances need to be calibrated by unusual theatrical metrics since the performances are unexceptional, but unexceptional by design. Excepting the shows during the Actors' Renaissance Season (considered in the next chapter), the Blackfriars pursues a policy of non-surprise, even anti-novelty. If you have been to the Blackfriars, you know what you'll get at the Blackfriars. Cued to evaluate the 'singularity and coherence of the director's vision', this reviewer decided instead that, 'When you put on Shakespeare the way Shenandoah Shakespeare does, you may not get it right every time, but you're never going to get it wrong'. This is both high praise and a mixed blessing, but productions at the Blackfriars are 'seldom exceptional' while being 'consistently accomplished' because what they're striving to accomplish is consistency. Another word for 'exceptional' could be 'inconsistent'.

This critic was not alone in her confusion since reviews of ASC often seem unclear about exactly what they've seen. But then the typical targets of critical focus don't mark the spot where Blackfriars' performances live. When the light is universal, it's hard to know what to focus on since, as Ralph Alan Cohen implies when he traduces the spotlight, the audience can look wherever they please. (It is a central company tenet that audiences enjoy seeing other audience members enjoy themselves; though of course audience members can also see the opposite.) Whether they are disappointed or enthused, benumbed by consistency or delighted by it, theatre reviewers of ASC productions nearly always address the light, or the audience engagement, even community, it helps foment. For critics as well as for the ASC, it is the constituting feature of Blackfriars performativity.

Paradoxically, the universal lighting makes the shows hard to read. Its universality – the consistent glow it throws on shows day after day, night after night – means that though costumes will vary all shows look the same. At least at the Blackfriars, the 'set' never changes. This means that shows can be simultaneously distinguished but indistinguishable. This seems by design. One reviewer pointed out that the company 'isn't about the business of creating fiery, memorable performances, and the details of this show aren't likely to stick in your mind. Still, the play – common, majestic, terrifically humane – makes its marks, and that probably suits the players just fine'.[33] The details won't stick, but the common humanity will. Indeed, when the company does foray into a noticeable 'reading' of a play, the critics respond as though to an affront. A guest director produced a modern day, boardroom *Lear* in 2003 – mobile phones, pistols, swivel chairs, the lot – which prompted a reviewer to ask, 'Isn't this the sort of overwrought thematic bludgeoning which the company has built its reputation on avoiding?'[34] The praise can feel either faint or damning – the company is lauded by these two critics for avoiding thematic pointing or memorable performances – but the curious case of the ASC is that they have built a reputation not for but *against* interpretation. Yet another paradox of the ASC enterprise is that what would sound like a damning assessment of another theatre company comes as high praise when it is concerned.

Schechner opposes 'realization' to 'interpretation' or 'adaptation' or 'deconstruction', and critics or audiences seeking an 'interpretation' or for that matter a 'deconstruction' or a 'reading' of this or that play will come away disappointed. When the ASC does occasionally put a foot outside the lines, it's usually down to exigency rather than interpretation. A 2015 *Dream*, for example, found Allison Glenzer trebling Hippolyta, Mustardseed and Snug the lion. When it came time for the lion's part in 'Pyramus and Thisbe', Snug was nowhere to be found, since he – or in this case she – was playing Hippolyta. 'Let me play the lion', said Hippolyta, echoing Bottom, and she did, addressing the lion's prologue about how easily women are frightened to Hermia and Helena with her tongue firmly in cheek. This created an interpretive 'through line' from Hippolyta's noticeable (and by now conventional) disapproval of Theseus' act-one sanction of Hermia (she marched off stage, unamused, which prompted Theseus' 'What cheer my love?') In other words, this lightly applied 'feminist' reading of the play – which artfully disarmed Snug's condescension to 'you ladies' – grew out of a theatrical exigency. Here, 'interpretation' grew out of the 'fact' that 'Shakespeare's traveling troupe may have had fewer than fifteen actors' and therefore the ASC only eleven, meaning that the 'ASC doubles parts, with one actor' – Bottom like – 'playing as many as seven roles in a single show'. Having Hippolyta take upon her the lion's part – Amazonian queen showing her lioness' heart – might *seem* like a directorial interpolation but it grew out of Shakespeare's staging conditions. History produced this 'interpretation' not the director's vision, or – dread word – 'concept'. Ultimately, a reviewer nails the effect when she concludes that 'Shenandoah's directors haven't been expected to impose their own visions, but to tease a collective idea of the play out of the ensemble'.[35] The 'ensemble' here must extend to the audience. The critic diagnoses the fact that what the ASC is 'realizing' is not even the intention of the playwright – *pace* Schechner – but a 'collective idea' not of *the* play, but of playing. Against interpretation, the ASC ranges a realization of a theatrical culture, one it envisions as interactive, accessible, joyful, and fun.

Given the emphasis on 'comic mooding' it is unsurprising that critics consistently praise comedies at the Blackfriars but are more reserved in assessing tragedies there, as though universal lighting works less well with dark material. Perhaps the solipsistic dramaturgy of Shakespeare's tragedies, which estrange individuals from communities of kin and kind, are not as at home as comedies in the Blackfriars' communitarian ecology. The *Philadelphia Enquirer* allowed that universal lighting 'does tend to lessen the emotional distance between audience and performers, but it also quite effectively diffuses the illusion that a world with its own reality is being created on stage'.[36] Tragedy asks of both actor and audience to consider and even produce estrangement, alienation and discomfort. If it is charming it can also be jarring, after the agonies of Lear or the torture of Othello, to be asked to pull out your ticket to see if you've won an autographed poster. After all, audience contact is designed to 'break down the barrier' – in another instance of revolutionary rhetoric. (The idea of breaking the barrier or down the 'fourth wall' is always at least slightly fatuous since it's the barrier that gives the action meaning by giving it something to break.) Tragedy can require that barriers be put up, however, that estrangement be courted or at least considered. The relentless regard for audience comfort – the insistence that they have fun – at the Blackfriars is sometimes at odds with the material on display, which produces a generic divergence in the critical response to performance in the house. As the Blackfriars company continues to refine their practices, the question remains whether 'audience contact' can be squared with tragic isolation.

It may be that universal lighting makes tragedy difficult to effect. Addressing the lighting, *The Christian Science Monitor* observed that 'audiences have to work harder to feel the murderous tension of "Macbeth" or "Richard III"'.[37] This has less to do with 'mood' or the 'tone' set by gloomy lighting, a cue established by film or the gothic sense that things can only go bump in the dark. (Though Warren observed in 1997 that he wouldn't 'necessarily want to do "Macbeth"' outside, by the universal light of day.)[38] It is obviously possible to produce tragedy under the brightest of spotlights. The more pressing question is whether a universally lit audience is capable of being carried out of comedy into a tragic disposition given the ASC's emphasis on 'fun'. Borrowing Henri Bergson's work on laughter and comedy as derived from juxtaposition, Caldwell argues that the historical difference visible at reconstructed playhouses is inherently comic: 'The juxtaposition of these two images [the architecture of the interior and that of the modern spectator] creates a special comic tension "off stage," one that our laughter frequently releases when our attention is drawn to it by the actor.'[39] Laughter is the sound that audience contact produces, as modern audience members collide with the past. The mood of the Blackfriars is, in these terms, always comic, always festive, and only fitfully at home with tragedy. If there's something odd about seeing a chandelier by the light of a spot, there's also something inherently funny. In these terms, a 'playhouse' is the opposite of a dark one, a dark house being the ASC's ideological and economic foe.

Due to this consistent house style – aided and abetted by universal light – the Blackfriars is more or less critic proof. This is financially as well as theoretically the case, since the ASC is almost wholly unreliant on the reviews of local – or even remote – papers other than for purposes of selective blurbing. The local newspaper, *The Staunton News-Leader*, routinely reviews, or possibly 'covers' the ASC, but rarely lays a glove on it. Like many regional theatres, the ASC relies on subscriptions and group sales, and so it is as often the titles of the plays or the reputation of the company rather than the opinion of reviewers that drive traffic to the corner of New Market Street. Recalling the *Staunton Advertiser*'s warning to actors not to condescend to audiences – lest they desert you for a cakewalk – the ASC works hard to ensure that whether they are talking to or with an audience, they are never talking down to them.

Coda

'We do it with the lights on' is a punchline to an old joke that various vocations tell on themselves. Scientists 'do it' repeatedly. Economists 'do it' with models. Professors 'do it' in patches. Whatever humour abides in this joke – or remains it it after this brief analysis – comes from the playfully vague antecedent of the pronoun 'it', which can obviously mean both sexual intercourse and the principal vocation of a scientist, economist, professor, what have you.

What, however, is the principal 'it' that the ASC does with the lights on? All actors do it with the lights on, after all, if only on themselves. The light by which the ASC does 'it', however, is shared by actors and audience alike. Since the audience isn't acting exactly – whatever 'roles' Shakespeare wrote 'for them' – the 'it' being done is something apart, something like engagement, something like community, something like communion. However cheeky, 'We do it with the lights on' is a more polite version of a more accurate motto: 'We do it with an audience.' In the end, Shakespeare is not the antecedent of 'it'; he is the occasion for it.

4

Time Bomb – The Actors' Renaissance Season (ARS)

For roughly nine months of the year, the ASC practices the arts of smooth elision. As treated in this book's first three chapters, the company has developed over the years a number of para- and intra-performative techniques to skilfully, casually and winningly finesse the seams between the times and places in which and at which they play. 'Blackfriars Performativity' – as detailed in the previous chapter – is comprised, above all, by the actors' mastery of the various scales of time and place at work in their playhouse. What this produces for the ASC, night after night, season after season, is a Shakespeare that seems to float free of time (though not place), a self-fulfilling prophecy of the author's 'timelessness'. The actors of the Virginia company are well-known for their musical chops, but perhaps their instrumental talent is a total mastery of competing time signatures.

Then, for three months every year, the ASC strikes a discordant note. The 'Actors' Renaissance Season' (ARS, an acronym that plays differently to American and British readers, or 'The Ren Season' in company shorthand) represents the ASC's most hardcore recursion to early English theatrical practice. Spanning the first three months of every calendar year, the season dispenses with a number of modern conventions (directors, designers, ample rehearsal time, full scripts) to embrace a Renaissance theatrical aesthetic. The season also essays non-canonical early modern plays, including the darker corners of the Shakespeare canon (while leading off with a popular Shakespeare title mounted with just a few days of rehearsal). This explicit bid for acute historical accuracy and the deep dive into the dramatic canon of the English Renaissance has produced surprising results since the season's inception in 2005, not least that the return to old practices and antique plays produces performances that feel brand new. As detailed in the chapter which follows, the raw vitality of the Renaissance season seems largely the result of the company's commitment to the rebirth of early performance practices, not material ones, so that what one sees on stage, January through April, is theatre less beholden to heritage than the heat of the theatrical event.

If the ASC is adept at folding history on itself so carefully that it hides the seams, during the Actors' Renaissance Season the seams show and the folds fray (but never tear). The exposed stitching of the Ren Season reveals the oddities of the ASC's engagements with history, but exposure is just what many of the plays deserve. It is easier to occupy the oddity of the ASC, in short, watching the *Blind Beggar of Alexandria* on a rainy Tuesday in February than when taking in *A Midsummer Night's Dream* on a midsummer's night. The latter will be wonderful; the former will be weird. It is, then, during the Actors' Renaissance Season where the eccentricities of the project fully manifest, when far from being transported beyond juxtapositions of time and place one will be hyper-aware that they're watching a 1596 George Chapman comedy that never played at the original Blackfriars in London being performed at the recreation Blackfriars in Staunton, Virginia. The Actors' Renaissance Season is a time bomb at the heart of the organization, but when it goes off, it utterly disarms.

The rhetoric around the ARS is largely one of deficits – a 2011 promo for the season reads, 'Gone are the directors, the designers, the months of group rehearsals that Shakespeare's company never knew. What's left? Raw energy of the

Renaissance theatre.'[1] The chapter that follows argues that the conventions of the ARS are best understood not as deficit but as surplus. It is within the season that the ASC becomes more than itself, more than merely revivalists, or conservationist, and more than merely a 'regional' theatre consistently producing quality Shakespeare. Particularly in its emphasis on unfamiliar plays, the ARS makes theatre history not just by pursuing early modern theatrical practices but by introducing old plays to new audiences. In so doing, the company literally alters theatre history, makes it, by extending the run of long-dormant plays. (The performance history of *Blind Beggar* now runs from 1601, when it was first, and last, revived, to 2011, when it was revivified in Staunton, again, for the first time.) In these terms, the Renaissance Season offers the richest plunder from the ASC's 'revolution', an intervention in history that recovers the past, changes the present, and alters the future of Shakespeare and performance (and scholarship and pedagogy) in yet unpredictable ways. Through its most rigorous engagement with the past, the Actors' Renaissance Season challenges – and changes – the present and future of Shakespeare and performance.

If the ASC most often courts continuity and consistency – a sort of 'timeless Shakespeare' – the Actors' Renaissance Season romances inconsistency and jarring juxtapositions, which play out in any number of ways, as this chapter explores. (A critic asked, in 2008, 'how the company's occasionally baffling blend of tradition and innovation works as well as it does'. This book, and this chapter, in particular, wonder the same thing.[2]) Curiously, the ASC's promotional materials reveal that, for at least three months, the company trades 'Shakespeare's Staging Conditions' for 'Renaissance' ones, while simultaneously staging its own insurrection since the ARS offers a self-contained subversion of the ASC's institutional practices. Above all, the multiple temporalities exponentially multiply from January through April, a season in which the Blackfriars does not so much harmonize discrepant time signatures as trumpet them. To come to terms with what goes on in the

ARS – to understand the way that the 'it' of 'We do *it* with the lights on' changes in this season – this chapter offers four brief impressions of ARS productions over the last decade, since Associate Artistic Director Jay McClure innovated the season in 2005. The chapter then concludes with a brief examination of ARS's history, in particular its history with academia, asserting that the ASC has fully realized the dream of an academic theatre, which J. L. Styan and others like him, envisioned during their revolutionary call in the mid-1970s. Ten years on, the Actors' Renaissance Season at the Blackfriars emblematizes the company's major intervention in their greatest enterprise – the making of history.

'Always Where I Need To Be' – *The Blind Beggar of Alexandria* (2009)

Like all decadent comic forms, the Shakespeare industry has its standard gags, one-liners sure to raise a chuckle from nodding academics. Ben Jonson's famed irascibility, the eccentric emendations of eighteenth-century editors and the self-evident badness of semi-obscure plays. This last chestnut loses none of its flavour if the audience (or joker for that matter) has not read, seen, or heard of the play to which they condescend. The more respectable form of this phenomenon is gravely to judge a drama fine for its time but unplayable today. In his 2012 book on the Admiral's men, Andrew Gurr describes the *Blind Beggar of Alexandria* as a star vehicle for Edward Alleyn in which the great tragedian shuffled through a pack of disguises that lampooned his more famous roles – Barabas, Tamburlaine, etc. Audiences today, lacking the requisite frame of reference, 'cannot appreciate the extent of Chapman's ingenious farce'. For Gurr, the play is 'brilliant but unrepeatable'.[3]

On a rainy Tuesday night in February 2011, I sat in the worst seat in the house and watched Gregory Jon Phelps belt out an acoustic cover of the Kooks' rave-up, 'Always where I need to be', from the Blackfriars' balcony. From out of the discovery space crept John Harrell, tatter-clad, blindfolded, lugging a rock that his arms could barely reach around. Disguised as Cleanthe, the titular role, his figure compounded Tiresias, Sisyphus and every poor wretch of blind-beggardom from the ancient Greeks to the modern street. Setting down his rock as the music stopped, Harrell prophesied from his knees to the virgins that he would soon seduce them. At their departure, he leapt to his feet, ripped his blindfold off and casually tossed the rock to his factotum. The moment got a real laugh from the crowd. We knew the rock was fake – a patently papier mâché phony – but we bought it for the play's sake. (We were just being polite since the play has asked us nicely, just as we took Phelps' acoustic cover in place of the real rock of the Kooks' original.) If Harrell's gesture was flip, its meaning was not. It put to the audience the following proposition about theatrical pleasure: it isn't enough to *reveal* the apparatus; you have to be willing to *revel* in it. Once Harrell tossed the rock the gag was afoot and a spirited one-and-a-half hours later (yes, one-and-half-hours *with* intermission) as the Blackfriars troupe took a final bow, it was clear that, at that moment, on that night, the *Blind Beggar of Alexandria* was the greatest play of the English Renaissance, the greatest play we had ever seen and the greatest play you will never see. After watching Cleanthe, the serial seducer, successfully cuckold himself with his own wife – and then do it again the next night with his *other* wife – we were willing to believe anything. Because that is what brilliant plays in performance do, make you believe anything, and among the many things that they might make you believe is that their pleasures are unrepeatable. We were, in that place, at that time, exactly where we needed to be.

Revelling in the apparatus often requires, but does not demand, revealing it. The Ren season often does both. The *Blind Beggar*'s phony rock was a local instance of a blanket approach. Performances during the Renaissance season do not court, and less rarely achieve, stylistic uniformity in their

FIGURE 1 *Miriam Donald Burrows, John Harrell and Alyssa Wilmoth in* The Blind Beggar of Alexandria. *American Shakespeare Center, 2009. Photo by Tommy Thompson. Used by permission.*

design, for instance. Actors pull their own costumes and so frequently look to, and like they, occupy different worlds. If we seek authority for this lack of uniformity, we could reference the plays themselves. *Blind Beggar*, for instance, is a pastiche of early English farce, *commedia dell'arte*, and Chapman's classical learning. For that matter, the text contains its own oddities – tellingly not apparent in performance – including a shadow of an undeveloped plot. The writer may, in fact, have been alluding to *Blind Beggar* when in the dedication to Chapman's *All Fools* he complains of 'wits' who have 'patch'd' his earlier plays. The hurly burly of the text, its multiple disguises, its juxtapositions of native comedy, European traditions and classical allusiveness seemed right at home in the hands of the Blackfriars actors, alive to inconsistency, bizarre juxtapositions and vaudevillian shifts in register from high drama to low farce. Seeking uniformity, a coherent 'world' in which to set this play, might not, after all, do justice to Chapman's comic dramaturgy. In 2011, at the Blackfriars, the world of Chapman's play was in a world of play, where fake rocks are more real than real ones and the only plausible things that can happen are things that can happen in a play.

During 2011's *Blind Beggar*, then, the 'apparatus' in its largest sense – the playhouse, the company, the actors, the institutional auspices – was ostentatiously apparent, as evident as the prompter who sat stage right, with the 'patch'd' text that the tattered actors gave exuberant life to in their production of Chapman's disguise comedy. The play's generous joke allowed audiences to enjoy the hero's multiple impressions, even, *pace* Gurr, as they failed to recognize their origins (but then the Blackfriars has proven among other things that people can enjoy a cover version even if they don't know the original). The other characters might have been in the dark, but leaving the lights on, in this instance, allowed the audience to see right through the various guises of the ASC project, and they were all the happier for being the less deceived.

'Little Bitch' – *The Custom of the Country* (2013)

Left to their own devices, actors can get up to some funny business, particularly when those actors are named Daniel Kennedy, an Australian actor who worked with the ASC from 2007–12. Cast in multiple roles in Fletcher and Massinger's baroque tragi-comedy, *The Custom of the Country*, Kennedy stood out, or crawled out, as one of the male whores employed in Sulpitia's brothel. Exhausted by his labours, Kennedy snaked on stage propelled only by his elbows, entirely dead from his waist down. Earlier, as Zenocia's father, he offered up his body to the Count Clodio, whose 'custom of the country' is *droit du seigneur*, which causes Zenocia to bolt the land with her espoused on her wedding night. Left behind, her father sought to ease the wrath of the *seigneur* whose *droit* had been thwarted. His willingness to substitute his body for his daughter's – to offer a non-procreative proxy to the magnifico, whose custom has blurred lines of property and propriety – was a witty, even fiercely intelligent reading of the play's exposure of the incestuous logic of patriarchal rule. 'Kings and fathers', as Milton wrote, 'are very different things.'[4]

Kennedy's performance drew on 'physical theatre' – an odd name, since what theatre worth the name isn't – and the practices of clowning, a tradition in which he has worked extensively. Every bone in Dan Kennedy's body is a funny bone and he infused *Custom* with a performance not exactly at odds with the Blackfriars norm, but a more insistently physical one than often seen there. He describes the evolution of his offer to Clodio in telling terms:

'Funnily enough, I never intended to offer my ass to Clodio. I originally got down on my hands and knees to offer him my neck, but the way I stoically stretched my neck suggested buggery; a much better gag. We kept it.'[5]

In other words, the original impulse was not 'funnily enough', and so he stretched it out. It was exemplary, moreover, of the zany acting employed during the ARS, where actors underline the theatrical truism that the body always precedes the text, if not supersedes it. During the summer and fall seasons, by contrast, the acting is characterized by inert bodies and highly expressive faces. (There's a lot of eyebrow acting at the Blackfriars, not least because the scale of the playhouse rewards it. A critic noted in 1994 that 'Per the SSE formula [...] *Othello* downplays physical activity ... in favor of a comfortably conversational delivery of dialogue'.[6]) Kennedy's reading of the play – and it *was* a reading – was a reading with and through his body, a physical interpretation of character,

FIGURE 2 *Tracie Thomason and Ben Curns in* The Custom of the Country, *American Shakespeare Center, 2013. Photo by Lauren D. Rogers. Used by permission.*

situation, and play, one as intelligent as it was hilarious. It was, moreover, mutely articulate. The Blackfriars may be, as the official line has it, a place one goes to 'hear a play', and actors often seem intent upon emptying their verbal arsenals as rapidly as possible. Kennedy's performance made the proposal that sometimes meaning lies not just between the ears but also below the belt. Above all, Kennedy discovered the physical life of the play, one that lies simultaneously within but also beyond the 'text itself'.

The composition of the acting company does not deviate much from the ARS into the summer/fall line up (the spring season sees the touring company take the stage while the resident troupe goes into rehearsal), but the *style* of performance takes a significant detour. It is more difficult to talk about '*the* style' of performance during the ARS than throughout the rest of the year, however, since it's a style marked by diversity, diversity not just from play to play but from actor to actor, act to act, even scene to scene. This can prompt the too easy criticism that ARS actors are 'in different plays' from one another. That is largely a function of process. Actors learn the parts from 'cue scripts', which convey only dialogue and their cues. Learning in isolation, actors might understandably imagine themselves to be 'in different plays' than their peers (what kind of play did the original Osric think he was in?) This phenomenon is exacerbated by unfamiliar titles and the lack of a director. Indeed, the Shakespeare title with which the season opens routinely demonstrates the greatest stylistic uniformity of the plays in the three-month repertory. Enfranchised by unfamiliarity, enabled by alien preparation practices, actors during the Renaissance season make autonomous choices and if an audience is startled by incongruities they also know whom to blame. 'Gone are directors ...' who might otherwise bear the brunt for the lack of uniformity within a given show.

Caveats aside, *the* style of acting during the Renaissance season is noteworthy for the exuberant physicality of Daniel Kennedy's performance. Moreover, the diversity of histrionic idioms foregrounds the fact that the actors are acting autonomously, not as automatons. Whatever the audience may think of a performance, *that* performance is what *that* actor thought *that* particular moment, scene, act, play, character required. As Andrea Stevens wrote in a 2008 *Shakespeare Bulletin* review:

> it is precisely [the] diffusion of directorial authority that shows this company at its best. Possibly because the absence of a director required the actors to lean more heavily on their individual training, the Renaissance Season displayed more sustained and innovative use of music, space, and certainly of dance and movement.[7]

In addition to autonomy, the absence of a director generates the impression that this group of talented men and women simply took it upon themselves to put on a version of *Custom of the Country*, almost as though they were not contractually obligated to do so. Daniel Kennedy's readiness to put his body on the line informed his performance and pointed up the significance of the season's working title: what is reborn during the ARS is responsibility, which begins and ends in the actor's flesh. For the actors that means there's nowhere to hide, which is just one more thing that universal lighting exposes.

'The Season of the Witch' – *The Witch* (2008)

And then one night, the lights went out. Or dimmed, at least, as Alli Glenzer, riveting as Hecate in Thomas Middleton's tragic-comic *The Witch*, called down the night. As she chanted '*Cum volui, ripis ipsis mirantibus*' (5.2),[8] willing rivers to run backwards and clouds to do her will, the house lights – which we had been promised would stay on, as we are promised every night – went dark, or at least dim. I happened to be seated next to long-time company member René Thornton. He had taken the season off but a busman in need of a holiday had come to watch his erstwhile colleagues work. It was pretty dark, but even by owl light I could see his reaction. He looked like a parishioner who had just heard heresy from the pulpit.

Diegetically, at least, the idea was that Hecate had pulled a cloud over the sun. In fact, an actor had passed a poster board in front of the scoop that lit the house from behind the rose window. The phenomenon was that history had stopped, paused to take a breath, or at least let in a shadow to remind us not to take it for granted. Even a universally lit theatre can go dark. Just as Middleton's Hecate controls the tides and dims the sun, theatre also answers to a higher authority. I wondered, only for a flicker, if in the next moment the parliamentary guards might batter down the doors and frog march the actors over to the courthouse. Or, less dramatically, if management might pull the plug on the show.

You have occasionally to turn off the lights to remind us that they're always on. Orthodoxy, that is, requires the occasional heterodoxy, a moment of night to remind us it's day. The Renaissance season serves this function within the ASC's larger endeavour. The heterodoxies are mild, of course; Hecate's dark period lasted only for an instant. But it reminded us not to believe everything we hear – that the lights will stay on for instance – or everything that we see. However many redundancies in the belts-and-suspender lighting system – chandeliers, sconces, spotlights, rose window – the Blackfriars could still go dark. This was more than merely metaphor. During *The Witch*'s pre-show, Allison Glenzer, the titular witch herself, had asked us to 'invest in imagination' by giving to the ASC's annual fund, which would ensure that 'these lights keep burning for future generations'. Hecate's curse – cobbled out of Ovid by way of Reginald Scot – made the point that the Blackfriars is always a burned-out bulb away from going dark for good, or worse.

Given the autonomy of the actors during the Renaissance

FIGURE 3 *Tyler Moss and Allison Glenzer in* The Witch, *American Shakespeare Center, 2008. Photo by Tommy Thompson. Used by permission.*

Season, it was fitting to later discover that it was an actor who passed in front of the light and caused the house to dim. The actors could have asked a stage manager to lower the spotlights or the chandeliers with a twist of a rheostat. Hecate was dimming the sun, however, not the chandeliers or the spotlights that 'she' did not know were there. To make a point to the Duchess who wanted her husband dead, Hecate dimmed the Italian sun, played in this case by a scoop of light behind the rose window that stood for the Virginia sun that reflected the light of the early modern London one (which are the same, of course; the Virginia sun and the London one are not in different places, they're in different times). However layered this particular light, by passing a hand over the bulb, the actors reminded us that whatever light we took them in we did so at their pleasure. Hecate-like, the actors declared the ARS the season of the witch. It was brief insurrection against house policy, reminding us of who pulled the strings but not who writes the checks.

However heterodox, the actors had to seek permission to let a shadow creep into the Blackfriars. Furthermore, whatever autonomy the actors might claim, whatever ownership they might possess – 'Gone are the directors, the designers, the months of rehearsals ...' – they do not choose the season's titles, they do not cast the plays, they do not schedule the repertory. The season seeks an equilibrium between management and labour, artistic autonomy and ideological control. But if the actors want to monkey with the lights, they have to ask the zookeepers.

Anyone trained up on theories of containment and subversion – or who did graduate work in English from 1988 on – might be tempted to read in this an allegory, Michel Foucault comes to New Market Street. The ASC stages its own subversion 'so as to use it to its own ends', as Louis A. Montrose describes it.[9] The 'time bomb' at the heart of the organization was installed by the organization, and it's scheduled to never go off. But the ARS looks more like an incubator than a contained subversion of ASC policy. The ARS is where the ASC explores its limits, even lets a shadow fall across its brightest ideology. It is where the ASC grows its own future and articulates its understanding that the *status quo* can become a *terminus ad quem* if an institution's practices and policies are not called into question, if only by a witch cursing in Latin at the lights.

'I Only Have Eyes for You' – *'Tis Pity She's a Whore* (2006)

Taste is a funny thing, since everybody has it except other people. It may not be to everyone's taste then – in fact there are some who might find it tast*eless* – to perform a cover of the Flamingos' 1959 doo-wop hit 'I Only Have Eyes for You' right after Putana's eyes are gouged out in John Ford's *'Tis Pity She's a Whore*. It might further seem in questionable taste for Vanessa Morosco, an elegantly languorous, cerebral actor, to feed grapes with chopsticks to her fellow Banditta while her confreres sang the song, chopsticks she had just pointedly withdrawn from her hair as she escorted a screaming Putana off-stage. It transformed the refrain 'I only have eyes for you' into a gruesome pun, but also recast the romantic song as a murder ballad, one of fixation. You could do worse than gloss Giovanni's obsession with the lyric: 'My love must be a kind of blind love / I can't see anyone but you.'

If pace was of 'a special aesthetic essence' for the SSE, music is the essential aesthetic essence at the Blackfriars, at no time more so than during the ARS, which frequently nests contemporary songs – broadly understood – into the drama of the sixteenth and seventeenth centuries. The actors appropriate tunes based upon thematic connections both witty and banal. This might mean Okkervill River's ode to sequels 'Plus Ones' before *2 Henry VI* or Spoons' 'The Two Sides of Monsieur Valentine' during the anonymous disguise farrago *Look About You*. For *'Tis Pity* this meant embedding the Flamingos' hit into John Ford's masterpiece. This not

FIGURE 4 *Vanessa Morosco and René Thornton, Jr in* 'Tis Pity She's a Whore, *American Shakespeare Center, 2006, Photo by Tommy Thompson. Used by permission.*

only introduces one classic to another – John Ford, meet the Flamingos – but elasticizes the meaning of the word 'classic' itself, democratizing the definition and elongating it as well. At such times, the actors seem less like actors than pop artists, making free with material from the popular repertory with a giddy abandon.

Recalling the ASC's precis of 'Shakespeare's Staging Conditions', we remember that the ASC sets the many songs of Renaissance drama 'in contemporary style'. Even when music and lyrics from the period do survive, the ASC does not use them, for instance, Robert Johnson's extant settings for the *Tempest*'s 'Where the bee sucks' or *Cymbeline*'s 'Hark, hark the lark'. The tactic is 'emblematic of our approach', the programme goes on, but the treatment of music is even more broadly emblematic than the programme intends. For despite their historical commitments, the ASC has never demonstrated any interest in Renaissance music, even during the Actors' Renaissance Season, where other features of the early theatre are explicitly pursued. Not only does the ASC not employ a group of professional musicians – as the original Blackfriars did, as the new Globe does – it devoutly avoids sackbuts and hautboys, motets and madrigals (but see the interview with Jim Warren in Chapter 5). This is broadly 'emblematic', since, in an actor's words, the company 'chooses the elements we think are cool and ignores the ones we think are lame'.[10] This extends beyond the setting of extant lyrics in contemporary styles. During the Renaissance season, pop songs are interpolated into plays, where they serve as interludes that – as with *'Tis Pity* – editorialize upon the events of the drama, converting plays into multi-medial collages of the now and then, the here and there.

Indeed, at times during the Ren Season it can feel like you've gone to a pop concert and a Massinger play broke out. It is obvious that a considerable portion of the actors' limited time has gone to rescoring an AC/DC hit for fiddle and mandolin, whereas the putative purpose of the ARS is to present to twenty-first century audiences the hidden gems of the seventeenth. Nevertheless, pop music is vital to the season's project since it sets the clock to what Greil Marcus calls 'pop time', which cribs from history and doesn't footnote: 'It is a curving time made [...] by the way songs and movies cannibalize history and rewrite it according to a logic of their own.'[11] In 'pop time, chronological integrity bows before the popular canon, which, though it may eat its own, effortlessly digests the most exotic ingredients. 'I Only Have Eyes for You' and *'Tis Pity She's a Whore* are both on the menu during the Actors' Renaissance Season. The music means the Renaissance season never looks dated. Music is not a symbol of the past, but rather a sign of its presence.

In addition to the medley of modern music and early modern texts, to the melange of costume styles and periods, to the mixture of acting styles, there is also the occasional fist-bump and high-five, which in an attempt to seem modern only end up looking dated. By and large, however, the actors weave pop material into 400-year-old verse drama not at the expense but to the enrichment of both. The weave reveals rather than disguises the various threads, however, which only rarely tangle in the hands of the Blackfriars actors. It may be that one thing directors do is ensure that the actors keep time. Among the virtues of a director's omission, then, is that left to their own devices actors will have their own anarchic way with time, substituting the pop kind for an imposed uniformity that ensures all theatrical elements punch the same clock.

A frequent question about productions of Renaissance drama is to ask in what period a show is set. During the Actors' Renaissance Season the answer is 'all of them'. The Flamingos did not make Ford 'feel new' anymore than Ford made the Flamingos feel old. (A short quiz, a pop one. Which is a play by John Ford and which a song by the Flamingos: 'Chances', 'The Vow', 'Would I be Crying', 'The Broken Heart', 'The Ladder of Love', 'Love's Sacrifice', 'The Lover's Melancholy'? Lightning round: Was John Ford England's oldest teenager or the Flamingos America's youngest Jacobeans?) The effect of the Flamingos' song in the midst of Ford's play is ultimately best conveyed by the opening line to the final stanza, a taut expression of pop's *cogito ergo sum*: 'You are here and so am I.'

Like the ASC rendition, The Flamingos' version – with its spooky-ethereal, shimmery production – is also not original. The song was written by Harry Warren and Al Dubin for the 1934 film *Dames* (the working title of Middleton's *Women Beware Women*). There, Dick Powell sings it to Ruby Keeler, her bangs curled diacritically over her intermittently interested eyes. Dubious at the outset, by the end of the song she's convinced: 'Gee Jimmy, that's swell', as Annabella said to Giovanni. 'I Only Have Eyes for You' has since been covered by a boggling array of artists, from Rosemary Clooney and Art Garfunkel to the Fugees, who sampled it for 'Zealots' on 1996's *The Score*. The ambition of every 'cover' is to conceal the original and, by so doing, become it. Thus we say, 'The Flamingos' "I Only Have Eyes for You" and the apostrophe doesn't even flinch. When the Flamingos lip-synched their version of what subsequently became their song on American Bandstand in the late 1950s, a reflective Dick Clark introduced them with a meditation on Renaissance drama: 'Of all of the songs around, sometimes the old ones I think are interesting, especially when they're redone in a different manner.' America's oldest teenager didn't mention who did the original. If you do it right, it's new every time.

Renaissance history

Like so many successful artistic endeavours, the Renaissance Season was born out of need when Associate Artistic Director Jay McClure suggested in 2003 that the company innovate something to fill the lag that stretches from January through April.

Fairly early in the running of the Blackfriars Playhouse,

we realized that winter programming was going to be challenging [...] I came up with the idea of the Actors' Renaissance Season based on what Shenandoah Shakespeare already did with Renaissance Runs and on my experience in summer stock (short rehearsal periods, sides, actors making big decisions by necessity and having the agency to do so).[12]

According to McClure, 'Renaissance Runs' were a technique Jim Warren developed in the early 1990s: 'At the start of rehearsal for each play, the actors rehearse, without the director, for about eight hours before performing the play for the director and artistic team.'[13] Only subsequently was the season rationalized as an answer to a specific question: 'what would happen if our resident troupe at the American Shakespeare Center tried producing the works of the Renaissance stage using Renaissance staging practices?'[14] As McClure explains, 'The idea of the Ren Season was not inspired by the work of any particular scholar. I had read Gurr's books before I came up with the idea. I read Stern's *Rehearsal From Shakespeare to Sheridan* and Bentley's *The Profession of Player in Shakespeare's Time, 1590–1642* quite a while after, in the fall of 2004.' The season was born then out of exigency and is as beholden to modern rehearsal protocols (of summer stock, of those Warren employed) as to those of the past. The season developed a belated academic rationale for its performance practices and thus the ASC continued to revise history, which is one of its talents, along with developing doctrines that do not sound doctrinaire.

As McClure notes, the ARS practices were pilfered from the present as well as the pages of theatre historical works, particularly Stern's, Gurr's and Bentley's. Despite its non-academic origins, it seems safe to say that no theatre has more directly observed the 'page to stage' mandate of those scholars calling for stage-centred criticism than the ASC during the Renaissance Season. The company's approach, at least from

January through April, is strictly by the book, particularly the books of Tiffany Stern, though other theatre historians had a hand in the making of the ARS (including Andrew Gurr, who gave the company a general benediction, and Roslyn Knutson, whose work on repertory informed ARS programming). In doing so the ASC answered the spirited calls of '76 that sought a Shakespearean stage where theatre and scholarship might finally marry. Perhaps all this time actors and academics had just been looking for the right venue. The Actors' Renaissance Season is what the 'Shakespeare Revolution' looks like with capital, scholarship and talent.

Arguably, not since John Russell Brown replaced Kenneth Tynan as dramaturg for the Royal National Theatre in 1973 has a professional Shakespearean had more influence upon the commercial theatre than Tiffany Stern has upon the ASC (the lone parallel would be Farah Karim-Cooper's influence at the Globe, particularly in shepherding the construction of the Sam Wanamaker indoor theatre, opened in 2014). Stern's influence is on display during the Ren Season, which deploys her research into rehearsal duration and cue scripts in particular. Which is to say Stern's impact is actually *not* on display during the Ren Season since it manifests itself in the rehearsal room, behind closed doors (this is a euphemism; the ASC offers open rehearsals, and scholars – see below – as well as the general public are welcome to watch). Following Stern, the ASC limits rehearsal time to 20–48 hours a show, which includes table work, costuming, musical prep and more. Furthermore, since 2006 the actors have learned their lines from cue scripts, which contain only their own lines and cues. This practice follows through on the work that Stern and Simon Palfrey collected in their *Shakespeare in Parts* (2007). Whatever other scholarship lurks behind the scenes, the ASC's official website gives Stern sole credit for the season: 'inspired by Tiffany Stern's *Making Shakespeare*, our actors got even closer to Renaissance staging conditions by using partial scripts that contained only their lines and a few words of the preceding cue'.[15] The season owes its origins to Jay McClure's innovative thinking – or reinnovated thinking – but it credits its scholarly underpinnings to Tiffany Stern's research.

The Ren Season therefore participates in a give-and-take relationship with academia. Or take-and-give, since it takes its scholarship from Stern but gives back to others interested in retro-rehearsal procedures. Scholars such as Stern, Allison Lenhardt, Rhonda Knight and Evelyn Tribble have observed rehearsals and folded their observations into their work.[16] To date, Tribble's *Cognition in the Globe: Attention and Memory in Shakespeare's Theatre* offers the most sophisticated analysis of ARS rehearsal practices, as she applies her work on 'distributed cognition' to explain the company's ability to quickly master a density of materials. She offers this as an analog to, not evidence of, the work of early modern playing companies, in part to explain those companies' seemingly inexplicable ability to process massive repertorial churn. She is particularly attentive to the 'exigencies of the inevitable mismatch between contemporary cognitive ecologies of acting and those of the past', not least that what the actors of the ARS experience as 'deficit' was, to their forebears, taken as read.[17] Tribble's sensitivity responds to the ASC's equally tempered 'inspired by Tiffany Stern's *Making Shakespeare*' – not governed, dictated, or even led by – as well as the actors themselves, who live in the nick of time between the 'contemporary' and the 'past', both taking and making history.

The fluid reciprocity between actors and academics during the ARS not only fulfills the mandate of the 'Spirit of '76', it also realizes an early dream of the ASC's founder. In what was possibly the first news feature on what would become Shenandoah Shakespeare Express, and eventually the ASC, Cohen describes the goals of the *Henry V* he put on as a seminar project with a group of students, including co-founder Jim Warren, who played Henry: '"I'm hoping that a whole new confidence in certain aspects of academic theater comes out of the seminar and production," Cohen said. "'Henry V' will be academic theater at its most academic but also at its most theatrical."'[18] Cohen's confidence, at least, emerged intact from the production since four years later he prophesied in the press that, '"Already one of three Shakespeare scholars anywhere in America have heard of us. By the end of this year, two of them will have heard of us. Two years from now all of them will have heard of us."'[19] His early ambition has probably been met, in that the ASC or at least the Blackfriars is well known among academics. Of course, since 1992 Cohen and Warren have amplified their ambition. In the intervening years, their work has been to turn the antithesis – 'academic' *but* 'theatrical' – into the apposite. The SSE was born out of an academic seminar, and now bears fruit for academics everywhere who can take in its bounty both in books and on the boards. The Ren Season gives them theatre at its most academic but also at its most theatrical.

Among working theatres, only the Globe has more closely embraced theatre history, and theatre historians, than the ASC. The Globe's two theatres stand on the shoulders of Andrew Gurr, John Orrell, Peter Greenaway, Farah Karim-Cooper and many others. Furthermore, since its inception, the Globe has explored music, costumes, make up, and more through research with Jenny Tiramani, Claire van Kempen, Farah Karim-Cooper and others. The Globe has evolved away from the Original Practices remit, and distanced themselves from the term as surely as has the ASC. (It's a sure sign that the Globe has put 'OP' behind it when they invited their founding artistic director, Mark Rylance, in as a guest to produce two 'authentic' pieces within their larger season.) Nevertheless, under the leadership of Farah Karim-Cooper, the Globe's research into early English theatrical practices has not just continued, but expanded and deepened and the Globe's commitment to such work is unparalleled, as evidenced in the Sam Wanamaker playhouse, lit purely by real candlelight: nowhere more so than at the Globe does scholarly research materialize the theatrical practices of the English Renaissance.

True to their origins, the ASC has always been more interested in methods than materials, in theatrical practice as opposed to theatrical stuff. As pointed out above, the company was not formed to build a playhouse and so has investigated *practices* like abbreviated rehearsals rather than *materials* like authentic costumes. For instance, though the Blackfriars' chandeliers are designed to hold real candles, the company has never put on a candle-lit performance in its first decade-plus of productions. And though the Blackfriars has a trap 'above', the heavens remain closed at the Blackfriars (at least until they can purchase a winch. God is in the funding.) 'Authenticity' has always been relatively low on the ASC's 'to do' list, regardless how closely the Blackfriars resembles the original. Perhaps enfranchised by their distance from the site of the original, the company engaged in best-guess scholarship but, once the building was opened, they've made their own way. To make a musical analogy inspired by the company's practices, the ASC has an original instrument, an 'old' one, but they use it to play the songs of Thomas Dolby, not Thomas Campion, of Robert Plant, not Robert Johnson. Again, to quote the programme, this is 'broadly emblematic' of the ASC's approach, which is a commitment to connect old texts with new audiences, not rigidly imitate the material practices of their theatrical forebears. The Ren Season, claims the ASC, 'adds to our overall understanding of the way these plays worked', but what delights them more is that the Renaissance Season 'was a bigger hit with our audiences than we imagined'.[20] However historical, however academic, the Renaissance season is more interested in awakening modern audiences than resurrecting theatrical origins.

The Actors' Renaissance Season has evolved over its ten-year history (as of the writing of this book), although its ten-year anniversary went unmarked; in contrast, the company made hay over both the Blackfriars' tenth-birthday in 2011 and the company's twenty-fifth in 2013. This has perhaps to do with the season's experimental status. Introduced out of expediency, the season may not have been built to last. Threading the needle, as ever, of historical practice and modern performance, the season began 'in 2005, [when] the American Shakespeare Center decided to try an experiment in modern staging'.[21] Experimentation has more to do with trying things out than blowing out candles, with trial-and-error not pomp-and-circumstance. The alterations to the season – its techniques adjusted, its programming tweaked, its repertory shifted – signals its possible impermanence as part of the ASC's overall programming, or at least its evolution. At least in its currently recognizable form, the 'Renaissance Season' may turn out to have been only for a season,

Indeed, as befitting its *ad hoc* origins, the ARS is an impure art. Since 2006, for instance, non-Renaissance plays have appeared in the Renaissance season – *The Rover*, *Cyrano*, *The Country Wife*, etc. – but while the Ren season has looked forward – to the Restoration and beyond – it has never looked back. No *Gorboduc*, no *Mankind*, not even the *Spanish Tragedy*. *Mother Bombie* is the earliest play the ARS has produced and *Tamburlaine* the 'earliest' written play that the ASC has ever produced. Possibly they want to avoid the fate of William Poel. One irony of the Elizabethan Stage Society is that their greatest success was with *Everyman*. More likely the ASC subconsciously understands that a search for a 'purity of origins' – in Roach's terms – requires a belief that there *is* an origin, and that its name is Shakespeare. A return to the pre-Shakespearean stage would emphasize the contingency of the idea of a Shakespearean origin for drama.

Thus the Ren season pushes forward into history, part of its experiment in what is – in the end – 'modern staging'. Indeed there are efforts afoot to produce new work during the Ren Season, fulfilling the founders' mandate that one reason to recreate old conditions is to produce new work. This salutary effort – to produce *avant* works under antique conditions, which Cohen has called for, echoing Poel – contributes to a tension that prevails across the institution. The company's general remit is that 'Shakespeare's plays work best under Shakespeare's staging conditions', which might suggest the same for Goldsmith, Molière, Congreve, Behn, Sheridan, Shaw and others, all of whom have had their plays produced under 'Shakespeare's Staging Conditions'. If there's a tension between a deterministic policy that believes that Shakespeare prospers under Shakespearean conditions and a belief that other playwrights will as well, it is an easy one, though an unintended consequence of this idea is the suggestion that Shakespeare's plays are *less* amenable to adaptation than the plays of 'lesser' playwrights. The ASC has always been adept at easing tensions between their stated mission and their staged products, however. All it takes is talent. Audiences can forgive or at least forget anything during a terrific show, even being told that the ASC follows Shakespeare's staging conditions while watching a play by one of the score of talented playwrights not named William Shakespeare. The Virginia company has a talent for diffusing tensions, even the raw energy of Renaissance drama or an experiment in modern staging that could have blown up in their face.

In the nick of time

This chapter has pursued an obvious paradox: when the ASC most explicitly engages with history, it becomes the least beholden to it. The ARS does not seem remotely 'Renaissancy'; it seems remotely modern. There is a cod profundity to this argument by paradox ('everything is its opposite!'), but it is nevertheless the fact that when the ASC adheres strictly to the practices of early modern playmaking its performances are at their most modern, even their most 'popular'. It is no paradox, in any event, to signal out the Actors' Renaissance Season as the ASC's apotheosis, when the Virginia company becomes most fully itself by occupying their alterity.

What the ARS exposes is the company's considerable time-management skills. That extends from the ASC's intricate programming, to the company's deft way with its historical retail, to the actors of the Renaissance season who have to make the best of what limited time they have. The season nevertheless occupies an interesting rift since what the company experiences – and advertises – as aberrant for today was, originally, standard operating procedure. ARS actors experience their resources largely as a lack – of directors, designers, time, and text – but they are (re)producing a theatrical culture where that 'lack' was not a deficit but was everything that is, or was, the case. The time the ARS actors lack was the time that 'Shakespeare's actors' had, or didn't, as the rhetoric around the season has it. Of course, even Stern would point out that it is impossible to determine *precisely* how much rehearsal went on, but the ASC is making history, not strictly following it, and so have amplified their deficits to capitalize upon them.

The introduction to this book argued that during the pre-show the actors attempt to find a cut in time to hang out for a while. If the ASC generally seeks a cut in time, the ARS operates in the nick of it. The actors are given various deficits – deficits of directors, designers, texts – but the lack of time is obviously the most daunting in the scarcity economy that is the ARS. The opening show receives twenty hours of rehearsal. It is, as noted, invariably a familiar title, and so the actors have often appeared in at least one production of the play, giving them a considerable leg-up on the play clock. While 'past performance is indicative of future results' in many fields, the same is not the case with drama. Theatre is hostage to a thousand contingencies, and just because an actor has been in a dozen *Shrew*s that doesn't mean he or she, especially she, has to like it. Whatever text the company works from, they're not performing *The Shrew*, they're performing *A Shrew*. The pressures of time – in particular its lack – are only partly assuaged by familiarity. A theatre might be a place where nothing takes place for the first time, but tell it to an actor on opening night.

The pressure under which the actors operate produces a sense of arch agony, an expressive feeling that the actors are fighting an unfamiliar play and the restraints of time that they are up against. That agony is played for laughs, however.

When an actor dries and calls upon the prompter, it is an occasion not for shame but shenanigans. Lines are called for with an air of exasperation, italicizing the challenging circumstances under which the actors operate. Every call to the prompter has a subtext of 'you-try-memorizing-350-lines-of-*Mother Bombie*-in-a-week'. (As an instance of the way that remembering can cause an actor to forget himself, a young performer named Grant Davis once called for a line near the end of *Custom of the Country*. The prompter reminded him that his line began 'Grant me ...'.) Though the actors vary considerably in their respective approaches to characterization, then, there is a collective sense of spirited exhaustion and physical labour that overrides idiosyncrasies. Watching the Blackfriars company put on a play during the Actors' Renaissance Season is like watching beavers build a dam.

Since the ASC is less interested in materials than methods, they face the challenge of making apparent to the audience the circumstances under which the actors have been labouring, which theatre otherwise tries to hide. If one didn't know a thing about the 'Actors' Renaissance Season' – and failed to read the programme, or listen to the pre-show talk – one might wander into a March 2015 performance of Lyly's *Mother Bombie* and marvel at the algorithmic excellence of Lyly's comedy as expertly handled by a group of adept actors. You wouldn't know that they had had just hours to prepare and learned their lines of this unfamiliar play from cue scripts. The company therefore goes to some lengths to detail in spoken and written materials the circumstances of the production, which has the planned effect of folding the auspices of the operation into the event of performance. The visible prompter is one main way in which the apparatus is revealed, a surplus body that stands for the deficits under which the actors laboured. Even when not called upon, the prompter is stage left, not just to help the actors remember their lines but to remind the audience that the actors have remembered them even though they were not given sufficient time to do so.

In closing, the 'Time Bomb' of the Renaissance Season

does not explode things, it exposes them. It also roughly sorts the ASC's full calendrical repertory into Shakespeare vs Renaissance Drama. As noted above, by establishing a three-month Renaissance Season, the ASC sets up an internal divide that is nonetheless not divisive. They might seem to be staging their own insurrection, but the effect is otherwise. Far from riving the Center, the ASC has created a canonical season of plays and playing dominated by Shakespeare's plays and 'Shakespeare's Staging Conditions' and a shorter 'Renaissance' season dominated by Renaissance plays and 'Renaissance' playing practices. It is telling, in this regard, that in its brief for the 'Renaissance Season' the ASC asks, 'what would happen if our resident troupe at the American Shakespeare Center tried producing the works of the *Renaissance* stage using *Renaissance* staging practices?'[22] (emphasis added). In other words, the standard programme refers to 'Shakespeare's Staging Conditions', but the company's plump for the ARS calls them 'Renaissance' practices of the 'Renaissance' stage just as though Shakespeare was of but not part of the Renaissance. The company, in few, sees the Renaissance season as just that, an investment in a contiguous canon, adjacent but not identical to the Shakespearean one.

The 'raw energy of Renaissance drama' – an apt description of what's on offer from January through April – both critiques and canonizes the material that occupies the stage for the majority of the year, then. The ASC kicks off every new year with a Renaissance repertory and playing style, bifurcating the plays of the late sixteenth and early seventeenth century into 'Shakespeare' and 'Renaissance Drama', a bifurcation that mirrors the anthology projects of the Shakespeare academy, which publishes adjunct volumes of Renaissance plays but does not mix Shakespeare's among them.[23] As a student once aptly put it, there is 'Shakespeare' and there is 'Renaissance Drama' and while the two are mutually constitutive, they are not, like Milton's kings and fathers, the same thing.

One unintended effect might be to make Shakespeare look staid by comparison with the 'raw energy' of Renaissance drama, of the Renaissance Season itself. If the virtue of omitting directors, designers and extended rehearsal is to release this 'raw energy', what is the vice of adding them? Inertia? Entropy? Still, it's brave of the Artistic Director – himself a director – to produce an annual season that proves directors are not always necessary. By the inherent logic of such things, of course, the aesthetic turbulence of the three-month season throws into contrast the uniform quality of the other nine. The Renaissance season therefore has a veneer not just of Canonical vs Non-canonical, but also of labour vs management and thus it restages some of the conflicts upon which the ASC built their work. Much of the early rhetoric vilified directors, concepts, and cumbersome sets. And yet, the ASC is a directors' theatre (in that they use them), and very much invested in concept. Could anything be more conceptual than building a $3.7 million reproduction of a seventeenth-century indoor playhouse? The ASC has a cumbersome set, so cumbersome that they can never change it. By staging their own insurrection, however, by giving the actors three months of anarchic reign, the ASC puts its own history on the stage. It ultimately reaffirms the dominance of the Shakespeare canon, a dignified guarantor of controlled quality unthreatened by the raw energy of a coterminous canon. 'Renaissance' drama might be exciting from time to time, but Shakespeare is forever.

Any division of the Blackfriars season into canon and anti-canon, actors and management, entropic versus energetic simplifies the situation considerably, however, since the Blackfriars season is tripartite. The touring company comes off the road and takes over the playhouse after the Actors' Renaissance Season wraps up. And thus the ASC remembers – and stages – the company's own origins. In fact, as the year unfolds, a pageant of the Virginia company's history unfurls. A scrappy group of rawly energetic, under-rehearsed actors exploring Shakespeare's staging conditions gives way to a polished touring company adeptly adjusting to a new space. They in turn give way to the summer/fall season of mature actors in sumptuous costumes wholly at home in their own playhouse. The company's move from an Express – one that performs in the nick of time – gives way to the stability of a company of centred actors who perform in the cut of it. But even this tripartite division doesn't *quite* capture the whole journey. In a fitting historical irony, the season has a coda, since it culminates at the end of the calendar year with an extended run of *A Christmas Carol*. And thus the revolution the ASC stages capitulates in the end to a Victorian icon. But only for a time, since, in a by-now predictable rhythm of iconicity and iconoclasm, not long after *Christmas Carol* takes its final bow, the revolution starts all over again with a revival of Shakespeare under Elizabethan conditions, as if for the very first time.

5

'But wait, there's more …!'

If 'something strange and boring' happens before every show at the Blackfriars Playhouse in Staunton, Virginia, something equally surprising happens at the end of every one. Shortly following a curtain call – entirely conventional but for the want of a curtain – and following a standing ovation – as de rigueur as the opening litany – an actor bursts through the arras and hollers at the audience's backs, 'But wait, there's more …!' The actor is announcing the results of a ticket raffle, the winner of which takes home a signed poster of the company's actors (second prize, a trip to the Renaissance). The ceremony of chance feels lifted from the casino world, another venue that blocks out the daylight to make sure no one knows what time it is. Beyond the immediate purpose of the announcement, the actor's cry, 'But wait, there's more …' stands for the ASC's eagerness to explain themselves, to bracket their performances with threshold events. Above all, the actors get to have the last word, just as soon at their characters have stopped talking.

This final chapter follows form and gives the last word not to the actors, but rather to the founders of the American Shakespeare Center, Jim Warren and Ralph Alan Cohen. I sat down with the co-founders separately, but they responded to more or less the same prompts, quotes excerpted from this book's first draft. The idea was to let Warren and Cohen respond to claims I made about their history, principles, practices and ambition. I explicitly invited them to challenge, query, emend or embroider upon the various claims this book makes about their enterprise. Except where they corrected falsities in the first draft, I have not revised the book to accommodate those places where they draw different conclusions than I have about the ASC's operation. Rather, I hope that the following, edited transcription of the two interviews introduces a dialectical dynamic into the book, building into it some of the enabling contradictions that galvanize the ASC itself. I have cleared the transcriptions that follow with both Warren and Cohen. Both interviews were conducted in late July and early August, 2015.

Talking with an audience: An interview with ASC co-founders Ralph Alan Cohen and Jim Warren

Jim Warren, Artistic Director

But for a brief period in the late 1980s, Jim Warren has been with the American Shakespeare Center for its entire existence. He was a charter member of the student seminar at James Madison University in spring 1988, when Ralph Alan Cohen convened a class around an exploration of *Henry V* and Shakespeare's staging conditions. The class culminated in a production in which Warren played Henry V, a production that planted the seed out of which the American Shakespeare Center has grown. Since then, he has directed over 120 shows, and he has been at the artistic helm of the company from the start. Jim Warren was, therefore, an early architect of the company's principles and has been the chief contractor in their construction, maintenance, and evolution ever since.

Warren is a passionate spokesman for the Virginia company's enterprise. As quick to laugh as he is eager to articulate the troupe's principles, his fervent belief in the company is undimmed across the quarter-of-a-century that he has been promoting, defending and implementing its goals. Though he has overseen – is largely responsible for – the company's evolution from a Converse-clad 'Express' to a sumptuously housed 'Center', he still sees the ASC as insurgents, outside the mainstream of twenty-first century Shakespeare and performance. Addressing at one point the company's personnel deficits, he said that he'd rather have too few bodies on the stage than the *wrong* bodies on the stage. Twenty-five years after the inaugural performance, Warren is still playing Henry V.

I interviewed Warren at the ASC offices in Staunton. The ASC has comfortable lodgings on the top floor of the R. R. Smith Center for History and Art. The building is an exquisitely renovated 1894 hotel in the French Second Empire style, designed by Staunton's most famous architect, T. J. Collins. The Smith Center houses the Staunton Augusta Arts Center, the Augusta County Historical Society and the Historic Staunton Foundation. Like this book, the building has many stories and the ASC sits at the top of them. (The Center for History and Art is on New Street. The irony is so neat that it satisfied my suspicion about this book's conceit and then made me suspicious of its neatness.) I arrived at Warren's office and was surprised to find him surrounded by packing boxes.

'Coming or going', I asked?

'I just haven't unpacked yet from the move', Warren replied, referring to the company's move to the Smith Center from their previous downtown offices. The move took place in 2012. The interview with the American Shakespeare Center's artistic director took place then amid signs of transience. He wore sneakers.

Author: *Why 'cite historical practice just to pick a fight with it'? Why 'build error into the apparatus of authenticity'? (p. 11).*

JW: I think that the inspiration for starting the company was the idea that Shakespeare was writing for a particular kind of theatrical environment. And the way that we do theatre today has changed a lot. What we do today is different than what he did 400 years ago [...] We thought that if we could recreate some of the staging conditions that he was writing for we could uncover some of the magic that he wrote into the plays that sometimes gets lost when you play with all the cool tricks we've invented. And so trying to figure out some of the guess work of, well, what sorts of things *was* he writing for and how can we do some of those things either in actuality or in the spirit of them to try and help the plays come alive in all the ways possible. So it was never about trying to recreate historical accuracy but rather to try and learn as much as we can about how they created theatre and what we can do to get that vibe [...] That puts us on both sides of the fence, which is let's research, let's see what we can discover or speculate about, and then interpret, recreate, but not replicate. So, for better or for worse, that puts us in neither the wholesale academic camp of, 'we are recreating as academically true as we can discover or rediscover in that academic search' nor are we just doing our own thing: creating cool theatre that we like; there's a foot in both camps.

Author: *One of your actors has said, anonymously, that the ASC 'does the stuff that we think is cool and not the stuff that we think is lame'. He was talking, I think, about Renaissance music, in particular, 'there are no hautboys or pavanes at the Blackfriars' –*

JW: Not yet.

Author: *That's actually interesting, I'd like to hear more about that. Music is so important at the Blackfriars and to the ASC. Music is so important, and so is history [...] but the history of Renaissance music has not been a big part –*

JW: That's a great microcosm and I would put costumes in a similar vein, in that, if you're trying to recreate what Shakespeare might have done, or the spirit of what he might have done, do you wear tights and pumpkin pants and play Renaissance music? One school of thought is, well, of course you should. And certainly that's what Mark Rylance and Jenny Tiramani [Director of Theatre Design at the Globe, 1997–2005] were exploring in those first years of the Globe: how *those* sounds from *those* instruments that were made at *that* time and in a particular way and how those clothes that were made at that time in a particular way, all have a *big* effect on how you perform those plays. If you try to recreate that kind of historical accuracy – for lack of better terminology – that puts you in a particular kind of camp. What we did when we started, because we had no money, was develop our own initial style with music and costume [...] I'll take music, because that's what you asked about. What Shakespeare's company played for their audience was contemporary for that audience. So we made the choice that we could do a better job of recreating the condition, the vibe, that they had by playing modern music on modern instruments. And wearing contemporary clothing is more like what Shakespeare did on some level, if your brain looks at it that way.

Author: *The development of costuming from the SSE to the ASC has been interesting. The costuming now is beautiful. It tends to skew more period than not, but tell me if I'm wrong about that.*

JW: It's ebbed and flowed. One of the things that I went hard core trying to find out if we could do was: can we make Elizabethan costumes sexy? Because in our younger days when we didn't have the money and it wasn't a choice, we were doing exclusively modern clothing. And we could feel good about doing that because Shakespeare wore contemporary clothes for his time, we're wearing

contemporary clothes for our time. But I also came from the
school of: most shows that I saw with tights and pumpkin
pants were dusty and boring and I didn't think we could
connect with a modern audience wearing those. At one point
I said, well, let's *try it*. And I think that we've developed an
aesthetic that – while I'm sure there are still some high school
kids who will come and see us in Elizabethan costumes and
think, 'well, that's not about me' – I believe strongly that we
have crossed barriers and we can do the best of both worlds
where something can be Elizabethan – Jacobean silhouettes
and / or clothing pieces and a high-school kid *can* still see
themselves in the show. So I want our costuming to be all
over the place: I want to be able to do Elizabethan. I want
to be able to do modern. I want to do medieval. I want to
do whatever the heck we want to do and still make that
connection with the audience. That's not what Shakespeare's
company did, probably, but I do think that we have enough
evidence of contemporary Elizabethan clothing being used
– we have the *Titus* woodcutting that shows some period
Romanesque pieces along with modern stuff – so I feel like
that's a principle we are embracing in our own way. But
back to that quote, I mean, I wouldn't quite put it that way
[laughs] but there are things like an all-male troupe that we
haven't done yet, and we know he did that. Why don't we
do that? In some of our materials I'm not particularly happy
with the way that it says, 'they did cross-gender casting,
with men playing women, so we get at that spirit by having
women playing men'.

Author: *It's slightly incoherent –*

JW: Yes, one of the basic tenets is, if we think Shakespeare
might have done something, then I want to try it. In some
way, shape, or form. So that is an instance where we have
not tried it yet.

Author: *You have to set priorities, and it sounded like from*

*what you were saying, exploring how to make Elizabethan/
Jacobean costuming sexy, that was a priority you guys have
obviously put resources towards over the last ten, fifteen
years, it's obvious on the stage. But as a hypothetical, you
chose that over, like, let's make Renaissance music 'sexy'.*

JW: Right.

Author: *Let's see if we can make great sounding
contemporary music on old instruments –*

JW: And that's a great example of, yes, we chose the one, we
have not chosen the other. Yet.

Author: *You've said a couple of times 'yet'. Are there things
you would like to [explore]? How to make Renaissance
music 'sexy'. How to make an all-male company 'sexy',
which other companies have done.*

JW: It's not hyperbolic when I say we want to try to do
anything we think they might have done in some way, shape,
or form. Yeah, I want to have Renaissance instruments
at some point. I would love to have, in sixteen plays over
fifty-two weeks in the Blackfriars – we won't talk about
where the Globe comes in – I would love to have enough
money, if money were not an object, and it was just about
'what is our aesthetic', I would love to have a show that
does what Mark and Jenny Tiramani did, and includes music
from the period.[1] Also, our actors are playing our music
rather than non-actor musicians, which is, I think, a piece of
our appeal, but it's not like we think Shakespeare probably
did it. That Blackfriars consort, those guys may have acted, I
mean, I think that those are probably the guys that had lines
in the *Romeo and Juliet* scene with the musicians. And they
might have done some double duty. But I think Shakespeare
had musicians that were not just the actors in the troupe.
And so, at some point, I want to be able to do that.

Author: *You've used the word a couple of times 'inspired by' certain practices, and I'm trying to sort of thread the needle 'what is a recreation', what is 'inspired by'. What about candlelight?*

JW: We're doing something in *Joan*[2] that we did when we staged Marlowe's *Edward II* where we've got candelabra on stage; today we did a run through of the first half, and it was the first time that we lit the candles. We've been rehearsing with unlit candles, and the candelabra were there so we were blocking around them. But it's *amazing to look at.* Just having those two live candelabra, five or seven candles lit on each one, that are part of the framing of what you see on stage, depending on where you're sitting is a whole different animal than the static, electric light bulbs that are simulated candles.

Author: *During a production of* Shakespeare's Joan of Arc, *your audience will see real candles –*

JW: Yes.

Author:: *They'll see chandeliers with fake candles –*

JW: Yes.

Author: *They'll see modern spotlights up above –*

JW: Yes

Author: *They'll be bathed in light from the 'Rose Window' –*

JW: Yes.

Author: *That's a* lot *of different kinds of light. In some ways, that really stands for a lot of these different kinds of –*

JW: Principles.

Author: *Principles that you're trying to make work altogether. And all that light comes together. It's a nice symbol.*

JW: Yes. Another microcosm. We knew when we built this recreation of the Blackfriars that there are no original blueprints of the Blackfriars. We did our best detective work to figure out, o.k., what *might* it have looked like. One of the things that is, again, speculation: the original Blackfriars probably had windows. We have a certain number of modern lighting instruments, and we thought the best way to use those instruments was to create the flavour of a clerestory, and that Rose Window is a good excuse to put some spotlights back there that will give some face lighting. Our approach has evolved; when we first opened, all the lighting was from up top.

Author: *Were the spotlights part of the original design of this Blackfriars or were they an add on?*

JW: They were an add on. When we first opened the place, we had the same chandeliers with artificial candles in there, and we just turned them up to eleven. And we tried to light the place the way one would light any room to a sufficient modern level. And so that's where we started. But, A) the artificial candles are blinding to look at when they are cranked up as bright as they can go. And B) that meant that we had to raise some of those chandeliers all the way up to the top so that nobody would have to look at them directly. But they would still bleed a bunch of light down to 'light up the room'. So it was a process of, well, what if we lowered the lumens on those artificial bulbs to make them more like real candles? If we do that, how do we then get 'light through windows'. Well, ok, we bought these instruments [the spotlights], at the time we did not think we'd be performing fifty-two weeks a year so we had other instruments that other companies might use. And so we tried to figure out a way we might position them that would make the most of the light they produced, and give us something that was not spotlights pointed down on the stage in a way that windows never could have done.

Author: *The building was designed for those spotlights to be where they are right now.*

JW: Correct. We put in a light grid. There are bars that we put in where those lights are hanging that are designed to hold those lights.

Author: *I have a theory about why this has not happened, [but] it will be interesting to hear what you think. You've never made an attempt to disguise those lights?*

JW: Right.

Author: *You don't mind your audience seeing that there are modern spotlights up there?*

JW: No.

Author: *What are your thoughts about that?*

JW: One of the things that we've talked about that we haven't tried yet is ... the technical term for what is in that Rose Window is one scoop ... and two 'licos'. What if we did that in all the bays?[3] So instead of having the lights out there where they are right now, what if we put them behind [the bays] and, if we had all the money in the world, and we could snap our fingers and we had all of those lights behind more window-type-shaped things to put them through, that *might* get us a better sun-through-window-simulation than what we've got. Anyway, we think Shakespeare performed during the day, so they had candles and sunlight ... Shakespeare joined the Lord Chamberlain's Men when they

were still at the Theatre and then they came across the river
and built the Globe. So he's writing plays for the outdoor
sun at the Theatre and the Globe that can't be turned off or
shuttered, and then late in Shakespeare's career they move
into the Blackfriars, and maybe they get to play with some
of that other stuff like shuttering the windows for lighting
effects. I'm a believer in kind of the opposite of where some
of the playing at the Wanamaker has gone in that I think
Shakespeare's indoor theatre had universal lighting, the same
way that the outdoor theatre had; I think they lit up their
whole room with candles and sunlight. And I think later in
the Jacobean period, some plays were written to mess with
that convention. But what we're trying to do right now in
our Blackfriars, what we're capable of doing right now is a
particular flavour of universal lighting that gives us the look,
the vibe, the feel of light from the chandelier candles, wall
sconce candles and sunlight. And we've tried to create that
using the materials we had available, not caring that it is not
museum-historically accurate.

Author: *Of all the principles adumbrated in the programme,
universal lighting is really at the heart of the heart of the
matter.*

JW: Absolutely. It's the biggest thing. It's the biggest thing ...
in going back to the future, trying to recreate 400-year-old
principles to make cool, modern theatre, having the lights on
the audience and the audience surrounding the stage, so that
we are all part of the world of the play is the biggest thing.

Author: *The programme talks about 'the basic principles
of Renaissance theatrical production' ... Basic principles
does not equal 'original practices'. And the institution has
– I think I'm right – quietly backed away – or maybe even
loudly backed away – from the term.*

JW: I've been loud about it. I haven't been loud about it *in* *print*, but I've been loud about it anytime anybody brings it up.

Author: *What for you is the difference between 'basic principles' and 'original practices'?*

JW: We helped coin that term 'original practices'. We were part of a group that was trying to figure out, well, is there a way to refer to – and we at the ASC had used 'Shakespeare's staging conditions' before that – but is there a way of talking about what we do that feels like it covers a bunch of things, and so 'original practices' was something that we and the Globe and … the New America Shakespeare Tavern used, and they trademarked the phrase 'original practices theatre', I think. The problem with a term like that, at least I felt, which became a problem, was that everybody had their own definition of what the term meant. What does 'original practices' mean? And as soon as I saw in print somebody saying we don't do original practices the way they thought we should be doing it, I said, 'well fuck that term'. We're not beholding to anybody's definition of what that stuff is. And where we put our focus is different than where Mark Rylance and Jenny Tirmani did, they thought it meant original materials, you know, you dye that thing in urine and I wasn't interested in dying things in urine. So, 'Shakespeare's staging conditions' is a vague umbrella because I don't think what we're doing follows a particular formula … in part, going back to the lighting or the instruments or the costumes: what does original practices mean in those categories?

Author: *Did you feel straight-jacketed by other people's definitions and just wanted to tailor your own?*

JW: Yes. Yes. If you say that your theatre tries to recreate Shakespeare's staging conditions and I say my theatre's trying to do it too, I think there's something about the inherent nature of those words put together that doesn't sound like a formula. It doesn't sound like an academic agenda ... I felt like the term 'original practices' was trying to marry a theatrical thing with an academic thing and I just didn't like being in that pool anymore, and so I thought we needed to get out.

Author: *Would it be a valid criticism, or even something that you would take on board, if I came to you and said, 'Jim, I've got evidence that when Shakespeare's company played at the Blackfriars, for* The Tempest *they had eighteen actors and you've got twelve, so this is somehow an invalid experience' ... What would be your reaction?*

JW: Well, the first thing I would say is that I feel pretty confident that Shakespeare had more than twelve – and I would like to have more than twelve – and when my budget can do it, I would like to do that.

Author: *Fair enough.*

JW: Especially when you can show me the evidence and I think, yeah, I agree with that evidence.

Author: *You're feeling your way through these things given the resources you have, to kind of create or re-create certain principles and conditions—*

JW: Based on what we have done over these twenty-seven years [...] I feel like eleven [actors] gets me to the point that I feel like I can recreate the vibe that Shakespeare's company had – even though I'd prefer fifteen – because I want to be able to cast all the roles and not have to do some of the extreme doubling that we have to do, I know that when I get below eleven [...] it's a different animal, a different kind of artform, that I'm not as interested in for this company. That's where, to use blunt terms and the broad strokes, I feel pretty confident that we are inaccurate with eleven and twelve [actors] but I feel close enough that I can get the vibe, so that the guy who has the last line of this scene as one character does not also have the first line in the next scene as a different character. Which, again, can create some great art, but it's a different animal, and not our animal.

Author: *I'm going to transition and ask a couple of questions about things you've probably spent less time thinking about [...] the connection of the SSE/ASC to Virginia and Staunton.*

JW: My first reaction is we lucked out. We got lucky in eight billion different ways. Had it not been in Virginia, it might not have worked out to get us where we are now. We did not sit down and create the company in '88 thinking much about Virginia. Or much about beyond Virginia. It was, 'if we recreate Shakespeare's staging conditions, we can create some cool theatre, and let's show the world that stuff, let's show anybody that will buy a ticket, or let us play in their space, let's show them that great stuff'. And so we didn't have aspirations to be a Harrisonburg company, we didn't have aspirations to be a Virginia company, or a regional company or national or international, it was 'how can we sell this idea? How can we get people to see it? How can we get people to love Shakespeare like we do, performed like this? And how can we play as many places as possible and make enough money to pay actors to keep doing it over and over again?' The first tour was fourteen performances in mostly rural Virginia and we had no aspiration beyond that. It was, let's just go wherever we can. And we just kept getting asked to play further and further away. If only Virginia venues had booked us, we would be solely a Virginia company, if Harrisonburg had helped us build a theatre, we'd probably be in Harrisonburg today.

Author: *And Richmond was on the map, early, as a potential site on which to build the Blackfriars.*

JW: By the time we got to the mid- and late-nineties, we still didn't have a desire to build a theatre. We were a touring troupe, and by the mid-nineties we'd been to forty-seven states, and five other countries, and one US territory, because that's where we could book performances. And then people came to us, starting to talk about building a theatre, and so the guy from Richmond [Virginia] that wanted to build a recreation of the Globe overlooking the James River sought us out and said, 'we want you to be the anchor company for that'. At the same time, we had people from Staunton come to us and say, 'you know, we want you to move your base of operations here, so that Staunton will be your home'. And because the Richmond Globe wanted us to be the anchor company there we were thinking, 'Ok, Staunton wants us to move our base of operations to Staunton, what would we build in Staunton?' We looked at buildings, existing buildings, thought about, you know, a black box. We needed a place to play in the summer when we weren't on the road. And as we started thinking about it, we thought: we try to turn every hole-in-the-wall we play into feeling like an Elizabethan or Jacobean playhouse. You know what we should do? We should build Shakespeare's indoor theatre, and try to make the *physical* space more of a recreation of Shakespeare's [theatre]. And so at one point, we were going to have his indoor theatre here in Staunton, and his outdoor theatre in Richmond. And when I tell this story I say 'Thank God for unanswered prayers'. The Richmond project fell apart. We were able to get the architect from that project [Tom McLaughlin] to work on our Blackfriars and we knew right away that we'd eventually build a Globe in Staunton too. And the weird thing is that had we sat down and said, 'Ok, we want to build a Blackfriars, a Globe, any theatre. What kind of theatre would we build, and where would we build it if we were starting from scratch and had everything open to us?' The idea of building a Blackfriars or Globe ma[de] so much sense based on the mission that we had started – with recreating Shakespeare's staging conditions – recreating the *physical* stages that he had makes perfect sense.

Author: *Sure.*

JW: As we looked at, well, where are the other big Shakespeare operations located and what are their operations like? They were destination theatres. Ashland, Oregon, is in the middle of nowhere. Cedar City, Utah, is in the middle of nowhere. Stratford, Ontario, is in a small place. It turned out that Staunton was the *perfect* place for us, because it's a small town, it's a get away for people to come here and get their theatre fix, do other things and the demographics within a four-hour drive are just out-of-this-world. So, had we scoured the country for a place, this place [...] in the beautiful Shenandoah Valley, with all the other kinds of things you can do here, it turned out to be perfect even though it was not a part of a perfect plan. So I feel like we got lucky. It turns out what fell in our lap, and what we pursued to make better was a Virginia-based thing. That wasn't because we had that brilliant idea from the beginning.

Author: *Building a theatre was never part of the original mission of the company. It was something that emerged or evolved, and it feels – as you said – like it makes perfect sense as an outgrowth of the original mission. But the Shenandoah Shakespeare Express was never formed as an architectural company with that particular kind of ambition.*

JW: No. I think pre-SSE, the all-student *Henry V* that we did in the black box theatre at James Madison University was a bit more geographically, architecturally based in that we built a set to try and recreate Shakespeare's staging conditions. But that show didn't tour. It gave us the ideas of, hey, we just put on a show using the stuff we found in a seminar where we were researching Shakespeare's staging conditions. And we did it, and it was fun, let's start a

professional company where we can recreate those staging
conditions anyplace that we can play. So the SSE was,
'we will come to you'. The 'Express' part of things was,
we're travelling and we *don't* have a home. Having a home
developed as we grew.

Author: *How important is it to you – leaving aside the
financial aspect of it – [to maintain] a touring company? Do
you consider that vital to the American Shakespeare Center's
identity and mission, quite apart from what it brings in
money?*

Author: Yes. The idea from the beginning that we can go
into somebody else's space and turn it into what I will call a
raucous, party atmosphere vibe by leaving the lights on the
audience and putting them around the playing area, that we
can turn their place into feeling like what we now have here
at home. And that will always be vital to us no matter how
big [we get]. We started as 'just' a touring troupe; now we
are a company that has several troupes and one of them goes
out on the road. Our tour is not just an educational add-on;
it's a part of the DNA of who we are.

Author: *You're now the American Shakespeare Center, with
an international reputation, do you feel yourself to be a
Virginia institution in a meaningful way?*

JW: Our home is in Virginia. And our home is in a
beautiful part of a beautiful state. That allows us to create a
destination-theatre experience for people. They get to come
here and see great theatre. And partake in an amazing local
community and a wider regional community. And when we
go out on the road, we are the Blackfriars Playhouse on the
road, we are ambassadors for the Blackfriars and Virginia.
Because Virginia, and this part of Virginia, has been integral
in the initial creation of our Blackfriars and the success of it,
I feel like Virginia is now just as much a part of our DNA as

Shakespeare's staging conditions, so yeah, we want people to come to Virginia from other countries and other states to see our corner of the world. The Virginia beers, the Virginia wines that we sell, the Virginia products in our gift shop, the connection we have to the tourism in this area is [all] now a huge part of who we are.

Author: *A local question, and a timely one: somebody coming to your playhouse comes to the Blackfriars between the Stonewall Jackson Hotel and the now-closed, but still-on-the-marquee Dixie Movie Theatre – you have no control over those things, but you are literally in the shadow of southern American history – do you ever feel that weight of local history upon your audience's experience?*

Author: What's funny – not funny, we'll use 'interesting' – it was a student of Ralph's who helped buy and revitalize that hotel next door that was called the Stonewall Jackson Hotel in its earlier days. Then it got redone, refurbished, after the Blackfriars was built, so it was a project that came into existence because of us. That hotel might not have gotten done when it got done if it hadn't been for us. We were hoping they were going to change the name, but they had these big lights up that were already on top of the building and they decided to keep the old name. I think if I could snap my fingers it would be named something else and the Dixie would be named something else. I don't feel like we have to run away from or hide from the southerness of where we are, but I don't fly the rebel flag because I feel the Virginia heritage requires me to do so and defend that. I think there are things in our community that are a part of history that aren't necessarily the parts of history that I would like to be associated with if it were my call.

Author: *I've often thought that a lot of the pre-show stuff is about bringing the audience across certain thresholds.*

JW: Yes.

Author: *There are thresholds of history that somebody encounters coming to the Blackfriars. You're walking through an almost geological cut of different times, you know, negotiating between nineteenth-century American architecture in Staunton, past the Dixie movie theatre, into a playhouse that's presenting sixteenth and seventeenth century plays ... there are a lot of time signatures at work there. One of the things I write about is that over twenty-five years the company has developed very skilful ways of managing those different kinds of competing histories, multiple temporalities. But your actors have a beautifully casual way of bring the audience across those thresholds. Is the pre-show stuff in any conscious way to help buffer the various competing time signatures?*

JW: I think it's a bit more basic than that. In my brain, that pre-show stuff is mostly about trying to set a tone that is relaxed, welcoming, not your crushed velvet Shakespeare experience –

Author: *If I could interrupt here, I've been looking through the old reviews and 'crushed velvet' comes up a lot and so it must means something metaphorically because there's definitely some crushed velvet on your stage these days –*

JW: I tend to think of it as the seats, that are made of crushed velvet and that term represents ... it's an umbrella term for the kind of Shakespeare that is, for my taste, hoity-toity, that is Shakespeare that is 'Culture' with a capital 'C', and has really big sets and lighting effects and modern technological tricks that put the audience in the dark and allows the audience to observe a live movie. So I think of 'crushed velvet' as precious Shakespeare, as Shakespeare that is elitist on some level. I think 'crushed velvet' as upper class and therefore exclusionary to the lower classes. And part of what we're trying to do is recreate the vibe that Shakespeare's company was able to have. Shakespeare wrote stuff for those groundlings who were uneducated and paying a penny, and the people in the Lord's Rooms that were the richest and the most educated. His material appeals to a wide demographic and we hope by recreating these staging conditions, it is accessible to that wide demographic. And I think that Shakespeare in America in the twentieth and twenty-first century has often been seen as elitist and crushed velvet for the upper classes or the well-to-do and it's good for you whether it's good or not, whether you like it or not.

Author: *If you go to the Royal Shakespeare Company now, their theatre spaces are all –*

JW: Yeah!

Author: *– In some way, you guys have won. In some ways.*

JW: No, but, yeah, I think that's awesome. And before us Tyrone Guthrie.

Author: *Great transition. I wanted to ask about that, too. Other people before you. Tyrone Guthrie, William Poel, other revivalists. The reason I ask is that going through all of the ASC archival stuff – which I am part of – early grants, early promotional stuff, William Poel never comes up.*

JW: No.

Author: *Tyrone Guthrie never comes up. There's a lot of rhetoric of 'we have revived this' and looks back to the early modern period –*

JW: And skips over those people.

Author: *And skips over those guys.*

JW: My first, crass answer to that is, if we thought it could have made us more money, get us more grants, we would have included that. Not that we wanted to deliberately ignore them in the narrative but it didn't necessarily help us in a way that felt tangible. I think that from the beginning, we – and that included you – were certainly aware of those things, we just didn't put a focus there because it didn't seem like it was going to be helpful to tell our story.

Author: *'We're setting out to revive the theatrical principles of William Poel' doesn't have quite the same traction.*

JW: Right. I also think, that what I know of Poel and what I know of Guthrie, it was a little bit like what Sam [Wanamaker] was doing in that some of their interests seemed to be more about the architecture and not about the performance principles we use [...] I don't recall reading about either one of them saying that using their own flavour of recreating Shakespeare's staging conditions will allow the plays to come alive in a way that they won't otherwise. It was, if we recreate that thrust stage, that will do certain things that a proscenium stage cannot do that are closer to what Shakespeare did. I think it was architecturally centred rather than performance-environment centred.

Author: *One of the things I'm interested in is that there are sporadically these Shakespeare revolutions, which are always about going back. You revolve to earlier times to try and get back to certain principles that we've lost. The American Shakespeare Center is now the American Shakespeare Center. You're no longer outsiders; you're institutional. You're a big, operating, successful North American theatre company. What's the next Shakespeare revolution look like?*

JW: This relates to the Guthries and the Poels on some level, in that I don't ever remember reading about them ever wanting the audience to be part of the play. It's not just that the lights are on for us. It's that the lights are on and the audience surrounds the space, and the actors and directors are looking for places to engage the audience and include them in the play. What we call 'universal lighting' – that the lights are lighting up the stage and the audience – by itself isn't enough. Certainly there's a lot of Shakespeare being done outdoors, under the sunlight, and usually in North America they start the play with the sun still out and there are lighting instruments there so that when the sun goes down you can see the lighting effects, but they're not using the audience as part of the world of the play when the sun is out. So … I still – as big as we are and as successful as we've been – I still do feel like an outsider in that I don't think any of the other major companies are interested in that part of Shakespeare's staging conditions. Even at the Globe, they have trouble even acting to the sides, and to the audience on the side. I'll never forget the production … it was *Titus Andronicus*, and I generally liked the show. I could not get a ticket to stand in the yard as a groundling because they only sold a few of those so they could bring those movable set pieces carrying people in through the audience. So I had a seat on the side, in the front of the lower level, where not a single actor *ever* looked my way through the course of the whole show until the bow. I *so* wanted to put my middle finger up. 'Now you acknowledge me?!' So even in a space like London's Globe today, and I think the Wanamaker Playhouse too, because they built architecture first and then had to come up with companies and productions to fill that space, they are not operating on the same principles that we are. They are not trying to get the same thing, so I still feel like the RSC space and Chicago Shakespeare Theatre, and all of these thrust spaces being built are a great step forward. But it's still not the same thing that we're doing, and so I feel like part of what's next for us is building a Globe so that we can have shows in Shakespeare's indoor theatre and outdoor theatre that recreate his staging conditions, which include making the audience part of the play. I also want those shows to change venue ... I think the idea of having a show, the same production, be in the Globe, move to the Blackfriars, *and* go on the road is a huge artistic thing that I want us to be able to do.

Author: *In terms of situating the ASC in the contemporary landscape of Shakespeare and performance, [is there] any work out there that you love?*

JW: I love pieces of a whole bunch of companies. I've seen shows in Oregon that I love. And I'd say the same thing about the Globe and the Wanamaker. The National Theatre in London produces great stuff, too, and stuff that I don't care for. Theatre for a New Audience has a great new space in Brooklyn and is doing some awesome things. So I go see shows that don't have anything to do with using Shakespeare's staging conditions and can be thrilled and delighted. I don't feel like Shakespeare *has to* be done the way we do it to be great. Most theatre companies for me are hit and miss, in a way that inspires me to try and be more consistent. So if you come to one of our shows and you hate it, I'm not sure you're going to come the next night and love it. And that's both a positive and a negative.

Author: *That's almost an exact paraphrase of something I've been talking about, which is that the sheer impressive consistency of the shows at the Blackfriars can be, critically, a mixed blessing. It's not going to be radically different, show to show, play to play. The experience I mean.*

JW: Sure, and certainly there are people who come see us and they think 'I want to sit on one of those stools on that stage. I wasn't there this last time, but the next time that's where I want to be'. And there are other people who say 'you could not pay me to be in that seat, but I like what they do'. I'm sure there are people who come and say, 'they don't turn off the lights? Why are they talking to the audience?

What is this acoustic mix of music with a banjo and a violin. Not my thing.' Those people who come and experience it and don't like it, I don't know if we can win them over.[4]

Author: *You have really done what a lot of theatres have frequently given lip service to which is you've created a community of actors, a pretty stable company of actors – people do come and go – but a committed core of actors who are here a lot. Was that part of the original mission? Or something that has evolved?*

JW: We knew from the beginning that what we wanted to do with our shows was different than the way most theatre companies do stuff. I tend not to use this word a lot because it's packed with different meanings for different people, but we basically have to *train* actors to perform like we perform. Once you do that, you're creating a useful entity. Every time we get a new person, we have to go through that process. So our current Summer/Fall Season has all vets. It's the very first time outside of a Ren Season that we've done that. I will cut my left hand off before I hire someone who's never worked for us for the Ren Season. You need to learn who we are and what we do before I put you in a situation where you're directing yourself on stage. We knew that from the beginning that having actors that we like who knew how to perform in our style was a huge benefit. But, I also want to be a place where we are constantly getting new people, new voices, new ways of thinking, so that in my ideal troupe, every single troupe – again outside of the Ren Season – is filled with vets who have been with us for a long time, vets who have gone away and come back, and new folks. I want to keep building that ... We're trying to create that balance between, yeah, let's find ways to use this group of veteran actors who want to be here again, but let's be smart about how we cast them. And if it's not right for that particular set of plays, then let's find a nice way to say, 'not this time'. And we also try to make that a two-way street ... You can say no to a contract offer, you can go away, and it's still a relationship that will continue beyond that. So hopefully we're also sending actors into other places that have our aesthetic in their brains and in their bodies, even if they're going to perform differently for someone else.

Ralph Alan Cohen, director of mission

Ralph Cohen's career baffles conventional academic templates. Trained by George Walton Williams at Duke University, Cohen took up an Assistant Professorship at James Madison University in Virginia where he became a decorated teacher, winning the State Council for Higher Education for Virginia Outstanding Faculty Award in 1987. He founded the university's study abroad programme and frequently took students on semesters to London. Playgoing formed a central plank in the London curriculum, yet his students' dissatisfaction with the productions they saw eventually prompted Cohen's immersion in active theatre-making at James Madison University. Housed in an English department, Cohen encountered predictable territoriality from theatre colleagues but persevered (Cohen always perseveres; 'tireless' should be listed under 'special talents' on his CV) and developed his own collegiate acting group, which transitioned into a para- then fully fledged professional company in 1993. The incorporation of the 'Shenandoah Shakespeare Express' in the early 1990s also signalled Cohen's break from the parameters of what the English profession had codified as the formal professional boundaries of academic American life in the late twentieth century.

Since he proved an uneasy fit in a traditional English department, Cohen customized a home for himself, co-founding, at Mary Baldwin University, in Staunton, the Shakespeare and Performance graduate programme, which is dedicated to the exploration of Renaissance drama through the medium of performance. He continues to teach there, write about pedagogy and evangelize for the American Shakespeare Center, where, as of 2016, he is Director of Mission. He also continues to direct at least one show a year for the company and has directed over thirty-five productions over the last twenty-five years, twenty-eight for the ASC alone. An entrepreneur at heart – he happily described himself as a 'huckster' (though not a 'charlatan') at one point in our discussion – he remains a catalyst, a builder, a passionate, almost zealous advocate for the efficacy and energy of Shakespeare in performance.

I interviewed Cohen at his home in Bridgewater, Virginia, about fifteen miles outside Staunton. He calls the house 'Gadshill', and one drives up a steep road, 'Shenandoah Lane', to get there. Even in Virginia, for Cohen, all roads lead to Shakespeare.

Author: *Ok, so here's a quote from the book that is actually a question: 'Why cite history just to pick a fight with it? Why that is, does the ASC build error into the apparatus of their claim to authenticity?'*

RC: Whatever error was there was not any kind of intentional picking of a fight.

Author: *Let me clarify, I'm not suggesting it's intentional. What I'm trying to get after is the way the SSE and then the ASC have toggled between the historically accurate allegiance to certain practices and its departure from others. You know, the programme copy that reads: 'Shakespeare's travelling company had fewer than twelve so ...'*

RC: Ok. This is interesting because this has always fascinated you. And I've never been quite able to get at the missing link for me about it. I love the moments when we discover that we are doing something interesting onstage, and that what we are doing isn't new. As opposed to, knowing that something was done and then doing it because something was done. I am, you know, I'm a teacher and

my biggest thing is that I really think that – and you know
how much I love other playwrights – there's just something
kind of remarkable about this particular playwright. But
I've also spent a lot of time admiring other playwrights of
the time and the period itself and sort of the arrangement
of the room, whatever that room was, and the sort of
aesthetic that was always there, that seems to have been
there, very much there, between a really engaged audience
[and the actor].

Author: *Ok.*

RC: But over the many years of watching students yawn
their way through what I would now say is overly produced
proscenium Shakespeare, I really began to notice when
they loved it. And they loved it when the audience was
recognized.

Author: *I think I know the answer to this, but you
don't really care … if someone came to you tomorrow with
something written in secretary hand from the early modern
period, that said 'on such and such[a] night at the Globe we
had eighteen actors …' you wouldn't be like, 'Well then, we
must have eighteen actors'?*

RC: Absolutely not.

Author: *That's not really what's at stake here.*

RC: Absolutely not. No, no, I actually think that the more
obstacles you give yourself, the more you create stuff. I think
twelve actors are good partly because it makes you figure
stuff out.

Author: *Reading reviews about the ASC – there's an
interesting thread about it being hard to locate directorial
interpretation. Like what's the director's vision? Where's*

*the director's hand? I think by design you guys submerge
the hand to the practice. But during that* A Midsummer
Night's Dream *[Summer/Fall 2015, directed by Cohen],
there is at least a kind of lightly feminist reading of the play
that comes out during* Pyramus and Thisbe, *but that rises
out of theatrical exigency. So it's as though history kind of
produces that interpretation of the play.*

RC: Here's what happened. I was cutting the script and
putting stuff back from what we'd done the last time. My
Hippolyta was Alli [Glenzer] and I had not noticed that in
our previous production, Hippolyta was doubled with Snug.
And when I got to that, then this is where the director and
the politics come in. I wanted my Queen still on the stage.

Author: *Yeah.*

RC: I wanted her there. And I didn't want her disappearing
offstage to come back as Snug … and I said, 'Ok', and 'I will
try to turn this into something'. And then, I really had exactly
the eureka moment that you see onstage [when Hippolyta says
'let me play the lion' and takes over the part] [*laughs*]. Now, if
we had had fifteen people that would never have happened. So
I can't be proud of that moment on *historical* grounds. But I
also know that every time Shakespeare wrote a play with fifty
characters in it, he was setting himself similar problems and
solving them in similar ways. And that's fun to know.

Author: *It's really a question about how, ultimately, how
important is history to you as the co-creator, the Director of
Mission of the ASC?*

RC: It's very important in this way: we are, I think,
contemptuous of history or condescending to history.

Author: *Who's the 'we' in that sentence?*

RC: I think most of us. You. Me. I think we all are a little condescending to what they achieved on a stage before us. I haven't continued to be, but I think there's a kind of what I call 'chronological chauvinism' or 'technological chauvinism' about the theatre. And so what I like is to find in history the reasons for why something might have been good and not bad.

Author: *Here's another quote, the programme details the 'basic principles of Renaissance theatrical production'. 'Basic principle' is not, it turns out, a synonym for 'original practices'. Is that correct?*

RC: Yes, I didn't write those things.

Author: *But you know what I'm asking about here?*

Author: Well first of all, you can't talk about us without talking about the Globe's huge success in '97, you know, which we are following ... there was so much energy around the Globe thing that we used that energy to build a Blackfriars. And I decided before you came that I did want to mention Vanessa Schormann during this interview. Vanessa Schormann wrote a book on the Globe. It's in German, sadly. I wish she'd translate it. [*Laughs.*] But I know what she's said, because she's a friend, and her thing at the end was I want: a theatre that's *like* the Globe in that people have to stand, and they can get rained on, and they're in a certain configuration, but I don't care about the oak. So, that's all I want. And I think, and I thought she was right then and I think she's kind of right now.

Author: *Fabulous.*

RC: However, nobody would have cared as much about us if we had done it in aluminum. I mean, it just wouldn't have mattered in the same way. And we wouldn't have been able

to claim a lot of the interest in what the theatre might have
been like. So every time that we have dared a theatre historian
to get it right for us, we've at the same time attracted twenty
people to the basic idea that this is something *like* what you
would have seen if you'd have gone into the Blackfriars.

And that the theatre that you're seeing, the things the
actors are doing – in terms of the amount of time they take,
in terms of the seamlessness between scenes, in terms of the
overall arrangement of audience and actor – is kind of what
the playwrights had in mind when they were writing things
down. And that's wonderful because there's just this great
moment when the door [to that first stage] opens [*laughs*],
and I feel like that every time a moment is good. That 'oh
look, the door opened, I must have gotten something right
because the door opened'.

Author: *What I'm trying to tease out here is what the ASC's
'historicism' is. Because if you visit the Blackfriars, in the
architecture, in the placard, in the programme, there are
certain historical claims being made, with some authority.
The authority is after all* the American Shakespeare Center.
*It does invite somebody to say … well, there's a kind of
incoherence, for instance, in saying 'they had all male
companies so we do whatever we do'. There is a slippage in
there between claims of historical accuracy …*

RC: There is … there is … I don't ever feel comfortable.
But to me, it's a very innocent question – it's a question of
innocence – innocent in every way, I suppose. You know,
gosh, the past might not be exactly like what we say and there
are historians who could say it's different. But for me, it's a
gesture towards the idea of an earlier stagecraft being, on the
whole, a healthier stagecraft for these shows. And it speaks
to my sense that theatre went off the rails at the end of the
eighteenth century. And in the next century, I think, driven by
movies, I think it went completely off the rails. I think what

we think of as a theatrical experience largely went away in the theatre that I grew up looking at in the '50s and '60s.

Author: *You mean the 1950s and 1960s.*

RC: Yeah, not the 1850s.

Author: *I wonder if some of the tension between historical claims and the basic principles you are more interested in is a result of the fact that the SSE was not formed to build a theatre.*

RC: No.

Author: *It's a huge difference with the Globe. The Globe, the whole great enterprise, was formed to ...*

RC: Building first.

Author: *Building first. You guys were built around some basic principle and about converting any room into the kind of experience, the atmosphere ...*

RC: Exactly. True.

Author: *The ecology in which an audience is part of it. That was the whole deal. And then, this opportunity came along.*

RC: Yep.

Author: *It sounds like you're saying, if you'd have just tried to build a good room for the kind of thing you guys did, if you had tried to build the Swan at the RSC, something that's kind of basically right ...*

RC: Yeah, yeah.

Author: *That would have been harder to do than something that had a kind of historical teeth to it. Do you think that's right?*

RC: It's almost right. It's almost right. I mean it would have been much easier and cheaper to build a Swan. But, we would not have been able to convince as many big donors that it was, that we were making an important theatre that way. And you know what? We wouldn't have been, you know?

Author: *Yeah.*

RC: Because in this way Vanessa was wrong, it really is because of the oak. Making it out of oak and making it look as it might have [looked] got us going; it got us, you know, noticed. You walk into that beautiful room and you think 'this must be an important place'.

Author: *You're in a kind of funny, but also cool position of being somebody who set out really to do the basic principles that now has on his hands a rigorously, studiously reconstructed Blackfriars playhouse. Because it allows you to do certain things.*

RC: I remember a moment, and I think this speaks to it … it reminds me of a conversation coming back from D.C. Now, Gina Gianbatista was my stage manager when we did *Henry V*, and …

Author: *In '88?*

RC: In '88. And Gina said, 'well, of course when you have the money, you'll use lights, right?' And I think that's a really interesting thing, and like what you said about the number of people in the cast, eighteen. If we had the money for more people to play more of the parts, I think eighteen people in a cast could make a worse Shakespeare production and make for a more cumbersome team. But more than that I think it would keep you from some of the energies that are in play that I think have to do with doubling ... I'm not saying we get the doubling or the lighting right every time, but once they are there, they work as a kind of spine for the whole show.

Author: *So even if Tiffany Stern comes to you tomorrow and says, 'I've discovered a document that says that Shakespeare's company had eighteen actors when they did* A Midsummer Night's Dream', *where would you find yourself in that? What's more important to you? Like, eighteen actors you say are too cumbersome, reduce the spirit, but then you've got this historical authenticity thing hanging out there?*

RC: My answer is, if I found out it was a number anywhere along the lines of 'everybody gets to play a part', I mean all the parts are played by different people, I think that would hurt it. If I found out that every single part was played by a different actor ...

Author: *No doubling.*

RC: There was no doubling, then I would think we have found a better way to do Shakespeare.

Author: [*Laughs.*] *Ok, that's great.*

RC: That's what I would think. Can I say something? I gotta say one thing about the gender thing right now. That I have always been uncomfortable with our statement about well, boys played girls, so girls can play boys. I mean I think that's ...

Author: *Jim Warren said the same thing, by the way.*

RC: Very uncomfortable with that. I mean it's facile and it's not honest. I've always thought that if we had actual boys, that would be a great thing. That's one of those things that I would like to look at because I think we haven't any idea how well it worked. Now I don't know what would happen politically if it went all male and three or four of those males were kids. But still it's interesting to me.

Author: *But to hammer that point then, why even bring up history in the programme when it comes to gender? I mean, why bother? Why not just say, 'we do what we want to do'?*

JC: Yeah. Great question. I think that once you start making decisions around that and selling yourself as an attempted early modern theatre, then you are looking for all the ways in which you are in fact like that.

Author: *Indeed.*

RC: What's wonderful is the early moderns were thinking about theatre outside our box. That's a good way to put it: we have been in a box since 1900, or earlier than that, 1850, whenever Irving and the rest of them helped put us in that box. And then the Lumière brothers nailed us in it for good because we start competing with movies. Ever since that moment, we have had our own box.

Author: *Well, you and Jim are Lumière brothers in your own way, because lighting is the most important thing to this whole enterprise, right? The universal lighting?*

RC: If I had to say one thing it would be that. Though it doesn't do you much good if everybody's on the same side of the stage. It doesn't help you as much.

Author: *So the universal lighting …*

RC: And thrust.

Author: *And the thrust. Because these things have to work together.*

RC: That's right. The return of the audience to the play is the most important thing, and I say this all the time.

Author: *I say this in the book: 'it is possible to leave the lights on the audience, and still leave them in the dark'. Right? By which I mean, leaving the lights on the audience is not enough. It's also, in addition to thrust staging, it's also an acting technique. So it's universal lighting ...*

RC: Right!

Author: *Universal lighting is not just about technology; it's about histrionic practice.*

RC: Exactly!

Author: *So can you speak to that?*

RC: A writer writing because he knew he had an audience he could use, and he had to fill two and half or three hours, whatever, and actors who were aware that if they don't engage an audience they will sort of lose them. And figuring out that balance [between the play on the stage and the play with the audience]; I have no clue exactly what the formula is, but I've seen it work. There's a balance, it's a really, really healthy balance. Because it's not very refreshing if every moment is an audience contact moment, if every moment is an engagement with the audience. You don't have to do much of it to make everybody feel they're a part of things. And if you do it at the right places, you know, it's really quite wonderful.

Author: *Yeah.*

RC: Somebody has to activate that audience since we've spent the last 180 years not being, not knowing, how to be audiences in that kind of environment. We have to be taught that again. But I also think that audiences are incredibly smart and incredibly fast and that you can teach them in about five seconds what the new rules are. It seems to me, it takes no time at all to teach them the new rules. So, so it's all recoverable, you know.

Author: *The ASC has a lot of threshold events to kind of get you into the show.*

RC: Yeah.

Author: *There's the theatre itself, there's the programme, then the actors' pre-show chat, which I've come to see as a kind of liturgy. Like, it's important to the company to recite these things before the show, not necessarily because they think audience doesn't know, but it's become part of the ASC's statement of belief and principle that 'we do it with lights on'.*

RC: We do still say that, don't we?

Author: *You do say it. But I'm saying you don't say it because you are actually worried about somebody thinking the lights are going to go off.*

RC: No, no. It's like the words don't much matter. It's part of 'welcome to our place, we do things differently here'. Nobody came out on the stage of the Globe and said, 'yeah, uh, the lights are gonna stay on'.

Author: *So let's talk about Virginia a little bit. And Staunton in particular. I write that, 'one could argue that the*

*Blackfriars is in Virginia because a graduate student named
Ralph Alan Cohen from Montgomery, Alabama ... landed
a job teaching in the English department at James Madison
University in Harrisonburg, Virginia. The rest as they say
is history ... While it can seem coincidental that the new
Blackfriars is in Virginia, viewed from a broader historical
perspective, the Virginia Blackfriars seems right at home'.
So it's a question about the aptness that the Blackfriars is in
Virginia.*

RC: It seems crazily apt. Do you want me to go in historical
terms?

Author: *Yeah.*

RC: I want to talk about two things. The way we found
aptness. And when we started looking for history. So the way
we made – didn't make, but found – that there's history that
supports the aptness. So first, let's start with what really came
first which is, in terms of this project, is the town of Staunton.
That really came first because whatever other aptness I've
found, I've found by looking for it. Ok, so, Staunton is a
remarkably wealthy town. It's a remarkably wealthy town
with a number of interesting cultural institutions. With the
railroad and the discovery of coal, the town became very
rich. So the town of Staunton is itself a special and interesting
place that was not destroyed in the Civil War ... So there's
a strange kind of combination of it being a Southern place
and it's not being. On the one hand, you've got a load of
Southern tradition – Jeb Stuart has a house here and VMI
[the Virginia Military Institute] is only 40 minutes south.
But we're not on the plantation side of the Blue Ridge and
there's a farming tradition brought down from Pennsylvania
into Augusta County by the non-slave owning Mennonites.
And then of course you've got the coal money, and what that
money did was create a remarkable collection of architecture.
So all of that gives us this interesting town, with a mix of

Appalachian, Southern and Anabaptist culture and a great destination. It also meant there was a lot of education and an enlightened city leadership. These were people who cared about plays and music and could be appealed to on that basis. Not a usual community.

Author: *Mm-hmm.*

RC: And there's some Englishness about it too.

Author: *Right*

RC: And we found that kind of wherever you go, that claiming the mother country. So starting up new in a town as proud of its Virginia heritage as Staunton is, wealthy enough and all those other things, but willing to take our word for it about the way a Blackfriars might have looked … was really lucky.

Author: *Yeah.*

RC: And apt. I kept wanting us to label this part of Virginia 'the heart of Virginia'. The heart of Virginia. Because it's central. And so it's a Super Virginia. And it was connected to that first name of ours, Shenandoah Shakespeare. There is something magical about Shenandoah as an idea of a river that runs through.

Author: *Let me have a follow-up question about the Anglocentrism of Virginia …*

RC: Yeah. It's definitely Anglophilic.

Author: *Which is part of the aptness that we talked about. So let me read you, and I should have said, of course I've chosen from the book sort of provocative quotes to try to get a rise out of you.*

RC: I hope you've chosen the most provocative, so I'll know the worst ...

Author: [Laughs.] *So here's a quote. 'In an early grant proposal circa 1990, [that I may have written], the author writes, "Say Shakespeare and most Americans think of tights and posturing, of British accents, and three and half hour productions." This is nearly a decade before the company decided to rebuild a Blackfriars, a project that required the Virginia company to recast its relationship to England from resistance to recapitulation. The transition from the SSE to the ASC isn't quite one from Anglophobia to Anglophilia, but the company at the new Blackfriars now don their tights without grudging'. Fair or unfair?*

RC: You oughta show the early logo, where we weren't sure what we were going to call ourselves yet, and we had 'Unroyal Shakespeare Company'.

Author: *Oh, I didn't know that.*

RC: 'The Unroyal Shakespeare Company'. With the shoe and the crown.

Author: *You still used that logo, though with a different name. Which is cheeky.*

RC: Right. And that was one of the names we thought about naming ourselves. You know that's dead on, about the move from Anglophobia to Anglophilia ... As soon as we thought we had earned the right to, we were happy to claim whatever we could that would excite the people.

Author: *One of the things that has come out of doing this project is realizing that the history of the ASC is really two histories. It's the history of the SSE and the history of the ASC/Blackfriars. You can cast it as a transition from*

'Express' to 'Center', transience to stability, but one of the stories that you can tell is a kind of anti-Englishness to a thorough Englishness in a very Anglophilic state.

RC: It kind of depends on what it is that we're claiming is English.

Author: *Good.*

RC: I mean, I'm still very bitter that I know deep in my heart that if our guys all had British accents we'd be better known. And we all know why. And it is the Anglophilia that rules the reviewers. And it makes me angry enough [*laughs*] to be pissed off at my English friends, though I love them dearly and it's not their fault they have English accents.

Author: *Isn't it?*

RC: But I also think that when you start and you are a bunch of students in tennis shoes and jeans, that the rhetoric of ... what did you call it? Rebellion?

Author: *Insurgency.*

RC: Insurgency. That rhetoric is necessary. As soon as you get adopted as the pet of the Shakespeare Association of America, as soon as Stephen Booth says this is the best thing going on if you want to see actors act, I mean, as soon as those things start to happen, you get a little less bellicose.

Author: *Mm-hmm.*

RC: Because you're secure. And you know you're doing good work.

Author: *As a 'Center', how do you maintain the energy, the audacity, the ambition, now that you're an institution that is a 'Center' that has a theatre?*

RC: It's easy because we're not really there yet. We are among scholars, I think we are a centre. I think scholars really care about what we are doing to some extent ...

Author: *Do you still see yourself as an outsider?*

RC: On the theatrical side of things? Yes. We will not be an outsider when the *Times* always sends someone down to cover the Actors' Renaissance Season. Then we'll be in. But until that happens, we are outsiders.

Author: *When you go to the RSC now, do you feel though like you've won? In architectural terms?*

RC: I would love after I'm dead for someone to mention Ralph Cohen in that victory, but the real thing is, as long as they realize Sam Wanamaker won, I've won. I mean, Wanamaker won. You look at Chicago Shakes. Look at any of those places and Wanamaker had it right.

Author: *It's actually rather hard to go find proscenium Shakespeare today. Or do you disagree with that? I mean, in the major theatrical venues producing Shakespeare, it's mostly thrusty.*

RC: I think that's true. I think that's interesting.

Author: *In reading lots of reviews of the SSE/ASC across the years, the phrase 'crushed velvet' comes up a lot, as a kind of metonymy or signifier for a particular tradition. Does it still exist? The crushed velvet Shakespeare? Or is it a kind of strawman?*

RC: You could have asked that question five years ago and

I would have said 'yes' because it not only existed, it was the Memorial Theatre in Stratford. And you can ask that question *now*, and I can sit trying to think of an important one.

Author: *Is the RSC the last barricade that's down? Is that the last 'hill to be taken'?*

RC: I honestly think it might have been. Well, it's the most important, right?

Author: *I think about the Actors' Renaissance Season as staging your earlier insurgency in some way.*

RC: I think it's that. One of the things I think you do is you keep bringing in outside stuff. And then what was an insurgency can become, I don't know, a long campaign.

Author: *Well, that's a version of the containment model. So you definitely want to bring in something subversive.*

RC: You definitely want to.

Author: *Back to Virginia just for a moment. I have heard you speak on this before and I want to hear your thoughts on it. The Blackfriars is between the Dixie Movie Theatre and the Stonewall Jackson Hotel.*

RC: I very much wanted them to change the name of the hotel. And at that time, I was enough in the counsels of the city so that I could say that in front of the people that might have been able to change it. And they said to me, 'No, Ralph. You know, that sign is so famous, we'd lose all our support. We cannot get rid of that sign. It's gotta be the Stonewall Jackson'. I do hope that whatever happens to the Dixie they change the name of it. God, I hope they do. I think they will.

Author: *Ok. Here's my transition. You're going to love this. From a name that is remembered next door to the Blackfriars, here's a name that is in some ways obscured at the Blackfriars. Why is there not a statue of William Poel in the lobby at the Blackfriars? Or Nugent Monck in the courtyard at the Globe? Why does revivalism forget its own history?*

RC: Have you looked at pictures of his [Poel's] productions?

Author: *Yeah.*

RC: Pretty proscenium, aren't they? [*Laughs.*]

Author: *Everything looks proscenium in a photograph.*

RC: Because nobody would know who Poel was, that's why. It wouldn't help us, you know. It wouldn't even help us to have a picture, I mean, a statue of Burbage. Which would be so good, actually, if we had a statue of Burbage.

Author: *You're not going to get out there and say, 'we do Shakespeare a little bit like William Poel did Shakespeare'.*

RC: [*Laughs.*] If William Poel had written plays, we would do that.

Author: *He did write plays.*

RC: Well, if he'd written plays we put on.

Author: [*Laughs.*] *Ok. But I'm interested in your intellectual genealogy, thinking about the mid-70s and books like Styan's* The Shakespeare Revolution. *Stuff John Russell Brown was also writing about with* Free Shakespeare. *Stuff that Dessen in the early years, some of the books he was doing.*

RC: Dessen came and talked to that seminar.

Author: *In '88?*

RC: Yes.

Author: *Because he was doing work on theatrical vocabulary at that point?*

RC: Yeah, he came and talked about that.

Author: *But you didn't read J. L. Styan's* The Shakespeare Revolution *and think like, yes, he's right? He says we should build a Shakespearean stage to get after Shakespearean …*

RC: No, no. I did read Styan and think he was right. I read Beckerman and loved it.

Author: *Beckerman's* Shakespeare's Globe?

RC: Yes. Yes, I loved it. I loved it.

Author: *So the stage-centred criticism?*

RC: I particularly loved it. The NEH Seminar that I was in in '87…

Author: *With Michael Goldman?[5]*

RC: With Goldman. It was a really remarkable time for me because this is kind of right after I met Patrick [Spottiswoode, Director, Globe Education].

Author: *Where were you in 1976?*

RC: In '76 [*laughs*]? I was nowhere near any of this.

Author: *Were you in graduate school or were you an assistant professor?*

RC: No, I was an assistant professor. I came here in '73.

Author: *Ok.*

RC: And I took my first group to Europe, Christmas of '75.

Author: *Ok.*

RC: And we saw things that, had I known more about theatre, I would be bragging the whole time. We saw *No Man's Land* with Ralph Richardson and John Gielgud.

Author: *Oh my god.*

Author: Boom. I got the students great tickets. And I didn't know a thing. Except I like theatre. And I was, you know, I was the lead, well, I was the second lead in my high school play.

Author: *[Laughs]*

RC: I played the Gig Young role in *Ask Any Girl*.[6] I had to wear lifts. That was my theatrical experience. No, I didn't believe in any of this stuff. My thinking about what makes Shakespeare work really came in when I was watching kids get bored at plays I had spent a huge amount of their money to see and get them good seats. And if I think about it, the reason I was spending the money on the good seats is connected to some sense I must have had that they need to be nearer or it's not as much fun, you know. It was just, the closer you are, the better; the more you'll like it.

Author: *Right.*

RC: And they didn't always like it. In the mid-80s the RSC was going through a huge change of management. But when I first started to go, Trevor Nunn was in charge. The Trevor Nunn production of *The Alchemist* I saw in the Other Place, in 1977. The very first time. It was the preview performance of it. [There were] 20 kids with me; they hadn't read the play. Told 'em not to read the play. Told 'em this show was just for me. I had spent, because it was a preview show, all of a pound fifty a ticket, so I didn't really give a shit. You know, a pound fifty a ticket. And they went wild. And it was three-quarters thrust. And I mean, now I look back, it was thrust, three-quarters, 150 people. And, yes, the lights were off, but you could see everybody.

Author: *I mean, that's it. That's all the stuff.*

RC: It was all the stuff. So all the components were there before there was any thinking in my mind about the Globe.

Author: *But you hadn't quite connected the dots yet.*

RC: Not at all. So I'm seeing that stuff and then getting to feel that I could direct something. So, you know, having strong ideas about it but again, not in these terms.

Author: *Good.*

RC: When I say 'not in these terms', I mean not at all in 'original practice' terms. But when I look at what my terms were – audience proximity, fast pace, words first – I see how they're cousins to these terms.

Author: [Laughs.] *Excellent. One of the things I'm trying to do is work a 'Spirit of '76' angle.*

RC: So why '76?

Author: *Styan's book is '76. John Russell Brown's* Free Shakespeare *is '77, Dessen's first book ...*

RC: See, I started reading these things only in the '80s.

Author: *That's actually what I'm getting at. You found the same thing but from a different ...*

RC: That's why I mentioned Michael Goldman.

Author: *Yeah.*

RC: And that's '87.

Author: *I see.*

RC: So that's when I start reading the things and caring about whatever Shakespeare might have been doing. You know, and Styan and Beckerman and then I invite Dessen to this seminar in the Fall of '87, I have the seminar on *Henry V* and then in spring of '88, we do it.

Author: *Ok.*

RC: And then we start the company. That's it.

Author: *This is a wind-up question – I mean to wind-up the conversation, not one to wind you up – because I'm now asking a future-oriented one.*

RC: Ok.

Author: *So now the American Shakespeare Center, the Globe and the RSC, most of the mainstream Shakespeare today, have at least a quasi-thrust stage. So if what was once marginal has become central, the logic of these things is that whatever the next big thing in Shakespeare and performance*

*is has to react against that. Maybe I'm wrong about that.
But what is your prediction of …*

RC: Well, what complicates your theory a little bit I think
is technology or the new technology. Because what I'm
always saying is that simultaneous presence is key to an
understanding of what makes theatre theatre and not movies.
So, that complicates your question.

Author: *It does – though 'simultaneous presence' is not
going to mean the same thing.*

RC: It's not going to be the same. So if I had to say right
now. I think devised theatre and the complete deconstruction
of Shakespeare is some of the most interesting things out
there right now. You know, *Sleep No More* and breaking
up the text. You know, I hate going to productions
of Shakespeare now that are 'regular' productions of
Shakespeare because most of the time I end up very upset
and I'll give you some examples. And I'll give you some
exceptions.

Author: *Good.*

RC: Ok. So an example of being very upset was at the *Two
Gents* I saw in Stratford [RSC 2014].

Author: *Yeah. I saw it.*

RC: And the two clowns weren't funny. It wasn't a very
good job. It was an Ok job. The house loved it because
it was an Ok job of a pretty good play in a thrust space.
And so the house loved it and that's fine, that's good.
But I was very unhappy because of all the things I could
tell they didn't do well because I know the play. You
know, we've done better. So, then we see that *Troilus and
Cressida –*

Author: *The Wooster Group [RSC 2014]?*

RC: Right, the Wooster Group. Which was on some level bosh, and we had an argument about it later –

Author: *Everyone had an argument about it later ...*

RC: ... but my point was, if Stratford is supposed to be where people meet Shakespeare, they weren't meeting him there. But I, like you, thought at least this is really interesting, because you and I both ...

Author: *We've already met Shakespeare.*

RC: We're Shakespeare weary. Now here's the one I saw and thought was good. I had just directed *Henry IV, Part 2*. Anyhow, I loved it. So I was watching Sher do it [Antony Sher played Falstaff in the RSC 2014 productions of both *1* and *2 Henry IV*]. And it wasn't 'great', but it was so good that I enjoyed it. But the only things that I have enjoyed without exception have been the deconstructed things.

Author: *Huh?*

RC: You can depress the hell out of me by having me go to D.C. and a not particularly good *Richard II* and hear everybody go nuts over it, and I'm just like, 'We can do better work than this', you know. So then my anger thing comes up. And I'd just rather avoid that nasty me and be happy. So I like to see shows I haven't seen before, early modern if possible. Or I'd like to see, like Synetic, where they use no words at all and dance out the play [Synetic Theatre, Washington, DC].

Author: *Right.*

RC: Totally do something different with it, you know. But

I would love to think that no matter what follows for the ASC we will be ... there's an expression I use that might not be a good one, but I call it 'bedrock Shakespeare'. That if you want to go someplace where concepts and notions and concerns for comfort and a bunch of modern things aren't too much interfering with the words, then there ought to be a place for that. I think we are still that place. That you can get a bedrock experience in the good way, in the best sense of it: a really solid experience of the words themselves and the feel of the audience and its connection with the play by going to our show. And not because that's time travelling, but because those two things together make good theatre. You know, and then you can leave and go: 'so that's what Shakespeare's like: Ok'.

Author: *Right.*

RC: I mean, maybe that's a really modest goal for us. But if we can keep that up and also refresh it. I think the best thing we've done since we built the Blackfriars is the Actors Renaissance Season. And if we were really smart we would turn the theatre over to an ensemble. We'd even try paying them out of receipts. We'd even try making them actually financially engaged in the decisions that we make. And you know, those are hard models to find.

Author: *That's really cool.*

RC: And then, to have a playwright maybe connected to that and then you're really looking at the dynamics. You know, the word 'original' that we talk about ...

Author: *Yeah.*

RC: I don't love it. I love 'practical origins'. But the thing I like best about the word 'original' is the sense of getting at that energy in the source. So, if we take the idea of source and a stream, a lot of questions that you and others who are critiquing the project bring are about the place where that stream comes out of, like the rocks around it or the topography around it. And some of the stuff is about, maybe, what comes out, like what's in the water and what's the mineral content and so on. But for me, if I could divide it in this way, what I want is the rush. I want to feel what that stream felt like, viscerally felt like. I can't prove that the minerals are the same and I can't prove that the topography is the same, or that the rocks around it are the same, but the sense that I am in that rush: that's what I mean by 'origin'. If we can get at that sense of an origin, then that's a huge thing. And sometimes, like in our production of the trivial little play *A Midsummer Night's Dream*, dammit, I feel like we do. And that makes me very happy.

One more thing …

The interviews with Warren and Cohen reveal that, although the company has dropped the 'Express' from their name, they remain committed to expediency. Time and again, Cohen and Warren invoke historical authenticity as a means to end. As Cohen has it, it would have been less expensive for the ASC to build a room like the RSC's Swan, a theatre that echoes the form and function but not the furnishings of an early modern indoor playhouse. However, 'we would not have been able to convince as many big donors that … we were making an important theatre that way … Making it out of oak and making it look as it might have [looked] got us going; it got us, you know, noticed. You walk into that beautiful room and you think "this must be an important place"'. In these terms, the Blackfriars is only accidentally authentic, with Cohen and Warren the unlikely but happy custodians of the 'world's only recreation of Shakespeare's indoor playhouse'.

The notion that the ASC would have struggled to attract 'big donors' had they wanted a playhouse with a less overt

historical claim can sound glib, even cynical. Perhaps it
is. If there's a 'Blackfriars Historicity' it is ultimately an
expedient one, then: strict adherence to the past in some
respects and blithe disregard in others. The ultimate aim is
not to 'time travel', as Cohen puts it, but to create a space,
even an occasion, for theatrical events that capture 'a sense
of an origin' if not its specifics. Above all, the authenticity
of the Blackfriars is in service of a greater end, to allow an
audience to 'meet Shakespeare' in the here and now. You'll
come for the past, but you'll stay for the present.

How ultimately do we evaluate the Blackfriars'
'importance'? For Cohen, at least, a deal of that importance
inheres in its authenticity. The oak, the chandeliers, the
elegantly painted *frons* articulate the playhouse's importance
before an actor has even stepped foot on the stage. The
playhouse is important irrespective of what happens there.
There is, therefore, an uneasy tension between Blackfriars'
'historicity' and Blackfriars' 'performativity.' The former can
make do without the latter, but not the other way around.
At worst, the building can supersede the plays put on there;
turn them into a pageant of living history. That this rarely
happens is a testament to the 'importance' of the kind of
playing the company has fomented, a form of playing that
has honed the art of speaking sincerely with its tongue in its
cheek.

APPENDIX

1988	Richard III
1989	The Taming of the Shrew
1990	Julius Caesar, A Midsummer Night's Dream
1991	Measure for Measure, Twelfth Night, A Midsummer Night's Dream
1992	Macbeth, The Merchant of Venice, The Comedy of Errors
1993	Antony and Cleopatra, Romeo and Juliet, A Midsummer Night's Dream
1994	Othello, Much Ado about Nothing, The Taming of the Shrew
1995	The Tempest, Twelfth Night, Hamlet, Rosencrantz & Guildenstern Are Dead
1996	Henry V, As You Like It, The Comedy of Errors, Julius Caesar
1997 1998	Richard III, Measure for Measure, Love's Labour's Lost, 1 Henry IV, A Midsummer Night's Dream, Macbeth, The Taming of the Shrew, Romeo and Juliet
1999	The Merchant of Venice, The Knight of the Burning Pestle, Macbeth, Much Ado about Nothing, Hamlet
2000	Richard II, Much Ado about Nothing, Doctor Faustus, Othello, Twelfth Night, The Roaring Girl
2001	A Midsummer Night's Dream, Hamlet, Rosencrantz & Guildenstern Are Dead, The Alchemist, The Winter's Tale, As You Like It, Romeo and Juliet, An American Christmas Carol: 1852

2002	Henry V, The Comedy of Errors, Saint Joan, The Merry Wives of Windsor, Love's Labour's Lost, Macbeth, Julius Caesar, Richard III, Twelfth Night, A Christmas Carol
2003	The Tempest, Coriolanus, The Taming of the Shrew, The Knight of the Burning Pestle, Much Ado about Nothing, King Lear, Tartuffe, A Christmas Carol
2004	A Midsummer Night's Dream, 1 Henry IV, The Two Gentlemen of Verona, The Importance of Being Earnest, The Merchant of Venice, Falstaff, Les Liaisons Dangereuses, The Santaland Diaries, A Christmas Carol
2005	The Complete Works of William Shakespeare (abridged), The Taming of the Shrew, A King and No King, The Tamer Tamed, Measure for Measure, She Stoops to Conquer, Twelfth Night, The Three Musketeers, The Comedy of Errors, Hamlet, All's Well That Ends Well, The Santaland Diaries, A Christmas Carol
2006	Greater Tuna, 'Tis Pity She's a Whore, Romeo and Juliet, Eastward Ho!, The Brats of Clarence, Richard III, Return to the Forbidden Planet, Much Ado about Nothing, Macbeth, As You Like It, The Tempest, Othello, The Santaland Diaries, A Christmas Carol
2007	The Duchess of Malfi, Hamlet (First Quarto), Pericles, The Brats of Clarence, The Devil is an Ass, Cyrano de Bergerac, A Midsummer Night's Dream, Julius Caesar, The Winter's Tale, Romeo and Juliet, Love's Labour's Lost, Antony and Cleopatra, The Santaland Diaries, A Christmas Carol
2008	Volpone, Macbeth, The Jew of Malta, Cymbeline, The Witch, The Taming of the Shrew, The Merchant of Venice, Henry V, King Lear, Twelfth Night, Measure for Measure,

Richard II, The Santaland Diaries, A Christmas
Carol

2009   The Revenger's Tragedy, A Midsummer
Night's Dream, The Changeling, 1 Henry
VI, The Blind Beggar of Alexandria, Hamlet,
Rosencrantz and Guildenstern Are Dead,
The Comedy of Errors, The Merry Wives of
Windsor, Much Ado about Nothing, Titus
Andronicus, 1 Henry IV, The Rehearsal, The
Santaland Diaries, A Christmas Carol

2010   Doctor Faustus, Twelfth Night, The Alchemist,
2 Henry VI, The Roman Actor, The Knight of
the Burning Pestle, All's Well That Ends Well,
Romeo and Juliet, The Taming of the Shrew,
Othello, Wild Oats, 2 Henry IV, The Fair Maid
of the West, The Twelve Dates of Christmas,
The Santaland Diaries, A Christmas Carol

2011   The Malcontent, The Comedy of Errors, Look
About You, 3 Henry VI, A Trick to Catch the
Old One, As You Like It, Macbeth, Measure
for Measure, Hamlet, The Importance of Being
Earnest, The Tempest, Henry V, Tamburlaine
the Great, The Twelve Dates of Christmas, The
Santaland Diaries, A Christmas Carol

2012   Philaster, or Love Lies a-Bleeding; Much Ado
about Nothing; Richard III; A Mad World,
My Masters; Dido, Queen of Carthage; A
Midsummer Night's Dream; The Winter's
Tale; 'Tis Pity She's a Whore; The Merchant
of Venice; The Lion in Winter; The Two
Gentlemen of Verona; Cymbeline; King John;
The Santaland Diaries; The 12 Dates of
Christmas; A Christmas Carol

2013   Julius Caesar, The Country Wife, Henry VIII,
The Custom of the Country, The Two Noble
Kinsmen, Twelfth Night, Love's Labour's Lost,
The Duchess of Malfi, Romeo and Juliet,

Return to the Forbidden Planet, All's Well That
Ends Well, Troilus and Cressida, She Stoops to
Conquer, The Twelve Dates of Christmas, The
Santaland Diaries, A Christmas Carol

2014
As You Like It; The Servant of Two Masters;
Timon of Athens; Epicene, or the Silent
Woman; The Maid's Tragedy; Othello;
The Merry Wives of Windsor; 1 Henry IV;
Macbeth; Cyrano de Bergerac; The Comedy
of Errors; Edward II; Pericles; The Twelve
Dates of Christmas; The Santaland Diaries; A
Christmas Carol

2015
The Taming of the Shrew, The Rover, The
White Devil, Every Man in His Humour,
Mother Bombie, Hamlet, Doctor Faustus,
Much Ado about Nothing, Wittenberg, Antony
and Cleopatra, A Midsummer Night's Dream,
The Winter's Tale, Shakespeare's Joan of Arc
(1 Henry VI), The Santaland Diaries, The
Twelve Dates of Christmas, A Christmas Carol

2016
The Tempest, Measure for Measure, Women
Beware Women, The Sea Voyage, Love for
Love, The Life of King Henry the Fifth, Julius
Caesar, The Importance of Being Earnest, Arms
and the Man, Bloody Bloody Andrew Jackson,
Twelfth Night, King Lear, The Rise of Queen
Margaret (2 Henry VI), The Twelve Dates of
Christmas, The Santaland Diaries, A Christmas
Carol

NOTES

Preface

1 'Birth Places: Shakespeare's Beliefs / Believing in Shakespeare,' *Shakespeare Quarterly* 65 (2014): 399–420, esp. 414.

2 Roland Barthes, *Camera Lucida: Reflections on Photography* (New York: Hill and Wang, 1982), 9.

3 http://www.americanshakespearecenter.com/v.php?pg=124 (accessed 1 September 2015).

4 The most thorough account is Ralph Alan Cohen's 'Shenandoah Shakespeare and the Building of the Third Blackfriars Playhouse,' *The Theater of Teaching and the Lessons of Theater*, eds Domnica Radulescu and Maria Stadter Fox (Oxford: Rowan & Littlefield, 2005), 143–60.

Introduction

1 Bert O. States, *The Pleasure of the Play* (Ithaca: Cornell University Press, 1994), 80.

2 Rebecca Schneider, *Performing Remains: Art and War in Times of Theatrical Reenactment* (New York: Routledge, 2011), 90. Schneider borrows the phrase 'again for the first time' from Andrew Benjamin's *Present Hope: Philosophy, Architecture, Judaism* (New York: Routledge, 1997): x.

3 States, *The Pleasure of the Play*, 81.

4 Schneider, *Performing Remains*, Foreword, *passim*.

5 W. B. Worthen, *Shakespeare and the Force of Modern*

Performance (Cambridge: Cambridge University Press, 2003), esp. Ch. 2, 'Globe Performativity'.

6   The idea and the phrase 'logic of the archive' is, of course, from Jacques Derrida's *Archive Fever: A Freudian Impression* (Chicago: University of Chicago Press, 1995). For the 'body-to-body' transmission, see Schneider, *Performing Remains*, 100.

7   This formulation paraphrases Richard Schechner's 'not not' idea of acting, articulated in 'Re-wrighting Shakespeare: A Conversation with Richard Schechner' in *Teaching Shakespeare through Performance*, ed. Milla Cozart Riggio (New York: Modern Language Association of America, 1999), 127–43, esp. 134.

8   ASC programme, 8; also available online: http://www. americanshakespearecenter.com/v.php?pg=49 (accessed 16 July 2015).

9   For a review of the scholarship on the size of touring companies, see Terence G Schoone-Jongen *Shakespeare's Companies: William Shakespeare's Early Career and the Acting Companies, 1577–1594* (Burlington, VT: Ashgate, 2008), esp. Ch. 3.

10   *Jamaica Plain/Roxbury Citizen*, 19 August 2003.

11   http://zynodoa.com/images/MediaKits/zyn_presspacket_ rev8_2013.pdf (accessed 15 April 2015).

12   Blackfriars Promotional Brochure, 2001. 'Light … After 359 Years of Darkness', Box A1, Control Folder F1, Washington and Lee University

13   Steve Hendrix, *Washington Post*, 2001.

14   'Light … After 359 Years of Darkness', Box A1, Control Folder F1.

15   'John Harrell', in *The Routledge Companion to Actors' Shakespeare*, ed. John Russell Brown (New York: Routledge, 2012), 78–9.

16   *Mid-Atlantic Country*, June 1995.

17   Thomas Paine, *Dissertations on Government, The Affairs of the Bank, and Paper Money* (Philadelphia: Charles Cist, 1838), 44.

18 *The Work of Art in the Age of its Technological Reproducibility and Other Writings on Media*, eds Michael W. Jennings, Brigid Doherty and Thomas Y. Levin (Cambridge: The Belknap Press of Harvard University Press, 2008), 21.

19 See Claire Colebrook, *Gilles Deleuze* (London:Routledge, 2002), 120.

20 See Henri Bergson, *Key Writings*, eds Keith Ansell Pearson and John Mullarkey (New York: Continuum, 2001), esp. 'The Idea of Duration', 49–80.

21 Rebecca Schneider, *Performing Remains*, 112.

22 Bob Anthony, Tuesday 18 May 1999, http://members.aol.com/review4u (accessed 15 July 2015).

Chapter 1

1   'Invocation of the Visual Image: Ekphrasis in "Lucrece" and Beyond', *Shakespeare Quarterly* 63 (2012): 175–98, esp. 187.

2   The company is believed to have first made landfall on 26 April 1607.

3   Quoted in Sonia Massai, 'Edward Blount, the Herberts, and the First Folio' in ed. Marta Staznicky, *Shakespeare's Stationers: Studies in Cultural Bibliography* (Philadelphia: University of Pennsylvania Press, 2013), 138.

4   See Wesley Frank Craven, *The Virginia Company of London, 1606–1624* (Williamsburg, VA: Virginia 350th Anniversary Celebration Corporation, 1957), 16.

5   Andrew Fitzmaurice, *Humanism and America: An Intellectual History of English Colonisation, 1500–1625* (Cambridge: Cambridge University Press, 2003), 62.

6   Craven, *The Virginia Company*, 19.

7   F. G. Fleay, *A Chronicle History of the London Stage, 1559–1642* (New York: Burt Franklin, 1890). See the entry for the play in the Lost Plays Database. https://www.lostplays.org/index.php?title=Main_Page (accessed 7 July 2015).

8   Craven, *The Virginia Company*, 57.

9   See Conway Robinson, *Abstract of the Proceedings of the Virginia Company of London, 1619–1624*, 8 vols (Richmond: Virginia Historical Society, 1879), esp. vol. 2.

10 Charlotte Carmichael Stopes, *The Life of Henry, Third Early of Southampton, Shakespeare's Patron* (Cambridge: Cambridge University Press, 1922), 446.

11 Stopes, *The Life*, 446.

12 Conway Robinson, *Abstract of the Proceedings of the Virginia Company of London, 1619–1624*, 8 vols (Richmond: Virginia Historical Society, 1879), vol. 1, vi–viii.

13 *The Staunton Spectator and Vindicator*, 29 April 1904, vol. 83, 1.

14 Ibid.

15 Ibid.

16 *The Staunton Spectator and Vindicator*, 21 September 1906, vol. 85, 1.

17 George Frederic Viett, *Pocahontas, the Virginia Nonpareil, A Drama of the 17th Century* (Richmond: C. W. Rex Co., 1907), 25.

18 Ibid., 41.

19 Ibid., 42.

20 Shakespeare's prescience evidently includes his having read Charles Kingsley's *Westward Ho!*, an 1885 historical novel set in the age of Elizabeth I, since the closing couplet closely paraphrases Kingsley's description of Sir Amyas Leigh, his adventuring hero, 'a symbol, though he knows it not, of brave young England longing to wing its way out of its island prison, to discover and to traffic, to colonize and to civilize, until no wind can sweep the earth which does not bear the echoes of an English voice.' *Westward Ho! or, the Voyages and Adventures of Sir Amyas Leigh, Knight* 2 vols. (London: Macmillan and Co., 1881), vol. 1, 16.

21 Stuart Anderson, *Race and Rapprochement: Anglo-Saxonism and Anglo-American Relations, 1895–1904* (Rutherford, NJ: Fairleigh Dickinson University Press, 1981), 12.

22 Reginald Horsman, 'Origin of Racial Anglo-Saxonism in

Great Britain before 1850', *Journal of the History of Ideas*, 37 (1976): 387–410, esp. 387.

23 Viett, *Pocahontas, the Virginia Nonpareil*, 40.

24 Ibid., 117.

25 Ibid., 14.

26 Ibid., 20.

27 Ibid., 20.

28 *The Staunton Spectator and Vindicator*, 21 September 1906, vol. 85, 1.

29 Viett, *Pocahontas, the Virginia Nonpareil*, 20.

30 Ibid., 37.

31 *The Staunton Spectator and Vindicator*, 21 September 1906, vol. 85, 1.

32 Viett, *Pocahontas, the Virginia Nonpareil*, 37.

33 Dave McNair, 'Erasing History: Wrecking Ball aiming for DeJarnette?', *The Hook*, 13 July 2006.

34 For further information on this horrific history, see Gregory Michael Dorr, 'Defective or Disabled? Race, Medicine, and Eugenics in Progressive Era Virginia and Alabama,' *History Cooperative* 5 (4) (October 2006); also Daniel Kevles, *In the Name of Eugenics: Genetics and the Uses of Human Heredity* (New York: Knopf, 1985).

35 George Frederic Viett, *'Thou Beside me Singing' and other poems, A Book of Verses* (Philadelphia: P. W. Ziegler & Co., 1900), xiii.

36 *The Staunton Spectator and Vindicator*, 16 December 1896, 1.

37 *The Staunton Spectator and Vindicator*, 16 December 1896, vol., 1.

38 Library of Congress Civil War Maps, 2nd edn, H332.

39 Railway traffic has declined, but Staunton sits at the elbow of two major US interstates, 81 and 64.

40 She would later join in life and art her famous husband Edward Sothern.

41 *Staunton Spectator*, Wednesday 7 October 1891, 1.

42 *Staunton Spectator*, Wednesday 14 October 1891.

43 Jno. B. Jeffrey's *Guide and Directory to the Opera Houses, Theatres, Public Halls, Bill Posters, etc. of the Cities and Towns of America.* 'Intended for the Use of Amusement Managers and their Agents," 5th and rev. edns. Chicago, 1882–3, 284.

44 *Staunton Spectator and Vindicator*, Friday 20 April 1906.

45 *Staunton Spectator and General Advertiser*, Tuesday 19 March 1867. Harry Langdon should not be confused with the star of silent films by that same name. The 'Harry Langdon' who stopped in Staunton in the 1860s would go on to work with Edwin Booth and Lawrence Barrett.

46 Folger Shakespeare Library Theatrical Scrapbook, B.30.2 'Hanford, Charles'.

47 Ibid.

48 *Staunton Spectator and General Advertiser*, 27 August 1872, 1.

49 *Billboard*, 29 March 1947, 8.

50 *Staunton Spectator and General Advertiser*, 12 September 1887.

51 *Staunton Spectator and General Advertiser*, 10 June 1873.

52 *Staunton Spectator and General Advertiser*, 17 April 1883. The history of the Masonic Lodge is long and fascinating in itself. Today, the graduate programme in Shakespeare and Performance at Mary Baldwin University, Staunton, VA, occupies the top two floors, so in the space where Alice King spoke students today honour her legacy.

53 *Staunton Spectator and General Advertiser*, Wednesday 14 November 1894.

54 Ibid.

55 *Staunton Spectator and General Advertiser*, Wednesday 4 April 1894.

56 *Miscellanies Selected from the Public Journals* (Boston: Joseph T. Buckingham, 1822), 244.

57 *Staunton Spectator and General Advertiser*, Wednesday 11 April 1894.

58 Edmund D. Potter, *A Guide to Historic Staunton, Virginia* (Charleston: History Press, 2008), esp. 107–9.

59 *Kate Field's Washington* 9 (1) (3 January 1894): 413.

60 Ibid., 413.

61 Staunton has a complex history with racist films. Its most
    famous son was Woodrow Wilson, twenty-eighth president
    of the United States. Among other things, Wilson became the
    first president to screen movies at the White House, including
    D. W. Griffith's *Birth of the Nation* in 1915. See Melvyn
    Stokes, *D. W. Griffith's 'The Birth of a Nation': A History of
    'The Most Controversial Motion Picture of all Time'* (Oxford:
    Oxford University Press, 2007), 111.

62 Celia Daileader, *Racism, Misogyny, and the* Othello
    Myth: Inter-racial Couples from Shakespeare to Spike Lee
    (Cambridge: Cambridge University Press, 2005), 138.

63 Quoted in Charles P. Roland, *An American Iliad: The Story
    of the Civil War*, 2nd edn (Lexington: The University Press of
    Kentucky, 2004), 218.

64 *American Heritage Dictionary of the English Language*, 4th
    edn (Boston: Houghton Mifflin, 2000).

65 Mary Anna Jackson, *Memoirs of Stonewall Jackson* (Louisville,
    KY: Prentice Press, 1895), 78.

66 James I. Robertson, *Stonewall Jackson: The Man, the Soldier,
    the Legend* (New York: Macmillan 1997), 169.

67 *The [Richmond] Daily Dispatch*, vol. VIII, no. 150, 24
    December 1855.

68 ASC archives, Washington and Lee University Library, Box A1,
    Control Folder F1.

Chapter 2

1 *Cities of the Dead: Circum-Atlantic Performance* (New York:
   Columbia University Press, 1996), 6.

2 For books and volumes that cover some of this territory,
   see Joe Falocco *Reimagining Shakespeare's Playhouse: Early
   Modern Staging Conventions in the Twentieth Century*
   (Cambridge: D. S. Brewer, 2010); Cary Mazer, ed., *Poel,
   Granville Barker, Guthrie, Wanamaker: Great Shakespeareans*,

vol. 15 (London: Bloomsbury Publishing, 2015); Robert Speaight, *William Poel and the Elizabethan Revival* (London: William Heinemann, 1954).

3 See Margreta de Grazia, *Shakespeare Verbatim: The Reproduction of Authenticity and the Apparatus of 1790* (Oxford: Clarendon Press, 1991).

4 See Terry Eagelton, 'Capitalism, Modernism, and Postmodernism', *New Left Review* 1.152 (1985): 136.

5 Michael Dobson analyses shrewdly the tendency to refer to the theatre of this time in such terms. He writes, 'the desire to represent Shakespeare and his colleagues as thoroughgoing self-established professionals may reflect not so much the state of the Elizabethan stage as that of twentieth-century universities, where the first generations of full-time academic theatre historians were perennially anxious to distinguish themselves from the mere dilettantes and enthusiasts who had hitherto chronicled the development of English drama', *Shakespeare and Amateur Performance* (Cambridge: Cambridge University Press, 2011), 6.

6 John Stockwoode, *A Sermon preached at Paules Crosse* (1579), 74.

7 See Julia Stone Peters, *Theatre of the Book 1480–1880: Print, Text and Performance in Europe* (Oxford: Oxford University Press, 2003).

8 *A New History of Early English Drama*, eds David Scott Kastan and John D. Cox (New York: Columbia University Press, 1997); see de Grazia, 13.

9 *The Arden Shakespeare: Complete Works*, eds Richard Proudfoot, Ann Thompson and David Scott Kastan (London: Thomson Learning, 2001), 4.

10 Glynne Wickham, *Early English Stages, 1300–1660*, 3 vols (New York: Routledge and Keegan Paul: 1959–81), vol. 1, xxix.

11 D. A. Brooks, *From Playhouse to Printing House: Drama and Authorship in Early Modern England* (Cambridge: Cambridge University Press, 2000). 153)

12 E. K. Chambers, *The Elizabethan Stage*, 4 vols (Oxford: Clarendon Press, 1923), vol. 2, 384.

13 E. K. Chambers, *The Elizabethan Stage*, 4 vols (Oxford: Clarendon Press, 1923), vol. 2, 384.

14 Marjorie Garber, *Sex and Real Estate: Why We Love Houses* (New York: Anchor, 2001).

15 Christie Carson and Farah Karim-Cooper, *Shakespeare's Globe: A Theatrical Experiment* (Cambridge: Cambridge University Press, 2008), 211.

16 See Cary Mazer, ed., *Poel, Granville Barker, Guthrie, Wanamaker: Great Shakespeareans*, vol. 15 (London: Bloomsbury, 2013).

17 ASC archives, Washington and Lee University Library, Box A1, Control Folder F1.

18 Nor has theatre history entirely forgotten Monck, see, e.g. Frank Hildy 'Playing Places for Shakespeare; The Maddermarket Theatre, Norwich', *Shakespeare Survey* 47 (1994): 81–90.

19 Robert Speaight, *William Poel and the Elizabethan Revival* (London: William Heinemann, 1954), 9.

20 Speaight, 12.

21 R. Shaughnessy, *The Shakespeare Effect: A History of Twentieth-Century Performance* (New York: Palgrave Macmillan, 2002), 17.

22 Cary Mazer, *Shakespeare Refashioned: Elizabethan Plays on Edwardian Stages* (Ann Arbor, MI: University of Michigan Press, 1981).

23 'William Poel' in *The Routledge Companion to Directors' Shakespeare*, ed. John Russell Brown (New York: Routledge, 2008), 356–73, esp. 366.

24 Speaight, 44.

25 Thomson, 359.

26 Ibid., 363.

27 Speaight, 95.

28 Quoted, in Paul Prescott, *Reviewing Shakespeare: Journalism and Performance from the Eighteenth Century to the Present* (Cambridge: Cambridge University Press, 2013), 90–1.

29 Prescott, *Reviewing Shakespeare*, 79.

30 Harcourt Williams, *Four Years at the Old Vic* (London: Edinburgh Press, 1935), 22.

31 Harley Granville Barker, *Prefaces to Shakespeare*, vol. 6 (London: B. T. Batsford, 1974), 36.

32 *The Saturday Review of Politics, Literature, Science, and Art*, 95 (1903): 776.

33 Folger Shakespeare Library Scrapbook, B.41.1 Literary societies (South Lambert, Elizabethan Stage).

34 Speaight, 101.

35 J. R. Planche, *The Recollections and Reflections of J.R. Plance, a Professional Autobiography*, 2 vols (London: Tinsley Brothers, 1872), vol. 2, 82.

36 Planche, vol. 2, 83–5.

37 Speaight, 51.

38 Lester Wallack, *Memories of Fifty Years* (New York: Scribers, 1889), 177.

39 Folger Shakespeare Library scrapbook B.113.6 Shakespeare (misc.).

40 Folger Shakespeare Library scrapbook B.56.1 Sh. Works, Introduction.

41 See, especially on Ben Greet, Michael Dobson, *Shakespeare and Amateur Performance: A Cultural History* (Cambridge: Cambridge University Press, 2011), esp. 172–82.

42 William Poel, *Shakespeare in the Theatre* (London and Toronto: Sidwick and Jackson, 1913), 204.

43 Speaight, 93.

44 Richard Flecknoe, *Love's Kingdom. A Pastoral Trage-Comedy. Not as it was Acted at the Theatre near Lincolns-Inn, but as it was written, and since corrected ... with a short Treatise of the English Stage, &c.* (London: 1664), (G7ᵛ).

45 Part of what drives this (re)discovery is that the myth of the minimalist early modern stage, described wittily by Alan Armstrong as the idea that a thin line can be drawn from James Burbage to Mies van der Rohe.

46 William Poel, 'Shakespeare's Profession', *Journal of the Royal Society of Arts* #3 250 (LXIII) (Friday 5 March 1915): 325–36.

47 Speaight, 148.

48 Cribbed from Keats 'Upon looking into Chapman's Home', which Tom Stoppard picks up in *The Real Thing*.

49 *The Monthly Chronicle, a National Journal of Politics, Literature, Science, and Art* 6 (London, 1840): 232.

50 *America's Theatre Guide*, vol. IV, 13 (August 1994).

51 Poel, *Journal of the Royal Society of Arts*, 336.

52 Thomson, 'William Poel', 359.

53 Ben Greet, *The Ben Greet Shakespeare for Young People and Amateur Players: As You Like It* (New York: Doubleday, 1912), 48.

54 Poel, *Shakespeare in the Theatre*, 204.

55 http://www.shakespearesglobe.com/discovery-space/adopt-an-actor/archive/claudio-played-by-alex-hassell/rehearsal-notes-3 (accessed 13 May 2015).

56 Speaight, 247.

57 Speaight, 246.

58 J. L. Styan, *The Shakespeare Revolution* (Cambridge: Cambridge University Press, 1977), 82.

59 Stephen Booth, 'Shakespeare at Valley Forge: The International Shakespeare Association Congress, 1976', *Shakespeare Quarterly* 27 (1976): 231–42, esp. 238.

60 Stephen Booth, 238.

61 Carson and Karim-Cooper, 20. Though the immediate attempt to franchise the project failed, these Depression era Globes did lead indirectly to an American tradition of Shakespeare festivals with quasi-Elizabethan theatres in Ashland, Oregon; San Diego; Odessa, Texas and Cedar City, Utah, among others.

62 Carson and Karim-Cooper, 15–16.

63 David Skinner, November/December 2007, 'Shakespearetown,' *Humanities* 28 (6): 104.

64 James Bulman's introduction to *Shakespeare, Theory, and*

Performance (New York: Routledge, 1996) outlines the lasting impact of the critical movement spearheaded by Styan.

65   Styan, 2.

66   John Russell Brown, *Free Shakespeare* (New York: Applause, 1974), 83.

67   Stephen Booth, *Shakespeare Quarterly* 43 (1992): 479–83, esp. 479–80.

68   *The Patriot-Ledger*, Thursday 12 August 1993.

69   I know this because I wrote much of this copy.

70   *JMU Breeze*, Thursday 26 August 2004.

71   *Metro Weekly*, 3 July 2003.

72   *JMU Breeze*, Thursday 11 September 1997.

73   Thursday 12 August 1993.

74   17 July 1992.

75   *Washington City Paper*, 1 July 1994.

76   *Curio*, Summer 1992.

77   *Daily Record*, Wednesday, 16 October 1999; *The Daily Record*, Friday 6 October 2000.

78   *EIR*, 29 September 2000; *The Monitor*, 6 October 1998; *The Winchester Star*, n.d.

79   *The Defender*, 1991.

80   *Mid-Atlantic Country*, June 1995.

81   *JMU Breeze*, n.d.

82   *JMU Breeze*, n.d.; *Daily News Record*, 11 July 1995.

83   *Washington Review*, 1992.

84   *The Scotsman*, 26 August 1992.

85   'Shenandoah Shakespeare and the Building of the Third Blackfriars Playhouse', *The Theater of Teaching and the Lessons of Theater*, eds Domnica Radulescu and Maria Stadter Fox (Oxford: Rowan & Littlefield, 2005), 143–60, esp. 150.

86   David Skinner, *Humanities* 28 (6) (November/December 2007).

87   Ibid.

88 *Washington City Paper*, 29 August 2003.

89 'Blackfriars Replica Opens in Virginia', *The Shakespeare Newsletter* (Winter 2001/2) 51.4 (251): 104.

90 J. L. Styan, *The Shakespeare Revolution*: 237.

91 'Shenandoah Shakespeare and the Building of the Third Blackfriars Playhouse', 143–60, esp. 156.

92 *Shakespeare Bulletin* 17 (1993).

Chapter 3

1   For W. B. Worthen, *Shakespeare and the Force of Modern Performance* (New York: Cambridge University Press, 2003).

2   'Blackfriars Playhouse Tour Script', 'updated 6/22/09', Washington and Lee University Library, ASC archive.

3   Speaight, 106.

4   Egan, Gabriel, 'Hearing or Seeing a Play?: Evidence of Early Modern Theatrical Terminology', available online: http://gabrielegan.com/publications/Egan2001k.htm (accessed 8 August 2015).

5   Douglas A. Brooks, *From Playhouse to Printhouse: Drama and Authorship in Early Modern England* (Cambridge: Cambridge University Press, 2000), 153.

6   Promotional Brochure, Washington and Lee University Library, ASC archive.

7   *Curio*, Summer 1992.

8   *On Stage*, Copley Newspaper, 31 August–6 September 1995.

9   'Blackfriars Playhouse Tour Script', 'updated 6/22/09'. Washington and Lee University Library, ASC archive.

10 Promotional Brochure, Washington and Lee University Library, ASC archive.

11 William Casey Caldwell, 'The Comic Structure of the Globe: History, Direct Address, and the Representation of Laughter in a Reconstructed Playhouse', *Shakespeare Bulletin* 31 (2013): 375–403, esp. 391.

12 Caldwell, 386.

13 Programme for the 2015 Blackfriars Playhouse Spring Season.

14 'Shenandoah Shakespeare and the Building of the Third Blackfriars Playhouse', 143–60, esp. 144.

15 Bridget Escolme, *Talking to the Audience: Shakespeare, Performance, Self* (Oxford: Routledge, 2005), 2.

16 Lia Razak Wallace, '"But I'll Catch Thine Eye": Direct Actor-Audience Eye Contact and the Creation of Social Theatre'. MLitt. Thesis, Mary Baldwin College, 2015.

17 Promotional Brochure, Washington and Lee University Library, ASC archive

18 William Casey Caldwell, 'The Comic Structure of the Globe: History, Direct Address, and the Representation of Laughter in a Reconstructed Playhouse', *Shakespeare Bulletin* 31 (2013): 375–403, esp. 377. For W. B. Worthen, see *Shakespeare and the Force of Modern Performance* (New York: Cambridge University Press, 2003), 107.

19 *The Christian Science Monitor*, Friday 20 May 1994.

20 See Robert Weimann, *Shakespeare and the Popular Tradition in the Theater: Studies in the Social Dimension of Dramatic Form and Function* (Baltimore: John Hopkins University Press, 1987).

21 Wallace, 'But I'll Catch Thine Eye'.

22 Ibid.

23 Ibid.

24 John Stephens, *Satyrial Essayes Characters and Others* (London, 1615).

25 Wallace, 'But I'll Catch Thine Eye'.

26 Ibid.

27 Escolme, 18.

28 Private communication with the author.

29 Sarah Werner, 'Audiences', in *Shakespeare and the Making of Theatre*, eds Stuart Hampton Reeves and Bridget Escolme (Basingstoke: Palgrave Macmillan, 2012), 165–80.

30 Escolme, *Talking to the Audience*, 15.

31 'Re-wrighting Shakespeare: A Conversation with Richard Schechner' in *Teaching Shakespeare through Performance*, ed. Milla Cozart Riggio (New York: Modern Language Association of America, 1999), 127–43, esp. 137.

32 *The Shakespeare Newsletter* 56.2 (269) (Fall 2006); Yvonne Bruce, 'More Matter with Less Art: *The Tempest* and *Macbeth* at Shenandoah Shakespeare', 51.

33 *The Washington Times*, Tuesday 28 May 1996.

34 *Washington City Paper*, 29 August 2003.

35 Ibid.

36 *Philadelphia Enquirer*, 7 August 1991.

37 *The Christian Science Monitor*, Friday 20 May 1994.

38 *The Breeze*, JMU student paper, Thursday 11 September 1997.

39 Caldwell, 475.

Chapter 4

1 http://www.americanshakespearecenter.com/search. php?content=results (accessed 8 July 2015).

2 Stephen Boykewich, *The Hook* (Charlottesville, VA) [full citation?].

3 Andrew Gurr, *Shakespeare's Opposites: The Admiral's Company, 1594–1625* (Cambridge: Cambridge University Press, 2012), 57.

4 *Eikon Basilike with selections from Eikonoklastes*, eds Jim Daems and Holly Faith Nelson (New York: Broadview, 2006), 37.

5 Private communication with the author.

6 *Chicago Reader*, 19 August 1994.

7 *Shakespeare Bulletin* 26 (2008): 181–6.

8 *Thomas Middleton: The Complete Works*, eds Gary Taylor and John Lavagnino (Oxford: Oxford University Press, 2010).

9   Louis A. Montrose, *The Purpose of Playing* (Chicago: University of Chicago Press, 1996), 8.

10 Private communication with the author.

11 Greil Marcus, *The History of Rock 'n' Roll in Ten Songs* (New Haven: Yale University Press, 2014), 53.

12 Private communication with the author.

13 Ibid.

14 http://www.americanshakespearecenter.com/v.php?pg=987 (accessed 16 June 2015).

15 http://www.americanshakespearecenter.com/v.php?pg=987 (accessed 16 June 2015).

16 See especially Allison K. Lenhardt, 'The American Shakespeare Center's "Actors' Renaissance Season": Appropriating Early Modern Performance Documents and Practices', *Shakespeare Bulletin* 30 (2012): 449–67; Evelyn B. Tribble, *Cognition in the Globe: Attention and Memory in Shakespeare's Theatre* (New York: Palgrave Macmillan, 2011).

17 See Tribble, 161.

18 *The Breeze*, James Madison University, April 7, 1988.

19 *Curio*, Summer 1992.

20 http://www.americanshakespearecenter.com/v.php?pg=987 (accessed 16 June 2015).

21 http://www.americanshakespearecenter.com/v.php?pg=987 (accessed 17 July 2015).

22 http://www.americanshakespearecenter.com/v.php?pg=987 (accessed 16 July 2015).

23 For a full history and critique of this practice, see Jeremy Lopez, *Constructing the Canon of Renaissance Drama* (Cambridge: Cambridge University Press, 2014).

Chapter 5

1   In fact, the early music movement at the Globe was spearheaded by Claire van Kampen, who continues to be

involved in the Globe project as they've expanded into the Sam Wanamaker Playhouse.

2   In 2015, the ASC marketed *1 Henry VI* as '*Shakespeare's Joan of Arc (Henry VI, Part 1)*'.

3   There are closed bay doors behind each spotlight.

4   Warren later offered the following expansion upon the question: 'Somebody referred to our work and style as "stale". Because we leave the lights on the audience and include them in the world of the play, because we use the Playhouse itself as our main "set," and because we don't do concept shows where *Richard III* is set in 1970s' Iran in order to show how the murderous King is like the Ayatollah Khomeini, this person said that our work was too similar play to play and, therefore, "stale". I can understand if you don't like what we do; we will not be everyone's cup of tea. But this comment was made in a season during which we were performing in true rotating repertory – with each of the actors in each show that changed every night – a modern-dress *Romeo and Juliet*, Shakespeare's lost rock-and-roll masterpiece *Return to the Forbidden Planet* which is a musical set on a space ship using lines from dozens of Shakespeare's plays, an Edwardian-looking *All's Well That Ends Well*, an eighteenth-century-looking *She Stoops to Conquer*, and in honour of our twenty-fifth anniversary, an SSE-throwback-style *Troilus and Cressida* in which the actors sat around the stage when they were not in the scene and one character wearing black high-top Chuck Taylor Converse tennis shoes like we did during the better part of our first decade. In just this one season, we had *huge* variety; maybe not quite Enobarbus's "infinite variety", but damn close. While we have a ton of elements in our staging style that are the same show to show, we still strive to create mini-banquets in each season where the plays themselves and the way they look provide our audiences with delicious and different meals on which to feast. The consistency of great work at the ASC from season to season, year after year, is a testament to the great people we hire to fulfill our unique mission. I think the example of these five shows in this one season shows how much variety we pack into our programming while being radically faithful to our mission.'

5   Michael Goldman ran a Folger Shakespeare Library seminar in 1987 titled 'Shakespeare and the Theatres of His Time'.

6   Gig Young (1913–78) was an American stage, film and television actor known mainly for second leads and supporting roles.

INDEX